THE 100

About the author

Kass Morgan received a BA from Brown University and a master's degree from Oxford University. She currently works as an editor and lives in Brooklyn, New York.

THE 100

KASS MORGAN

HODDER

First published in the United States of America in 2013
by Little, Brown and Company
An Hachette Book Group Company

First published in Great Britain in 2013 by Hodder & Stoughton
An Hachette UK company

20

A CIP catalogue record for this title is available from the British Library

Paperback 978 1 444 76688 2
Ebook 978 1 444 76689 9

alloyentertainment

Produced by Alloy Entertainment
1700 Broadway
New York, NY 10019
www.alloyentertainment.com

Printed and bound by CPI Group (UK) Ltd, Croydon, CR0 4YY

Hodder & Stoughton policy is to use papers that are natural, renewable and recyclable products and made from wood grown in sustainable forests. The logging and manufacturing processes are expected to conform to the environmental regulations of the country of origin.

Hodder & Stoughton Ltd
338 Euston Road
London NW1 3BH

www.hodder.co.uk

To my parents and grandparents, with love and gratitude

CHAPTER 1

Clarke

The door slid open, and Clarke knew it was time to die.

Her eyes locked on the guard's boots, and she braced for the rush of fear, the flood of desperate panic. But as she rose up onto her elbow, peeling her shirt from the sweat-soaked cot, all she felt was relief.

She'd been transferred to a single after attacking a guard, but for Clarke, there was no such thing as solitary. She heard voices everywhere. They called to her from the corners of her dark cell. They filled the silence between her heart-beats. They screamed from the deepest recesses of her mind. It wasn't death she craved, but if that was the only way to silence the voices, then she was prepared to die.

She'd been Confined for treason, but the truth was far worse than anyone could've imagined. Even if by some miracle she was pardoned at her retrial, there'd be no real reprieve. Her memories were more oppressive than any cell walls.

The guard cleared his throat as he shifted his weight from side to side. "Prisoner number 319, please stand." He was younger than she'd expected, and his uniform hung loosely from his lanky frame, betraying his status as a recent recruit. A few months of military rations weren't enough to banish the specter of malnutrition that haunted the Colony's poor outer ships, Walden and Arcadia.

Clarke took a deep breath and rose to her feet.

"Hold out your hands," he said, pulling a pair of metal restraints from the pocket of his blue uniform. Clarke shuddered as his skin brushed against hers. She hadn't seen another person since they'd brought her to the new cell, let alone touched one.

"Are they too tight?" he asked, his brusque tone frayed by a note of sympathy that made Clarke's chest ache. It'd been so long since anyone but Thalia—her former cell mate and her only friend in the world—had shown her compassion.

She shook her head.

"Just sit on the bed. The doctor's on his way."

"They're doing it here?" Clarke asked hoarsely, the words

scraping against her throat. If a doctor was coming, that meant they were forgoing her retrial. It shouldn't have come as a surprise. According to Colony law, adults were executed immediately upon conviction, and minors were Confined until they turned eighteen and then given one final chance to make their case. But lately, people were being executed within hours of their retrial for crimes that, a few years ago, would have been pardoned.

Still, it was hard to believe they'd actually do it in her cell. In a twisted way, she'd been looking forward to one final walk to the hospital where she'd spent so much time during her medical apprenticeship—one last chance to experience something familiar, if only the smell of disinfectant and the hum of the ventilation system—before she lost the ability to feel forever.

The guard spoke without meeting her eyes. "I need you to sit down."

Clarke took a few short steps and perched stiffly on the edge of her narrow bed. Although she knew that solitary warped your perception of time, it was hard to believe she had been here—alone—for almost six months. The year she'd spent with Thalia and their third cell mate, Lise, a hard-faced girl who smiled for the first time when they took Clarke away, had felt like an eternity. But there was no other explanation. Today had to be her eighteenth birthday, and the only present waiting for Clarke was a syringe that would paralyze her muscles until her heart stopped beating. Afterward, her lifeless body would be released into space, as was the custom on the Colony, left to drift endlessly through the galaxy.

A figure appeared in the door and a tall, slender man stepped into the cell. Although his shoulder-length gray hair partially obscured the pin on the collar of his lab coat, Clarke didn't need the insignia to recognize him as the Council's chief medical advisor. She'd spent the better part of the year before her Confinement shadowing Dr. Lahiri and couldn't count the number of hours she'd stood next to him during surgery. The other apprentices had envied Clarke's assignment, and had complained of nepotism when they discovered that Dr. Lahiri was one of her father's closest friends. At least, he had been before her parents were executed.

"Hello, Clarke," he said pleasantly, as if he were greeting her in the hospital dining room instead of a detention cell. "How are you?"

"Better than I'll be in a few minutes, I imagine."

Dr. Lahiri used to smile at Clarke's dark humor, but this time he winced and turned to the guard. "Could you undo the cuffs and give us a moment, please?"

The guard shifted uncomfortably. "I'm not supposed to leave her unattended."

"You can wait right outside the door," Dr. Lahiri said with exaggerated patience. "She's an unarmed seventeen-year-old. I think I'll be able to keep things under control."

The guard avoided Clarke's eyes as he removed the handcuffs. He gave Dr. Lahiri a curt nod as he stepped outside.

"You mean I'm an unarmed eighteen-year-old," Clarke said, forcing what she thought was a smile. "Or are you turning into one of those mad scientists who never knows what year it is?" Her father had been like that. He'd forget to program the circadian lights in their flat and end up going to work at 0400, too absorbed in his research to notice that the ship's corridors were deserted.

"You're still seventeen, Clarke," Dr. Lahiri said in the calm, slow manner he usually reserved for patients waking up from surgery. "You've been in solitary for three months."

"Then what are you doing here?" she asked, unable to quell the panic creeping into her voice. "The law says you have to wait until I'm eighteen."

"There's been a change of plans. That's all I'm authorized to say."

"So you're authorized to *execute* me but not to talk to me?" She remembered watching Dr. Lahiri during her parents' trial. At the time, she'd read his grim face as an expression of his disapproval with the proceedings, but now she wasn't sure. He hadn't spoken up in their defense. No one had. He'd simply sat there mutely as the Council found her parents—two of Phoenix's most brilliant scientists—to be in violation of the Gaia Doctrine, the rules established after the Cataclysm to ensure the survival of the human race. "What about my parents? Did you kill them, too?"

Dr. Lahiri closed his eyes, as if Clarke's words had transformed from sounds into something visible. Something grotesque. "I'm not here to kill you," he said quietly. He opened his eyes and then gestured to the stool at the foot of Clarke's bed. "May I?"

When Clarke didn't reply, Dr. Lahiri walked forward and sat down so he was facing her. "Can I see your arm, please?"

Clarke felt her chest tighten, and she forced herself to breathe. He was lying. It was cruel and twisted, but it'd all be over in a minute.

She extended her hand toward him. Dr. Lahiri reached into his coat pocket and produced a cloth that smelled of antiseptic. Clarke shivered as he swept it along the inside of her arm. "Don't worry. This isn't going to hurt."

Clarke closed her eyes.

She remembered the anguished look Wells had given her as the guards were escorting her out of the Council chambers. While the anger that had threatened to consume her during the trial had long since burned out, thinking about Wells sent a new wave of heat pulsing through her body, like a dying star emitting one final flash of light before it faded into nothingness.

Her parents were dead, and it was all his fault.

Dr. Lahiri grasped her arm, his fingers searching for her vein.

See you soon, Mom and Dad.

His grip tightened. This was it.

Clarke took a deep breath as she felt a prick on the inside of her wrist.

"There. You're all set."

Clarke's eyes snapped open. She looked down and saw a metal bracelet clasped to her arm. She ran her finger along it, wincing as what felt like a dozen tiny needles pressed into her skin.

"What is this?" she asked frantically, pulling away from the doctor.

"Just relax," he said with infuriating coolness. "It's a vital transponder. It will track your breathing and blood composition, and gather all sorts of useful information."

"Useful information for who?" Clarke asked, although she could already feel the shape of his answer in the growing mass of dread in her stomach.

"There've been some exciting developments," Dr. Lahiri said, sounding like a hollow imitation of Wells's father, Chancellor Jaha, making one of his Remembrance Day speeches. "You should be very proud. It's all because of your parents."

"My parents were executed for treason."

Dr. Lahiri gave her a disapproving look. A year ago, it would've made Clarke shrink with shame, but now she kept her gaze steady. "Don't ruin this, Clarke. You have a chance to do the right thing, to make up for your parents' appalling crime."

There was a dull crack as Clarke's fist made contact with the doctor's face, followed by a thud as his head slammed against the wall. Seconds later, the guard appeared and had Clarke's hands twisted behind her back. "Are you all right, sir?" he asked.

Dr. Lahiri sat up slowly, rubbing his jaw as he surveyed Clarke with a mixture of anger and amusement. "At least we know you'll be able to hold your own with the other delinquents when you get there."

"Get where?" Clarke grunted, trying to free herself from the guard's grip.

"We're clearing out the detention center today. A hundred lucky criminals are getting the chance to make history." The corners of his mouth twitched into a smirk. "You're going to Earth."

CHAPTER 2

Wells

The Chancellor had aged. Although it'd been less than six weeks since Wells had seen his father, he looked years older. There were new streaks of gray by his temples, and the lines around his eyes had deepened.

"Are you finally going to tell me why you did it?" the Chancellor asked with a tired sigh.

Wells shifted in his chair. He could feel the truth trying to claw its way out. He'd give almost anything to erase the disappointment on his father's face, but he couldn't risk it—not before he learned whether his reckless plan had actually worked.

Wells avoided his father's gaze by glancing around the

room, trying to memorize the relics he might be seeing for the last time: the eagle skeleton perched in a glass case, the few paintings that had survived the burning of the Louvre, and the photos of the beautiful dead cities whose names never ceased to send chills down Wells's spine.

"Was it a dare? Were you trying to show off for your friends?" The Chancellor spoke in the same low, steady tone he used during Council hearings, then raised an eyebrow to indicate that it was Wells's turn to talk.

"No, sir."

"Were you overcome by some temporary bout of insanity? Were you on drugs?" There was a faint note of hopefulness in his voice that, in another situation, Wells might've found amusing. But there was nothing humorous about the look in his father's eyes, a combination of weariness and confusion that Wells hadn't seen since his mother's funeral.

"No, sir."

Wells felt a fleeting urge to touch his father's arm, but something other than the handcuffs shackling his wrists kept him from reaching across the desk. Even as they had gathered around the release portal, saying their final, silent good-byes to Wells's mother, they'd never bridged the six inches of space between their shoulders. It was as if Wells and his father were two magnets, the charge of their grief repelling them apart.

"Was it some kind of political statement?" His father winced slightly, as though the thought hit him like a physical blow. "Did someone from Walden or Arcadia put you up to it?"

"No, sir," Wells said, biting back his indignation. His father had apparently spent the past six weeks trying to recast Wells as some kind of rebel, reprogramming his memories to help him understand why his son, formerly a star student and now the highest-ranked cadet, had committed the most public infraction in history. But even the truth would do little to mitigate his father's confusion. For the Chancellor, nothing could justify setting fire to the Eden Tree, the sapling that had been carried onto Phoenix right before the Exodus. Yet for Wells, it hadn't been a choice. Once he'd discovered that Clarke was one of the hundred being sent to Earth, he'd had to do something to join them. And as the Chancellor's son, only the most public of infractions would land him in Confinement.

Wells remembered moving through the crowd at the Remembrance Ceremony, feeling the weight of hundreds of eyes on him, his hand shaking as he removed the lighter from his pocket and produced a spark that glowed brightly in the gloom. For a moment, everyone had stared in silence as the flames wrapped around the tree. And even as the guards rushed forward in sudden chaos, no one had been able to miss whom they were dragging away.

"What the hell were you thinking?" the Chancellor asked, staring at him in disbelief. "You could've burned down the whole hall and killed everyone in it."

It would be better to lie. His father would have an easier time believing that Wells had been carrying out a dare. Or perhaps he could try to pretend he *had* been on drugs. Either of those scenarios would be more palatable to the Chancellor than the truth—that he'd risked everything for a girl.

The hospital door closed behind him but Wells's smile stayed frozen in place, as if the force it had taken to lift the corners of his mouth had permanently damaged the muscles in his face. Through the haze of drugs, his mother had probably thought his grin looked real, which was all that mattered. She'd held Wells's hand as the lies poured out of him, bitter but harmless. *Yes, Dad and I are doing fine.* She didn't need to know that they'd barely exchanged more than a few words in weeks. *When you're better, we'll finish* Decline and Fall of the Roman Empire. They both knew that she'd never make it to the final volume.

Wells slipped out of the hospital and started walking across B deck, which was mercifully empty. At this hour, most people were either at tutorials, work, or at the Exchange. He was supposed to be at a history lecture, normally his favorite subject. He'd always loved stories about ancient cities like Rome and New York, whose dazzling triumphs were matched only by the magnitude of their downfalls. But he couldn't spend two hours surrounded by the same tutorial mates who had filled his message queue with vague, uncomfortable condolences. The only person he could talk to about his mother was Glass, but she'd been strangely distant lately.

Wells wasn't sure how long he'd been standing outside the door before he realized he'd arrived at the library. He allowed the scanner to pass over his eyes, waited for the prompt, and then pressed his thumb against the pad. The door slid open just long enough for Wells to slip inside and then closed behind him with a huffy thud, as if it had done Wells a great favor by admitting him in the first place.

Wells exhaled as the stillness and shadows washed over him. The books that been evacuated onto Phoenix before the Cataclysm were kept in tall, oxygen-free cases that significantly slowed the deterioration process, which is why they had to be read in the library, and only then for a few hours at a time. The enormous room was hidden away from the circadian lights, in a state of perpetual twilight.

For as long as he could remember, Wells and his mother had spent Sunday evenings here, his mother reading aloud to him when he was little, then reading side by side as he got older. But as her illness progressed and her headaches grew worse, Wells had started reading to her. They'd just started volume two of *Decline and Fall of the Roman Empire* the evening before she was admitted to the hospital.

He wove through the narrow aisles toward the English Language section and then over to History, which was tucked into a dark back corner. The collection was smaller than it should've been. The first colonial government had arranged for digital text to be loaded onto Phoenix, but fewer than a hundred years later, a virus wiped out most of the digital archives, and the only books left were those in private collections—heirlooms handed down from the original colonists to their descendants. Over the past century, most of the relics had been donated to the library.

Wells crouched down until he was eye level with the *G*s. He pressed his thumb against the lock and the glass slid open with a hiss, breaking the vacuum seal. He reached inside to grab *Decline and Fall* but then paused. He wanted to read on so he'd be able to tell his mother about it, but that would be tantamount to arriving in her hospital room with her memorial plaque and asking for her input on the wording.

"You're not supposed to leave the case open," a voice said from behind him.

"Yes, thank you," Wells said, more sharply than he'd meant. He rose to his feet and turned to see a familiar-looking girl staring at him. It was the apprentice medic from the hospital. Wells felt a flash of anger at this blending of worlds. The library was where he went to forget about the sickening smell of antiseptic, the beep of the heart monitor that, far from a sign of life, seemed like a countdown to death.

The girl took a step back and cocked her head, her light hair falling to one side. "Oh. It's you." Wells braced for the first swoon of recognition, and the rapid eye movements that meant she was already messaging her friends on her cornea slip. But this girl's eyes focused directly on him, as if she were looking straight into his brain, peeling back the layers to reveal all the thoughts Wells had purposefully hidden.

"Didn't you want that book?" She nodded toward the shelf where *Decline and Fall* was stored.

Wells shook his head. "I'll read it another time."

She was silent for a moment. "I think you should take it now." Wells's jaw tightened, but when he said nothing, she continued. "I used to see you here with your mother. You should bring it to her."

"Just because my father's in charge of the Council doesn't mean I get to break a three-hundred-year rule," he said, allowing just a shade of condescension to darken his tone.

"The book will be fine for a few hours. They exaggerate the effects of the air."

Wells raised an eyebrow. "And do they exaggerate the power of the exit scanner?" There were scanners over most public doors on Phoenix that could be programmed to any specifications. In the library, it monitored the molecular composition of every person who exited, to make sure no one left with a book in their hands or hidden under their clothes.

A smile flickered across her face. "I figured that out a long time ago." She glanced over her shoulder down the shadowy aisle between the bookcases, reached into her pocket, and extracted a piece of gray cloth. "It keeps the scanner from recognizing the cellulose in the paper." She held it out to him. "Here. Take it."

Wells took a step back. The chances of this girl trying to embarrass him were far greater than the odds of her having a piece of magical fabric hidden in her pocket. "Why do you have this?"

She shrugged. "I like reading other places." When he didn't say anything, she smiled and extended her other hand. "Just give me the book. I'll sneak it out for you and bring it to the hospital."

Wells surprised himself by handing her the book. "What's your name?" he asked.

"So you know to whom you'll be eternally indebted?"

"So I know who to blame when I'm arrested."

The girl tucked the book under her arm and then extended her hand. "Clarke."

"Wells," he said, reaching forward to shake it. He smiled, and this time it didn't hurt.

"They barely managed to save the tree." The Chancellor stared at Wells, as if looking for a sign of remorse or glee—anything to help him understand why his son had tried to set fire to the only tree evacuated from their ravaged planet. "Some of the council members wanted to execute you on the spot, juvenile or not, you know. I was only able to spare your life by getting them to agree to send you to Earth."

Wells exhaled with relief. There were fewer than 150 kids in Confinement, so he had assumed they'd take all the older teens, but until this moment he hadn't been sure he would be sent on the mission.

His father's eyes widened with surprise and understanding as he stared at Wells. "That's what you wanted, isn't it?"

Wells nodded.

The Chancellor grimaced. "Had I known you were this desperate to see Earth, I could have easily arranged for you to join the second expedition. Once we determined it was safe."

"I didn't want to wait. I want to go with the first hundred."

The Chancellor narrowed his eyes slightly as he assessed Wells's impassive face. "Why? You of all people know the risks."

"With all due respect, you're the one who convinced the Council that nuclear winter was over. *You* said it was safe."

"Yes. Safe enough for the hundred convicted criminals who were going to die anyway," the Chancellor said, his voice a mix of condescension and disbelief. "I didn't mean safe for my *son*."

The anger Wells had been trying to smother flared up, reducing his guilt to ashes. He shook his hands so the cuffs rattled against the chair. "I guess I'm one of them now."

"Your mother wouldn't want you to do this, Wells. Just because she enjoyed dreaming about Earth doesn't mean she'd want you to put yourself in harm's way."

Wells leaned forward, ignoring the bite of the metal digging into his flesh. "She's not who I'm doing this for," he said, looking his father straight in the eye for the first time since he'd sat down. "Though I do think she'd be proud of me." It was partially true. She'd had a romantic streak and would have commended her son's desire to protect the girl he loved. But his stomach writhed at the thought of his mom knowing what he'd really done to save Clarke. The truth would make setting the Eden Tree on fire seem like a harmless prank.

His father stared at him. "Are you telling me this whole debacle is because of that girl?"

Wells nodded slowly. "It's my fault she's being sent down there like some lab rat. I'm going to make sure she has the best chance of making it out alive."

The Chancellor was silent for a moment. But when he spoke again, his voice was calm. "That won't be necessary." The Chancellor removed something from his desk drawer and placed it in front of Wells. It was a metal ring affixed with a chip about the size of Wells's thumb. "Every member of the expedition is currently being fitted with one of these bracelets," his father explained. "They'll send data back up to the ship so we can track your location and monitor your vitals. As soon as we have proof that the environment is hospitable, we'll begin recolonization." He forced a grim smile. "If everything goes according to plan, it won't be long before the rest of us come down to join you, and all this"—he gestured toward Wells's bound hands—"will be forgotten."

The door opened and a guard stepped over the threshold. "It's time, sir."

The Chancellor nodded, and the guard strode across the room to pull Wells to his feet.

"Good luck, son," Wells's father said, assuming his trademark brusqueness. "If anyone can make this mission a success, it's you."

He extended his arm to shake Wells's hand, but then let it fall to his side when he realized his mistake. His only child's arms were still shackled behind him.

CHAPTER 3

Bellamy

Of course the smug bastard was late. Bellamy tapped his foot impatiently, not caring about the echo that rang throughout the storeroom. No one came down here anymore; anything valuable had been snatched up years ago. Every surface was covered with junk—spare parts for machines whose functions had been long forgotten, paper currency, endless tangles of cords and wires, cracked screens and monitors.

Bellamy felt a hand on his shoulder and spun around, raising his fists to block his face as he ducked to the side.

"Relax, man," Colton's voice called out as he switched on his flashbeam, shining it right in Bellamy's eyes. He surveyed Bellamy with an amused expression on his long, narrow face.

"Why'd you want to meet down here?" He smirked. "Looking for caveman porn on broken computers? No judgments. If I were stuck with what passes for a girl down on Walden, I'd probably develop some sick habits myself."

Bellamy ignored the jab. Despite his former friend's new role as a guard, Colton didn't stand a chance with a girl no matter what ship he was on. "Just tell me what's going on, okay?" Bellamy said, doing his best to keep his tone light.

Colton leaned back against the wall and smiled. "Don't let the uniform fool you, brother. I haven't forgotten the first rule of business." He held out his hand. "Give it to me."

"You're the one who's confused, Colt. You know I always come through." He patted the pocket that held the chip loaded with stolen ration points. "Now tell me where she is."

The guard smirked, and Bellamy felt something in his chest tighten. He'd been bribing Colton for information about Octavia since her arrest, and the idiot always seemed to find twisted pleasure in delivering bad news.

"They're sending them off today." The words landed with a thud in Bellamy's chest. "They got one of the old dropships on G deck working." He held out his hand again. "Now come on. This mission's top secret and I'm risking my ass for you. I'm done messing around."

Bellamy's stomach twisted as a series of images flashed before his eyes: his little sister strapped into an ancient metal cage, hurtling through space at a thousand kilometers an hour. Her face turning purple as she struggled to breathe the toxic air. Her crumpled body lying just as still as—

Bellamy took a step forward. "I'm sorry, man."

Colton narrowed his eyes. "For what?"

"For this." Bellamy drew his arm back, then punched the guard right in the jaw. There was a loud crack, but he felt nothing but his racing heart as he watched Colton fall to the ground.

Thirty minutes later, Bellamy was trying to wrap his mind around the strange scene in front of him. His back was against the wall of a wide hallway that led onto a steep ramp. Convicts streamed by in gray jackets, led down the incline by a handful of guards. At the bottom was the dropship, a circular contraption outfitted with rows of harnessed seats that would take the poor, clueless kids to Earth.

The whole thing was completely sick, but he supposed it was better than the alternative. While you were supposed to get a retrial at your eighteenth birthday, in the last year or so, pretty much every juvenile defendant had been found guilty. Without this mission, they'd be counting down the days until their executions.

Bellamy's stomach clenched as his eyes settled on a second ramp, and for a moment, he worried that he'd missed

Octavia. But it didn't matter whether he saw her board. They'd be reunited soon enough.

Bellamy tugged on the sleeves of Colton's uniform. It barely fit, but so far none of the other guards seemed to notice. They were focused on the bottom of the ramp, where Chancellor Jaha was speaking to the passengers.

"You have been given an unprecedented opportunity to put the past behind you," the Chancellor was saying. "The mission on which you're about to embark is dangerous, but your bravery will be rewarded. If you succeed, your infractions will be forgiven, and you'll be able to start new lives on Earth."

Bellamy barely suppressed a snort. The Chancellor had some nerve to stand there, spewing whatever bullshit helped him sleep at night.

"We'll be monitoring your progress very closely, in order to keep you safe," the Chancellor continued as the next ten prisoners filed down the ramp, accompanied by a guard who gave the Chancellor a crisp salute before depositing his charges in the dropship and retreating back up to stand in the hallway. Bellamy searched the crowd for Luke, the only Waldenite he knew who hadn't turned into a total prick after becoming a guard. But there were fewer than a dozen guards on the launch deck; the Council had clearly decided that secrecy was more important than security.

He tried not to tap his feet with impatience as the line of prisoners proceeded down the ramp. If he was caught posing as a guard, the list of infractions would be endless: bribery, blackmail, identity theft, conspiracy, and whatever else the Council felt like adding to the mix. And since he was twenty, there'd be no Confinement for him; within twenty-four hours of his sentencing, he'd be dead.

Bellamy's chest tightened as a familiar red hair ribbon appeared at the end of the hallway, peeking out from a curtain of glossy black hair. Octavia.

For the past ten months, he'd been consumed with agonizing worries about what was happening to her in Confinement. Was she getting enough to eat? Was she finding ways to stay occupied? Stay sane? While Confinement would be brutal for anyone, Bellamy knew that it'd be infinitely worse for O.

Bellamy had pretty much raised his younger sister. Or at least he'd tried. After their mother's accident, he and Octavia had been placed under Council care. There was no precedent for what to do with siblings—with the strict population laws, a couple was never allowed to have more than one child, and sometimes, they weren't permitted to have any at all—and so no one in the Colony understood what it meant to have a brother or sister. Bellamy and Octavia lived in different group homes for a number of years, but Bellamy had always looked out for her, sneaking her extra rations whenever he "wandered" into one of the restricted storage facilities, confronting the tough-talking older girls who thought it'd be fun to pick on the chubby-cheeked orphan with the big blue eyes. Bellamy worried about her constantly. The kid was special, and he'd do anything to give her a chance at a different life. Anything to make up for what she'd had to endure.

As Octavia's guard led her onto the ramp, Bellamy suppressed a smile. While the other kids shuffled passively along as their escorts led them toward the dropship, it was clear Octavia was the one setting the pace. She moved deliberately, forcing her guard to shorten his stride as she sauntered down the ramp. She actually looked *better* than the last time he'd seen her. He supposed it made sense. She'd been sentenced to four years in Confinement, until a retrial on her eighteenth birthday that would very well lead to her execution. Now she was being given a second chance at a life. And Bellamy was going to make damn sure she got it.

He didn't care what he had to do. He was going to Earth with her.

The Chancellor's voice boomed over the clamor of footsteps and nervous whispers. He still held himself like a soldier, but his years on the Council had given him a politician's gloss. "No one in the Colony knows what you are about to do, but if you succeed, we will all owe you our lives. I know that you'll do your very best on behalf of yourselves, your families, everyone aboard this ship: the entire human race."

When Octavia's gaze settled on Bellamy, her mouth fell open in surprise. He could see her mind race to make sense of the situation. They both knew he'd never be selected as a guard, which meant that he had to be there as an impostor. But just as she began to mouth a warning, the Chancellor turned to address the prisoners who were still coming down the ramp. Octavia reluctantly turned her head, but Bellamy could see the tension in her shoulders.

His heart sped up as the Chancellor finished his remarks and motioned for the guards to finish loading the passengers. He had to wait for just the right moment. If he acted too soon, there'd be time to haul him out. If he waited too long, Octavia would be barreling through space toward a toxic planet, while he remained to face the consequences of disrupting the launch.

Finally, it was Octavia's turn. She turned over her shoulder and caught his eye, shaking her head slightly, a clear warning not to do anything stupid.

But Bellamy had been doing stupid things his whole life, and he had no intention of stopping now.

The Chancellor nodded at a woman in a black uniform. She turned to the control panel next to the dropship and started pressing a series of buttons. Large numbers began flashing on the screen.

The countdown had begun.

He had three minutes to get past the door, down the ramp, and onto the dropship, or else lose his sister forever.

As the final passengers loaded, the mood in the room shifted. The guards next to Bellamy relaxed and began talking quietly among themselves. Across the deck on the other ramp, someone let out an obnoxious snort.

2:48 . . . 2:47 . . . 2:46 . . .

Bellamy felt a tide of anger rise within him, momentarily overpowering his nerves. How could these assholes *laugh* when his sister and ninety-nine other kids were being sent on what might be a suicide mission?

2:32 . . . 2:31 . . . 2:30 . . .

The woman by the control panel smiled and whispered something to the Chancellor, but he scowled and turned away.

The real guards had begun trudging back up and were filing into the hallway. Either they thought they had better things to do than witness humanity's first attempt to return to Earth, or they thought the ancient dropship was going to explode and were headed to safety.

2:14 . . . 2:13 . . . 2:12 . . .

Bellamy took a deep breath. It was time.

He shoved his way through the crowd and slipped behind a stocky guard whose holster was strapped carelessly to his belt, leaving the handle of the gun exposed. Bellamy snatched the weapon and charged down the loading ramp.

Before anyone knew what was happening, Bellamy jabbed his elbow into the Chancellor's stomach and threw an arm around his neck, securing him in a headlock. The launch deck exploded with shouts and stamping feet, but before anyone had time to reach him, Bellamy placed the barrel of the gun against the Chancellor's temple. There was no way he'd actually shoot the bastard, but the guards needed to think he meant business.

1:12 . . . 1:11 . . . 1:10 . . .

"Everyone back up," Bellamy shouted, tightening his hold. The Chancellor groaned. There was a loud beep, and the flashing numbers changed from green to red. Less than a minute left. All he had to do was wait until the door to the dropship started to close, then push the Chancellor out of the way and duck inside. There wouldn't be any time to stop him.

"Let me onto the dropship, or I'll shoot."

The room fell silent, save for the sound of a dozen guns being cocked.

In thirty seconds, he'd either be heading to Earth with Octavia, or back to Walden in a body bag.

CHAPTER 4

Glass

Glass had just hooked her harness when a flurry of shouts rose up. The guards were closing in around two figures near the entrance to the dropship. It was difficult to see through the shifting mass of uniforms, but Glass caught a flash of suit sleeve, a glimpse of gray hair, and the glint of metal. Then half the guards knelt down and raised their guns to their shoulders, giving Glass an unobstructed view: The Chancellor was being held hostage.

"Everyone back up," the captor yelled, his voice shaking. He wore a uniform, but he clearly wasn't a guard. His hair was far longer than regulation length, his jacket fit badly, and his awkward grip on the gun showed that he'd never been trained to use one.

No one moved. "I said back *up*."

The numbness that had set in during the long walk from her cell to the launch deck melted away like an icy comet passing the sun, leaving a faint trail of hope in its wake. She didn't belong here. She couldn't pretend they were about to head off on some historic adventure. The moment the dropship detached from the ship, Glass's heart would start to break. *This is my chance*, she thought suddenly, excitement and terror shooting through her.

Glass unhooked her harness and sprang to her feet. A few other prisoners noticed, but most were caught up watching the drama unfolding atop the ramp. She dashed to the far side of the dropship, where another ramp led back up to the loading deck.

"I'm going with them," the boy shouted as he took a step backward toward the door, dragging the Chancellor with him. "I'm going with my sister."

A stunned silence fell over the launch deck. *Sister.* The word echoed in Glass's head but before she had time to process its significance, a familiar voice pulled her from her thoughts.

"Let him go."

Glass glanced at the back of the dropship and froze, momentarily stunned by the sight of her best friend's face. Of course, she'd heard the ridiculous rumors that Wells had been Confined, but hadn't given them a second thought. What was he doing here? As she stared at Wells's gray eyes, which were trained intently on his father, the answer came to her: He must have tried to follow Clarke. Wells would do anything to protect the people he cared about, most of all Clarke.

And then there was a deafening crack—*a gunshot?*—and something inside of her snapped. Without stopping to think, to breathe, she dashed through the door and began sprinting up the ramp. Fighting the urge to look back over her shoulder, Glass kept her head down and ran as fast as she'd ever run in her life.

She'd chosen just the right moment. For a few seconds, the guards stood still, as if the reverberation from the gunshot had locked their joints in place.

Then they caught sight of her.

"Prisoner on the run!" one of them shouted, and the others quickly turned in her direction. The flash of movement activated the instincts drilled into their brains during training. It didn't matter that she was a seventeen-year-old girl. They'd been programmed to look past the flowing blond hair and wide blue eyes that had always made people want to protect Glass. All they saw was an escaped convict.

Glass threw herself through the door, ignoring the angry shouts that rose up in her wake. She hurtled down the passageway that led back to Phoenix, her chest heaving, her breath coming in ragged gasps. "You! Stop right there!" a guard shouted, his footsteps echoing behind her, but she didn't pause. If she ran fast enough, and if the luck that had been eluding her all her life made a final, last-minute appearance, maybe she could see Luke one last time. And maybe, just maybe, she could get him to forgive her.

Gasping, Glass staggered down a passageway bordered by unmarked doors. Her right knee buckled, and she grabbed on to the wall to catch herself. The corridor was beginning to grow blurry. She turned her head and could just make out the shape of an air vent. Glass hooked her fingers under one of the slats and pulled. Nothing happened. With a groan, she pulled again and felt the metal grate give. She yanked it open, revealing a dark, narrow tunnel full of ancient-looking pipes.

Glass pulled herself onto the small ledge, then scooted along on her stomach until there was room to bring her knees up to her chest. The metal felt cool against her burning skin. With her last milligram of strength, she crept deeper into the tunnel and closed the vent behind her. She strained her ears for signs of pursuit, but there was no more shouting, no more footsteps, only the desperate thud of her heart.

Glass blinked in the near darkness, taking stock of where she was. The cramped space extended straight in both directions, thick with dust. It had to be one of the original air shafts, from before the Colony built their new air circulation and filtration systems. Glass had no idea where it would lead, but she was out of options. She started to crawl forward.

After what felt like hours, her knees numb and her hands burning, she reached a fork in the tunnel. If her sense of direction was right, then the tunnel on the left would lead to Phoenix, and the other would run parallel to the skybridge—onto Walden, and toward Luke.

Luke, the boy she loved, who she'd been forced to abandon all those months ago. Who she'd spent every night in Confinement thinking about, so desperate for his touch that she'd almost felt the pressure of his arms around her.

She took a deep breath and turned to the right, not knowing if she was headed toward freedom or certain death.

Ten minutes later, Glass slid quietly out of the vent and lowered herself to the floor. She took a step forward and coughed as a plume of dust swirled around her face, sticking to her sweaty skin. She was in some kind of storage space.

As her eyes adjusted to the darkness, shapes began to materialize on the wall—writing, Glass realized. She took another few steps forward, and her eyes widened. There were *messages* carved into the walls.

Rest in peace
In memoriam
From the stars to the heavens

She was on the quarantine deck, the oldest section of Walden. As nuclear and biological war threatened to destroy Earth, space had been the only option for those lucky enough to survive the first stages of the Cataclysm. But some infected survivors fought their way onto the transport pods—only to find themselves barred from Phoenix, left to die on Walden. Now, whenever there was the slightest threat of illness, anyone infected was quarantined, kept far from the rest of the Colony's vulnerable population—the last of the human race.

Glass shivered as she moved quickly toward the door, praying that it hadn't rusted shut. To her relief, she was able to wrench it open and began dashing down the corridor. She peeled off her sweat-soaked jacket; in her white T-shirt and prison-issue pants, she could pass for a worker, someone on sanitation duty, perhaps. She glanced down nervously at the bracelet on her wrist. She wasn't sure whether it would work on the ship, or if it was only meant to transmit data from Earth. Either way, she needed to figure out a way to get it off as soon as possible. Even if she avoided the passages with retina scanners, every guard in the Colony would be on the lookout for her.

Her only hope was that they'd be expecting her to run back to Phoenix. They'd never guess that she would come here. She climbed up the main Walden stairwell until she reached the entrance to Luke's residential unit. She turned into his hallway and slowed down, wiping her sweaty hands on her pants, suddenly more nervous than she'd been on the dropship.

She couldn't imagine what he'd say, the look he'd give her when he saw her on his doorstep after her disappearance more than nine months earlier.

But maybe he wouldn't have to say anything. Perhaps, as soon as he saw her, as soon as the words began to pour out of her mouth, he would silence her with a kiss, relying on his lips to tell her that everything was okay. That she was forgiven.

Glass glanced over her shoulder and then slipped out the door. She didn't think anyone had seen her, but she had to be careful. It was incredibly rude to leave a Partnering Ceremony before the final blessing, but Glass didn't think she'd be able to spend another minute sitting next to Cassius, with his dirty mind and even fouler breath. His wandering hands reminded Glass of Carter, Luke's two-faced roommate whose creepiness only slithered out of the darkness when Luke was out on guard duty.

Glass climbed the stairs toward the observation deck, taking care to lift the hem of her gown with each step. It'd been foolish to waste so many ration points collecting the materials for the dress, a piece of tarp that she'd painstakingly sewn into a silver slip. It felt utterly worthless without Luke there to see her in it.

She hated spending the evening with other boys, but her

mother refused to let Glass be seen at a social event without a date, and as far as she knew, her daughter was single. She couldn't understand why Glass hadn't "snatched up" Wells. No matter how many times Glass explained that she didn't have those types of feelings for him, her mother sighed and muttered about not letting some badly dressed scientist girl steal him away. But Glass was happy that Wells had fallen for the beautiful if slightly over-serious Clarke Griffin. She only wished she could tell her mother the truth: that she was in love with a handsome, brilliant boy who could never escort her to a concert or a Partnering Ceremony.

"May I have this dance?"

Glass gasped and spun around. As her eyes locked with a familiar pair of brown ones, her face broke into a wide smile. "What are you doing here?" she whispered, looking around to make sure they were alone.

"I couldn't let those Phoenix boys have you all to themselves," Luke said, taking a step back to admire her dress. "Not when you look like this."

"Do you know how much trouble you'll get in if they catch you?"

"Let them try to keep up." He wrapped his arms around Glass's waist, and as the music from downstairs swelled, he spun her through the air.

"Put me down!" Glass half whispered, half laughed as she playfully hit his shoulder.

"Is that how young ladies are taught to address gentlemen admirers?" he asked, using a terrible, fake Phoenix accent.

"Come on," she said, giggling as she grabbed his hand. "You really shouldn't be here."

Luke stopped and pulled her to him. "Wherever you are is where I'm supposed to be."

"It's too risky," she said softly, bringing her face up to his.

He grinned. "Then we better make sure it's worth our while." He placed his hand behind her head and brought his lips to hers.

Glass raised her hand to knock a second time when the door opened. Her heart skipped a beat.

There he was, his sandy hair and deep-brown eyes exactly as she remembered them, exactly as they'd appeared in her dreams every night in Confinement. His eyes widened in surprise.

"Luke," she breathed, all the emotion of the past nine months threatening to break through. She was desperate to tell him what had happened, why she'd broken up with him and then disappeared. That she'd spent every minute of the nightmarish last six months thinking of him. That she never stopped loving him. "Luke," she said again, a tear sliding down her cheek. After the countless times she'd broken down in her cell, whispering his name in between sobs, it felt surreal to say it to him.

But before she had a chance to grab hold of any of the words flitting through her mind, another figure appeared in the door, a girl with wavy red hair.

"Glass?"

Glass tried to smile at Camille, Luke's childhood friend, a girl who'd been as close to him as Glass was to Wells. And now she was here . . . in Luke's flat. *Of course*, Glass thought with a strained kind of bitterness. She'd always wondered if there was more to their relationship than Luke had admitted.

"Would you like to come in?" Camille asked with exaggerated politeness. She wrapped her hand around Luke's, but Glass felt as if Camille's fingers had plunged into her heart instead. While Glass had spent months in Confinement pining for Luke until his absence felt like a physical ache, he'd moved on to someone else.

"No . . . no, that's okay," Glass said, her voice hoarse. Even if she managed to find the words, it would be impossible to tell Luke the truth now. Seeing them together made it all the more ridiculous that she'd come so far—risked so much—to see a boy who had already moved on.

"I just came to say hello."

"You came to say *hello*?" Luke repeated. "After almost a year of ignoring my messages, you thought you'd just *drop by*?" He wasn't even trying to hide his anger, and Camille dropped his hand. Her smile hardened into a grimace.

"I know. I'm—I'm sorry. I'll leave you two alone."

"What's really going on?" Luke asked, exchanging a look with Camille that made Glass feel both desperately foolish and terribly alone.

"Nothing," Glass said quickly, trying and failing to keep her voice from trembling. "I'll talk to you . . . I'll see you . . ." She cut herself off with a weak smile and took a deep breath, ignoring her body's furious plea to stay close to him.

But just as she turned, she saw a flash of a guard uniform out of the corner of her vision. She inhaled sharply and turned her face as the guard passed.

Luke pressed his lips together as he looked at something just beyond Glass's head. He was reading a message on his cornea slip, Glass realized. And from the way his jaw was tightening, she got the sickening sense it was about her.

His eyes widened with understanding, and then horror. "Glass," he said hoarsely. "You were Confined." It wasn't a question. Glass nodded.

He shifted his gaze back to Glass for a moment, then sighed and reached out to place his hand on her back. She could feel the pressure of his fingers through the fabric of her thin T-shirt, and despite her anxiety, her skin thrilled at his touch. "Come on," he said, pulling her toward him. Camille stepped to the side, looking annoyed, as Glass stumbled into the flat. Luke quickly shut the door behind them.

The small living area was dark—Luke and Camille had been inside with the lights off. Glass tried to push the implications of that fact out of her head as she watched Camille sit down in the armchair that Luke's great-grandmother had found at the Exchange. Glass shifted uncomfortably, unsure whether to take a seat. Being Luke's ex-girlfriend somehow felt odder than being an escaped convict. She'd had six months in Confinement to come to terms with her criminal record, but Glass had never imagined what it would be like to stand in this flat feeling like a stranger.

"How did you escape?" he asked.

Glass paused. She had spent all her time in Confinement imagining what she would say to Luke if she ever got the chance to see him again. And now she had finally made her way back to him, and all the speeches she'd practiced felt flimsy and selfish. He was doing fine; she could see that now. Why should she tell him the truth, except to win him back and make herself feel less alone? And so, in a shaky voice, Glass quickly told him about the hundred and their secret mission, the hostage situation, and the chase.

"But I still don't understand." Luke shot a glance over his shoulder at Camille, who had given up pretending that she wasn't paying attention. "Why were you Confined in the first place?"

Glass looked away, unable to meet his eyes as her brain

raced for an explanation. She couldn't tell him, not now, not when he'd moved on. Not when it was so obvious he didn't feel the same way for her.

"I can't talk about it," she said quietly. "You wouldn't underst—"

"It's fine." Luke cut her off sharply. "You've made it clear that there are lots of things I can't understand."

For the briefest of moments, Glass wished she'd stayed on the dropship with Clarke and Wells. Although she was standing next to the boy she loved, she couldn't imagine feeling any lonelier on the abandoned Earth than she did right now.

CHAPTER 5

Clarke

For the first ten minutes, the prisoners were too rattled by the shooting to notice that they were floating through space, the only humans to leave the Colony in almost three hundred years. The rogue guard had gotten what he wanted. He'd pushed the Chancellor's limp body forward just as the dropship door was closing, and then stumbled into a seat. But from the shocked expression on his pale face, Clarke gathered that gunfire had never been part of the plan.

Yet for Clarke, watching the Chancellor get shot was less alarming than what she'd seen in the moments beforehand.

Wells was on the dropship.

When he'd first appeared in the door, she'd been sure it

was a hallucination. The chance of her losing her mind in solitary was infinitely higher than the chance of the Chancellor's son ending up in Confinement. She'd been shocked enough when, a month after her own sentencing, Wells's best friend, Glass, had appeared in the cell down the row from her. And now Wells, too? It seemed impossible, but there was no denying it. She'd watched him jump to his feet during the standoff, then crumple back into his seat as the real guard's gun went off and the imposter burst through the door, covered in blood. For a moment, an old instinct gave her the urge to run over and comfort Wells. But something much heavier than her harness kept her feet rooted to the floor. Because of him, she'd watched her parents be dragged off to the execution chamber. Whatever pain he was feeling was no less than he deserved.

"*Clarke.*"

She glanced to the side and saw Thalia grinning at her from a few rows ahead. Her old cell mate twisted in her seat, the only person in the dropship not staring at the guard. Despite the grim circumstances, Clarke couldn't help smiling back. Thalia had that effect. In the days after Clarke's arrest and her parents' execution, when her grief felt so heavy it was difficult to breathe, Thalia had actually made Clarke laugh with her impression of the cocky guard whose shuffle turned into a strut whenever he thought the girls were looking at him.

"Is that him?" Thalia mouthed now, tilting her head toward Wells. Thalia was the only person who knew everything—not just about Clarke's parents, but the unspeakable thing that Clarke had done.

Clarke shook her head to signal that now wasn't the time to talk about it. Thalia motioned again. Clarke started to tell her to knock it off when the main thrusters roared to life, shaking the words from her lips.

It had really happened. For the first time in centuries, humans had left the Colony. She glanced at the other passengers and saw that they had all gone quiet as well, a spontaneous moment of silence for the world they were leaving behind.

But the solemnity didn't last long. For the next twenty minutes, the dropship was filled with the nervous, overexcited chatter of a hundred people who, until a few hours ago, had never even thought about going to Earth. Thalia tried to shout something to Clarke, but her words were lost in the din.

The only conversation Clarke could follow was that of the two girls in front of her, who were arguing over the likelihood of the air on Earth being breathable. "I'd rather drop dead right away than spend days being slowly poisoned," one said grimly.

Clarke sort of agreed, but she kept her mouth shut. There was no point in speculating. The trip to Earth would be short—in just a few more minutes, they'd know their fate.

Clarke looked out the windows, which were now filling with hazy gray clouds. The dropship jerked suddenly, and the buzz of conversation gave way to a flurry of gasps.

"It's okay," Wells shouted, speaking for the first time since the doors closed. "There's supposed to be turbulence when we enter Earth's atmosphere." But his words were overpowered by the shrieks filling the cabin.

The shaking increased, followed by a strange hum. Clarke's harness dug into her stomach as her body lurched from side to side, then up and down, then side to side again. She gagged as a rancid odor filled her nose, and she realized that the girl in front of her had vomited. Clarke squeezed her eyes shut and tried to stay calm. Everything was fine. It'd all be over in a minute.

The hum became a piercing wail, punctuated by a sickening crush. Clarke opened her eyes and saw that the windows had cracked and were no longer full of gray.

They were full of flames.

Bits of white-hot metal began raining down on them. Clarke raised her arms to protect her head, but she could still feel the debris scorching her neck.

The dropship shook even harder, and with a roar, part of the ceiling tore off. There was a deafening crash followed by a thud that sent ripples of pain through every bone in her body.

As suddenly as it began, it was all over.

The cabin was dark and silent. Smoke billowed out of a hole where the control panel had been, and the air grew thick with the smell of melting metal, sweat, and blood.

Clarke winced as she wiggled her fingers and toes. It hurt, but nothing seemed to be broken. She unhooked her harness and rose shakily to her feet, holding on to the scorched seat for balance.

Most people were still strapped in, but a few were slumped over the sides or sprawled on the floor. Clarke squinted as she scanned the rows for Thalia, her heart speeding up each time her eyes landed on another empty seat. A terrifying realization cut through the confusion in Clarke's mind. Some of the passengers had been thrown outside during the crash.

Clarke limped forward, gritting her teeth at the pain that shot up her leg. She reached the door and pulled as hard as she could. She took a deep breath and slipped through the opening.

For a moment, she was aware of only colors, not shapes. Stripes of blue, green, and brown so vibrant her brain couldn't process them. A gust of wind passed over her, making her skin tingle and flooding her nose with scents Clarke couldn't begin to identify. At first, all she could see were the trees. There were hundreds of them, as if every tree on the planet had come to welcome them back to Earth. Their enormous branches were lifted in celebration toward the sky, which was a joyful blue. The ground stretched out in all directions—ten times farther than the longest deck on the ship. The amount of space was almost inconceivable, and Clarke suddenly felt light-headed, as if she were about to float away.

She became vaguely aware of voices behind her and turned to see a few of the others emerge from the dropship. “It’s beautiful,” a dark-skinned girl whispered as she reached down to run her trembling hand along the shiny green blades of grass.

A short, stocky boy took a few shaky steps forward. The gravitational pull on the Colony was meant to mimic Earth’s, but faced with the real thing it was clear they hadn’t gotten it quite right. “Everything’s fine,” the boy said, his voice a mixture of relief and confusion. “We could’ve come back ages ago.”

“You don’t know that,” the girl replied. “Just because we can breathe now, doesn’t mean the air isn’t toxic.” She twisted around to face him and held her wrist up, gesturing with her bracelet. “The Council didn’t give us these as jewelry. They want to see what happens to us.”

A smaller girl hovering next to the dropship whimpered as she pulled her jacket up over her mouth.

“You can breathe normally,” Clarke told her, looking around to see if Thalia had emerged yet. She wished she had something more reassuring to say, but there was no way to tell how much radiation was still in the atmosphere. All they could do was wait and hope.

"We'll be back soon," her father said as he slipped his long arms into a suit jacket Clarke had never seen before. He walked over to the couch where she was curled up with her tablet and ruffled her hair. "Don't stay out too late. They've been strict about curfew lately. Some trouble on Walden, I think."

"I'm not going anywhere," Clarke said, gesturing toward her bare feet and the surgical pants she wore to sleep. For the most famous scientist in the Colony, her father's deductive reasoning left something to be desired. Although he spent so much time wrapped up in his research, it was unlikely he'd even know that scrubs weren't currently considered high fashion among sixteen-year-old girls.

"Either way, it'd be best if you stayed out of the lab," he said with calculated carelessness, as if the thought had only just crossed his mind. In fact, he'd said this about five times a day since they'd moved into their new flat. The Council had approved their request for a customized private laboratory, as her parents' new project required them to monitor experiments throughout the night.

"I promise," Clarke told them with exaggerated patience.

"It's just that it's dangerous to get near the radioactive materials," her mother called out from where she stood in front of the mirror, fixing her hair. "Especially without the proper equipment."

Clarke repeated her promise until they left and she was finally able to return to her tablet, though she couldn't help wondering idly what Glass and her friends would say if they knew that Clarke was spending Friday night working on an essay. Clarke was normally indifferent toward her Earth Literatures tutorial, but this assignment had piqued her interest. Instead of another predictable paper on the changing view of nature in pre-Cataclysmic poetry, their tutor had asked them to compare and contrast the vampire crazes in the nineteenth and twenty-first centuries.

Yet while the reading was interesting, she must have dozed off at some point, because when she sat up, the circadian lights had dimmed and the living space was a jumble of unfamiliar shadows. She stood up and was about to head to her bedroom when a strange sound pierced the silence. Clarke froze. It almost sounded like screaming. She forced herself to take a deep breath. She should have known better than to read about vampires before bed.

Clarke turned around and started walking down the hallway, but then another sound rang out—a shriek that sent shivers down her spine.

Stop it, Clarke scolded herself. She'd never make it as a doctor if she let her mind play tricks on her. She was just unsettled by the unfamiliar darkness in the new flat. In the morning, everything would be back to normal. Clarke waved her palm across the sensor on her bedroom door and was about to step inside when she heard it again—an anguished moan.

Her heart thumping, Clarke spun around and walked down

the long hallway that led to the lab. Instead of a retinal scanner, there was a keypad. Clarke brushed her fingers over the panel, briefly wondering if she'd be able to guess the password, then crouched down and pressed her ear to the door.

The door vibrated as another sound buzzed through Clarke's ear. Her breath caught in her throat. *That's impossible.* But when the sound came again, it was even clearer.

It wasn't just a scream of anguish. It was a word.

"*Please.*"

Clarke's fingers flew over the keypad as she entered the first thing that came to her head: *Pangea*. It was the code her mother used for her protected files. The screen beeped and an error message appeared. Next she entered *Elysium*, the name of the mythical underground city where, according to bedtime stories parents told their children, humans took refuge after the Cataclysm. Another error. Clarke tore through her memory, searching for words she'd filed away. Her fingers hovered above the keypad. *Lucy*. The name of the oldest hominid remains Earthborn archaeologists ever discovered. There was a series of low beeps, and the door slid open.

The lab was much bigger than she'd imagined, larger than their entire flat, and filled with rows of narrow beds like in the hospital.

Clarke's eyes widened as they darted from one bed to another. Each contained a *child*. Most of the kids were lying there asleep, hooked up to various vital monitors and IV stands, though a few were propped up by pillows, fiddling with tablets in their laps. One little girl, hardly older than a toddler, sat on the floor next to her bed, playing with a ratty stuffed bear as clear liquid dripped from an IV bag into her arm.

Clarke's brain raced for an explanation. These had to be sick children who required round-the-clock care. Maybe they were suffering from some rare disease that only her mother knew how to cure, or perhaps her father was close to inventing a new treatment and needed twenty-four-hour access. They must've known that Clarke would be curious, but since the illness was probably contagious, they'd lied to Clarke to keep her safe.

The same cry that Clarke had heard from the flat came again, this time much louder. She followed it to a bed on the other side of the lab.

A girl her own age—one of the oldest in the room, Clarke realized—was lying on her back, dark-blond hair fanned out on the pillow around her heart-shaped face. For a moment, she just stared at Clarke.

"Please," she said. Her voice trembled. "Help me."

Clarke glanced at the label on the girl's vital monitor. SUBJECT 121. "What's your name?" she asked.

"Lilly."

Clarke stood there awkwardly, but when Lilly scooted back on her pillows, Clarke lowered herself to sit on the bed next to her. She'd just started her medical training and hadn't interacted with patients yet, but she knew one of the most important parts of being a doctor was bedside manner. "I'm sure you'll get to go home soon," she offered. "Once you're feeling better."

The girl pulled her knees to her chest and buried her head, saying something too muffled for Clarke to make out.

"What was that?" she asked. She glanced over her shoulder, wondering why there wasn't a nurse or a medical apprentice covering for her parents. If something happened to one of the kids, there'd be no one to help them.

The girl raised her head but looked away from Clarke. She chewed her lip as the tears in her eyes receded, leaving a haunting emptiness in their wake.

When she finally spoke, it was in a whisper. "No one ever gets better."

Clarke suppressed a shudder. Diseases were rare on the ship; there hadn't been any epidemics since the last outbreak they'd quarantined on Walden. Clarke looked around the lab for something to indicate what her parents were treating, and her eyes settled on an enormous screen on the far wall. Data flashed across it, forming a large graph. *Subject 32. Age 7. Day 189. 3.4 Gy. Red count. White count. Respiration. Subject 33. Age 11. Day 298. 6 Gy. Red count. White count. Respiration.*

At first Clarke thought nothing of the data. It made perfect sense for her parents to monitor the vitals of the sick children in their care. Except that *Gy* had nothing to do with vital signs.

A *Gray* was a measure of radiation, a fact she well knew as her parents had been investigating the effects of radiation exposure for years, part of the ongoing task to determine when it'd be safe for humans to return to Earth.

Clarke's gaze settled on Lilly's pale face as a chilling realization slithered out of a dark place in the back of Clarke's mind. She tried to force it back, but it coiled around her denial, suffocating all thoughts except a truth so horrifying, she almost gagged.

Her parents' research was no longer limited to cell cultures. They'd moved onto human trials.

Her mother and father weren't curing these children. They were killing them.

They'd landed in some kind of clearing, an L-shaped space surrounded by trees.

There weren't many serious injuries, but there were enough to keep Clarke busy. For nearly an hour, she used torn jacket sleeves and pant legs as makeshift tourniquets, and ordered the few people with broken bones to lie still until she found a way to fashion splints. Their supplies were scattered across the grass, but although she'd sent multiple people to search for the medicine chest, it hadn't been recovered.

The battered dropship was at the short end of the clearing, and for the first fifteen minutes, the passengers had clustered around the smoldering wreckage, too scared and stunned to move more than a few shaky steps. But now they'd started milling around. Clarke hadn't spotted Thalia, or Wells, either, although she wasn't sure whether that made her more anxious or relieved. Maybe he was off with Glass. Clarke hadn't seen her on the dropship, but she had to be here somewhere.

"How does that feel?" Clarke asked, returning her attention to wrapping the swollen ankle of a pretty, wide-eyed girl with a frayed red ribbon in her dark hair.

"Better," she said, wiping her nose with her hand, unintentionally smearing blood from the cut on her face. Clarke had to find real bandages and antiseptic. They were all being exposed to germs their bodies had never encountered, and the risk of infection was high.

"I'll be right back." Clarke flashed her a quick smile and rose to her feet. If the medicine chest wasn't in the clearing, that meant it was probably still in the dropship. She hurried back to the still-smoking wreck, walking around the perimeter as she searched for the safest way to get back inside. Clarke reached the back of the ship, which was just a few meters from the tree line. She shivered. The trees grew so closely together on this side of the clearing, their leaves blocked most of the light, casting intricate shadows on the ground that scattered when the wind blew.

Her eyes narrowed as they focused on something that didn't move. It wasn't a shadow.

A girl was lying on the ground, nestled against the roots of a tree. She must have been thrown out of the back of the dropship during the landing. Clarke lurched forward, and felt a sob form in her throat as she recognized the girl's short, curly hair and the smattering of freckles on the bridge of her nose. *Thalia.*

Clarke hurried over and knelt beside her. Blood was gushing from a wound on the side of her ribs, staining the grass beneath her dark red, as if the earth itself were bleeding. Thalia was breathing, but her gasps were labored and shallow. "It's going to be okay," Clarke whispered, grabbing on to her friend's limp hand as the wind rustled above them. "I swear, Thalia, it's all going to be okay." It sounded more like a prayer than a reassurance, although she wasn't sure who she was praying to. Humans had abandoned Earth during its darkest hour. It wouldn't care how many died trying to return.

CHAPTER 6

Wells

Wells shivered in the late afternoon chill. In the few hours since they'd landed, the air had grown colder. He moved closer to the bonfire, ignoring the snide glances of the Arcadian boys on either side of him. Every night he'd spent in Confinement, he'd fallen asleep dreaming about arriving on Earth with Clarke. But instead of holding her hand while they gazed at the planet in wonder, he'd spent the day sorting through burned supplies and trying to forget the expression that crossed Clarke's face when she spotted him. He hadn't expected her to throw her arms around him, but nothing could've prepared him for the look of pure loathing in her eyes.

"Think your father kicked the bucket already?" a Walden boy a few years younger than Wells asked as the kids around him snickered.

Wells's chest tightened, but he forced himself to stay calm. He could take one or two of the little punks without breaking a sweat. He'd been the undisputed champion of the hand-to-hand combat course during officer training. But there was only one of him and ninety-five of them—ninety-six if you counted Clarke, who was arguably less of a Wells fan than anyone on the planet at the moment.

As they'd loaded onto the dropship, he'd been dismayed not to see Glass there. To the shock of everyone on Phoenix, Glass had been Confined not long after Clarke, though no matter how many times he pressed his father, Wells had never discovered what she'd done. He wished he knew why she hadn't been selected for the mission. Although he tried to convince himself that she could've been pardoned, it was far more likely that she was still in Confinement, counting down the days until her fast-approaching eighteenth birthday. The thought made his stomach twist.

"I wonder if Chancellor Junior thinks he gets first dibs on all the food?" asked an Arcadian boy whose pockets were bulging with nutrition packs he'd collected during the mad scramble after the crash. From what Wells could see, it looked like they'd been sent down with less than a month's worth of food, which would disappear quickly if people kept pocketing everything they found. But that couldn't be possible—there had to be more in a container somewhere. They would come across it once they finished sorting through the wreckage.

"Or if he expects us to make his bed for him." A petite girl with a scar on her forehead smirked.

Wells ignored them, looking up at the endless stretch of deep-blue sky. It really was astonishing. Even though he'd seen photographs, he had never imagined the color would be quite so vivid. It was strange to think that a blanket of blue—made of nothing more substantial than nitrogen crystals and refracted light—separated him from the sea of stars and the only world he'd ever known. He felt his chest ache for the three kids who hadn't survived long enough to see these sights. Their bodies lay on the other side of the dropship.

"Beds?" a boy said with a snort. "You tell me where we'll find a *bed* in this place."

"So where the hell are we supposed to sleep?" the girl with the scar asked, looking around the clearing as if she expected sleeping quarters to magically appear.

Wells cleared his throat. "Our supplies included tents. We just need to finish sorting through the containers and collect all the pieces. In the meantime, we should send a few scouts to look for water so we know where to set up camp."

The girl made a show of glancing from side to side. "This looks good to me," she said, prompting more snickers.

Wells tried to force himself to stay calm. "The thing is, if we're near a stream or a lake, it'll be easier to—"

"Oh, good." A low voice cut him off. "I'm just in time for the lecture." Wells glanced to the side and saw a boy named Graham walking toward them. Aside from Wells and Clarke, he was the only other person from Phoenix, yet Graham appeared to know most of the Waldenites and Arcadians by name, and they all treated him with a surprising amount of respect. Wells didn't want to imagine what he'd had to do to earn it.

"I wasn't *lecturing* anyone. I'm just trying to keep us alive."

Graham raised an eyebrow. "That's interesting, considering that your father keeps sentencing our friends to death. But don't worry, I know you're on our side." He grinned at Wells. "Isn't that right?"

Wells glanced at him warily, then gave a curt nod. "Of course."

"So," Graham went on, his friendly tone at odds with the hostile glint in his eyes, "what was your infraction?"

"That's not a very polite question, is it?" Wells tried for what he hoped was a cryptic smile.

"I'm so sorry." Graham's face took on an expression of mock horror. "You have to forgive me. You see, when you've spent the past 847 days of your life locked in the bottom of the ship, you tend to forget what's considered polite conversation on Phoenix."

"847 days?" Wells repeated. "I guess we can assume you weren't Confined for miscounting the herbs you probably stole from the storehouse."

"No," Graham said, taking a step toward Wells. "I wasn't." The crowd fell silent, and Wells could see a few people shifting uncomfortably while others leaned in eagerly. "I was Confined for murder."

Their eyes locked. Wells kept his expression carefully devoid of emotion, refusing to give Graham the satisfaction of seeing the shock on his face. "Oh?" he said carelessly. "Who'd you kill?"

Graham smiled coldly. "If you'd spent any time with the rest of us, you'd know that *that* isn't considered a very polite question." There was a moment of tense silence before Graham switched gears. "But I already know what you did anyway. When the Chancellor's son gets locked up, word travels fast. Figures you wouldn't fess up. But now that we're having a nice little chat, maybe you can tell us exactly what we're doing down here. Maybe you can explain why so many of our *friends* keep getting executed after their retrials." Graham was still smiling, but his tone had grown low and dangerous. "And why now? What made *your father* decide to send us down all of a sudden?"

His father. All day, absorbed in the newness of being on Earth, Wells had almost been able to convince himself that the scene on the launch deck—the sharp sound of the gunshot, the blood blooming like a dark flower on his father's chest—had been a terrifying dream.

"Of course he's not going to tell us," Graham scoffed. "Are you, soldier?" he added with a mock salute.

The Arcadians and Waldenites who'd been watching Graham turned eagerly to Wells, the intensity of their gazes making his skin prickle. Of course, he knew what was going on. Why so many kids were being executed on their eighteenth birthdays for crimes that might have been pardoned in the past. Why the mission had been hastily thrown together and put in motion before there'd been time to plan properly.

He knew better than anyone, because it was all his fault.

"When will we get to go home?" asked a boy who didn't look much older than twelve. Wells felt an unexpected pang of pity for the brokenhearted mother who was still somewhere on the ship. She had no idea that her son had been hurtled through space onto a planet the human race had left for dead.

"We *are* home," Wells said, forcing as much sincerity as he could into the words.

If he said it enough times, perhaps he'd start to believe it himself.

He'd almost skipped the concert that year. It had always been his favorite event, the one evening musical relics were taken out of their oxygen-free preservation chambers. Watching the performers, who spent most of their time practicing on simulators, coax notes and chords out of the relics was like witnessing a resurrection. Carved and welded by long-dead hands, the only instruments left in the universe produced the same soaring melodies that had once echoed through the concert halls of ruined civilizations. Once a year, Eden Hall was filled with music that had outlasted humanity's tenure on Earth.

But as Wells entered the hall, a large, oval room bordered by a curved panoramic window, the grief that had been drifting through his body for the past week solidified in his stomach. He normally found the view incredibly beautiful, but that night the glittering stars that surrounded the cloud-shrouded Earth reminded him of candles at a vigil. His mother had loved music.

It was crowded as usual, with most of Phoenix buzzing around excitedly. Many of the women were eager to debut new dresses, an expensive and potentially maddening feat depending on what sort of textile scraps you found at the Exchange. He took a few steps forward, sending a ripple of whispers and knowing glances through the crowd.

Wells tried to focus on the front of the room where the musicians were gathering under the tree for which Eden Hall was named. The legend was that the sapling had miraculously survived the burning of North America and had been carried onto Phoenix right before the Exodus. Now it reached to the very top of the hall, its slender branches stretching out more than ten meters in each direction, creating a canopy of leaves that partially obscured the performers with a veil of green-tinged shadows.

"Is that the Chancellor's son?" a woman behind him asked. A new wave of heat rose to his already flushed cheeks. He'd never grown immune to the comet tail of double takes and curious glances he dragged behind him, but tonight it felt unbearable.

He turned and started walking toward the door, but froze as a hand grabbed his arm. He spun around and saw Clarke giving him a quizzical look. "Where are you running off to?"

Wells smiled grimly. "Turns out I'm not in the mood for music."

Clarke looked at him for a moment, then slipped her hand into his. "Stay. As a favor to me." She led him toward two empty seats in the back row. "I need you to tell me what we're listening to."

Wells sighed as he settled down next to Clarke. "I already told you they were performing Bach," he said, shooting a longing glance at the door.

"You know what I'm talking about." Clarke interlocked her fingers with his. "This movement, that movement." She grinned. "Besides, I always clap at the wrong time."

Wells gave her hand a squeeze.

There was no need for any sort of introduction or announcement. From the moment the first notes burst forward, the crowd fell silent, the violinist's bow slicing through their chatter as it swept across the strings. Then the cello joined in, followed by the clarinet. There were no drums tonight, but it didn't matter. Wells could practically hear the thud of two hundred hearts beating in time to the music.

"This is what I always imagined a sunset would sound like," Wells whispered. The words slipped out of his mouth before he had time to think, and he braced for an eye roll, or at least a look of confusion.

But the music had also cast its spell on Clarke. "I'd love to see a sunset," she murmured, resting her head on his shoulder.

Wells absently ran his hand through her silky hair. "I'd love to see a sunset with you." He bent down and kissed her forehead. "What are you doing in about seventy-five years?" he whispered.

"Cleaning my dentures," Clarke said with a smile. "Why?"

"Because I have an idea for our first date on Earth."

The light was fading, the bonfire flickering across the faces standing around Wells.

"I know this all seems strange and intimidating and, yes, unfair, but we're here for a reason," he told the crowd. "If we survive, everyone survives."

Nearly a hundred heads turned to him, and for a moment, he thought perhaps his words had chipped away at the layers of calcified defiance and ignorance. But then a new voice crashed into the silence.

"Careful there, Jaha."

Wells twisted around and saw a tall kid in a bloodstained guard uniform. The boy who'd forced his way onto the dropship—who'd held Wells's father hostage. "Earth is still in recovery mode. We don't know how much bullshit it can handle."

Another wave of snickers and snorts rippled around the fire, and Wells felt a rush of sudden, sharp anger. Because of this kid, his father—the person responsible for protecting the entire human race—had been *shot*, and he had the nerve to stand there and accuse *Wells* of bullshit?

"Excuse me?" Wells said, lifting his chin to give the boy his best officer's stare.

"Cut the crap, okay? Just say what you really mean. If we do exactly what you say, then you won't report us to your father."

Wells narrowed his eyes. "Thanks to you, my father is probably in the hospital." *Being given the best possible care, and on his way to a swift recovery*, Wells added silently. He hoped it was true.

"If he's even alive," Graham interjected, and laughed. For a second, Wells thought he saw the other boy wince.

Wells took a step forward, but then another voice yelled

out from the crowd, stopping him. "So you're not a spy?"

"A *spy*?" Wells almost laughed at the accusation.

"Yeah," the impostor guard agreed. "Spying on us just like these bracelets, right?"

Wells looked at the kid in the ill-fitting guard uniform more closely. Had he been told about the purpose of the bracelets, or had he figured it out on his own? "If the Council wanted to spy on you," he said, ignoring the comment about the transponders, "don't you think they'd choose someone a bit less obvious?"

The boy in the bloody uniform smirked. "We can discuss the pros and cons of your father's administration some other time. But for now, just tell us: If you're not a spy, what the hell are you doing here? There's no way anyone will believe you were actually Confined."

"I'm sorry," Wells said in a tone that conveyed anything but regret. "You appeared in a stolen guard's uniform and held my father hostage in order to break onto this ship. I think *you're* the one who owes us an explanation."

The boy's eyes narrowed. "I did what I had to do to protect my sister."

"Your *sister*?" Wells repeated. People broke the population laws more often on Walden than on Phoenix. But Wells had never heard of anyone having a sibling, not since the Cataclysm.

"That's right." The boy crossed his arms and met Wells's eyes with a challenging stare. "Now I'm going to ask you one more time, what are you really doing here?"

Wells took a step forward. He didn't owe anyone an explanation, let alone this criminal, who was probably lying about having a sister and who knew what else. But then a flash of movement caught his eye. Clarke was heading toward the fire from the other side of the clearing, where she'd been tending to the injured passengers.

Wells turned back to the tall boy and sighed, his anger draining away. "I'm here for the same reason you are." His eyes darted toward Clarke, who was still out of earshot. "I got myself Confined to protect someone I care about."

The crowd fell silent. Wells turned his back on them and started walking, not caring if their eyes followed him as he made his way toward Clarke.

For a moment, the sight of her overwhelmed his brain. The light in the clearing had changed as the sky grew darker, making the flecks of gold in her green eyes appear to glow. She was more beautiful on Earth than he'd ever seen her.

Their eyes locked, and a chill traveled down his spine. Less than a year ago, he'd been able to tell what she was thinking just by looking at her. But now her expression was inscrutable.

"What are you doing here, Wells?" she asked, her voice strained and weary.

She's in shock, Wells told himself, forcing his mind to wrap around the ill-fitting explanation. "I came for you," he said softly.

Her face assumed an expression that broke through the barriers, a mixture of sorrow, frustration, and pity that seemed to travel from Clarke's eyes straight into his chest.

"I wish you hadn't." She sighed and pushed past him, striding off without another glance.

Her words knocked the air out of him, and for a moment, all Wells could think about was remembering how to breathe. Then he heard a chorus of murmurs from the bonfire behind him, and turned, curious despite himself. Everyone was pointing upward at the sky, which was turning into a symphony of color.

First, orange streaks appeared in the blue, like an oboe joining a flute, turning a solo into a duet. That harmony built into a crescendo of colors as yellow and then pink added their voices to the chorus. The sky darkened, throwing the array of colors into even sharper relief. The word *sunset* couldn't possibly contain the meaning of the beauty above them, and for the millionth time since they'd landed, Wells found that the words they'd been taught to describe Earth paled in comparison to the real thing.

Even Clarke, who hadn't stopped moving since the crash, froze in her tracks, her head tilted up to better appreciate the miracle taking place overhead. Wells didn't have to see her face to know that her eyes would be widened in awe, her mouth slightly parted with a gasp as she watched something she had only ever dreamed about. Something *they* had only ever dreamed about, Wells corrected himself. He turned away, unable to look at the sky any longer, pain hardening into something dense and sharp in his chest. It was the first sunset humans had witnessed in three centuries, and he was watching it alone.

CHAPTER 7

Bellamy

Bellamy squinted up at the sunrise. He'd always assumed those ancient poets had been full of shit, or at least had much better drugs than he'd ever tried. But they were right. It was crazy to watch the sky go from black to gray and then explode into streaks of color. It didn't make him want to break out into song or anything, but then again, Bellamy had never been the artistic type.

He leaned over and pulled Octavia's blanket up over her shoulder. He'd spotted it sticking out of one of the supply containers the night before and had practically knocked out some kid's tooth in the ensuing tussle. Bellamy exhaled, watching as his breath crystallized in front of him, lingering far longer than it would on the ship, where the ventilation system practically sucked the air out of your lungs before it had a chance to leave your mouth.

He looked around the clearing. After that Clarke girl had finished evaluating Octavia and determined she only had a sprained ankle, Bellamy had carried her over toward the trees where they'd spent the night. They were going to keep their distance until he figured out how many of these kids were real criminals and how many had just been in the wrong place at the wrong time.

Bellamy squeezed his sister's hand. It was his fault she'd been Confined. It was his fault she was here. He should've known she'd been planning something; she'd been talking for weeks about how hungry some of the children in her unit had been. It had been only a matter of time before she did something to feed them—even if it meant stealing. His selfless little sister was sentenced to die for having too big of a heart.

It was his job to protect her. And for the first time in her life, he'd failed.

Bellamy threw his shoulders back and raised his chin. He was tall for a six-year-old, but that didn't stop people from staring as he made his way through the crowd at the distribution center. It wasn't against the rules for children to come on their own, but it was rare. He went over the list his mother had made him repeat back to her three times before she'd let him leave their flat. *Fiber meal—two credits. Glucose packets—one credit. Dehydrated grain—two credits. Tuber flakes—one credit. Protein loaf—three credits.*

He darted around two women who'd stopped to grumble in front of some white things that looked like brains. Bellamy rolled his eyes and kept moving. Who cared that Phoenix got all the good stuff from the solar fields? Anyone who wanted to eat vegetables probably had little, mushy white brains themselves.

Bellamy cupped his hands under the fiber dispenser, caught the packet that slid out, and tucked it under his arm. He started to make his way over to the tuber section when something bright and shiny caught his eye. Bellamy turned and saw a pile of red, round fruit inside a display case. Normally, he didn't care about the expensive things they locked away—twisted carrots that reminded Bellamy of orange witch fingers, and ugly mushrooms that looked more like brain-sucking black-hole zombies than food. But these were different. The fruit was a rosy pink, the same color that his neighbor Rilla turned when they played alien invasion in the corridor. Or used to play before Rilla's father was taken away by the guards and Rilla was sent to live in the care center.

Bellamy stood on his tiptoes to read the number on the data

panel. Eleven credits. That sounded like a lot, but he wanted to do something nice for his mother. She hadn't gotten out of bed for three days. Bellamy couldn't imagine being that tired.

"Do you want one?" an irritated voice asked. He looked up and saw a woman in a green uniform glaring at him. "Order it or step aside."

Heat rose to Bellamy's cheeks, and for a moment, he considered running away. But then a surge of indignation washed over his embarrassment. He wasn't going to let some sour-faced distribution worker stop him from getting his mother the treat she deserved. "I'll take *two*," he said in the haughty voice that always made his mother roll her eyes and ask, *I wonder who you got that from?* "And don't rub your fingers all over them," he added pointedly.

The woman raised her eyebrow before glancing at the guards behind the transaction table. No one on Walden liked the guards, but his mother seemed particularly afraid of them. Lately, she'd grab Bellamy's hand and turn in the other direction whenever she saw a patrol team approaching. Could she have done something wrong? Were the guards going to come take her away like they'd taken Rilla's father? *No*, he told himself. *I won't let them*.

He took his apples and marched over to the transaction table. Another distribution worker scanned his card, staring for a moment at the information on the panel before shrugging her shoulders and waving him forward. One of the guards shot him a curious look, but Bellamy kept his eyes straight ahead. He forced himself to walk until he'd left the distribution center and then broke into a run, clutching his packets to his chest as he tore down the walkway leading to his residential unit.

He palmed into their flat and shut the door carefully behind him. He couldn't wait to show his mother what he'd brought her. He stepped into the living space, but the lights didn't turn on. Was the sensor broken again? His stomach tightened slightly. His mother hated entering maintenance requests. She didn't like having strangers in their home. But how long could they spend in the dark?

"Mom!" Bellamy called, dashing into her room. "I'm back! I did it!" The lights were working here, and they buzzed to life as Bellamy ran through the door. But the bed was empty.

Bellamy froze as a wave of terror washed over him. She was gone. They'd taken her. He was all alone. But then a muffled stomp from the kitchen reached his ears. He sighed as his panic was quickly replaced by relief, then excitement. She was out of bed!

He ran into the kitchen. His mother was facing the small, round window that looked out into the dark staircase. One hand was placed on her lower back, as if it was hurting her. "Mom!" he called. "Look what I got you."

His mother inhaled sharply but didn't turn around. "Bellamy," she said, as though he were a neighbor dropping by for an unexpected visit. "You're back. Leave the food on the table and go to your room. I'll be right there."

Disappointment pressed down on him, weighing his feet to the floor. He wanted to see the look on his mother's face when she saw the fruit. "Look!" he urged, stretching his arms forward, unsure what she could see in the reflection of the dark, dusty window.

She twisted her head to look at him over her shoulder. "What are those?" She narrowed her eyes. "Apples?" She pressed her lips together and rubbed the side of her head like she used to do when she came home from work. Before she got sick. "How much did they—never mind. Just go to your room, okay?"

Bellamy's palms had begun to sweat as he placed the packets on the table near the door. Had he done something wrong? The lights flickered and then went out. "*Damn it*," his mother muttered as she looked up at the ceiling. "Bellamy, *now*," she commanded. Or at least, he thought it was his mother. She was facing away from him again, and her voice swirled through the darkness until it didn't sound like her anymore.

As he slunk away, Bellamy shot a quick glance over his shoulder. His mother didn't even look like herself. She'd turned to the side, and her stomach appeared huge and round, like she was hiding something under her shirt. He blinked and scampered off, convinced that his eyes had been playing tricks on him, ignoring the chill traveling down his spine.

"How's she doing?"

Bellamy glanced up to see Clarke standing above him, looking uneasily from him to his sleeping sister. He nodded. "I think she's okay."

"Good." She raised a slightly singed eyebrow. "Because it'd be a shame if you followed through on your threat from last night."

"What did I say?"

"You told me that if I didn't save your sister, you'd blow up the goddamn planet and everyone on it."

Bellamy smiled. "Good thing it's only a sprained ankle." He cocked his head to the side and surveyed Clarke quizzically. The skin under her eyes was bruised with exhaustion, but the purple shadows just made them look greener. He felt a twinge of guilt for being such a jerk to her the night before. He'd pegged her as another self-absorbed Phoenix girl who was training as a doctor because it gave her something to brag about at parties. But the strain in her delicate face and the blood matted in her reddish-gold hair made it clear she hadn't stopped to rest since they'd landed.

"So," Bellamy continued, remembering Wells's declaration at the bonfire yesterday, and the way Clarke had stomped away from him, "why were you so mean to little Chancellor Junior?"

Clarke looked at him with a mixture of shock and indignation. For a moment, he thought she might actually hit him, but then she just shook her head. "That's none of your business."

"Is he your boyfriend?" Bellamy pressed.

"No," Clarke said flatly. But then her mouth twitched into a questioning smile. "Why do you care?"

"Just taking a census," Bellamy replied. "Specifically, to determine the relationship status of all the pretty girls on Earth."

Clarke rolled her eyes, but then she turned back to Octavia and the playfulness drained from her face.

"What is it?" Bellamy looked from Clarke to his sister.

"Nothing," Clarke said quickly. "I just wish I had some antiseptic for that cut on her face. And some of the others are going to need antibiotics."

"So we don't have *any* medicine?" Bellamy asked, frowning in concern.

Clarke looked at him, startled. "I think the medical supplies kits were thrown out of the dropship in the crash. We'll be fine, though," she said quickly, the lie shooting out of her mouth before she had time to make her features match it. "We'll be okay for a while. The human body has a remarkable ability to heal itself. . . ." She trailed off as her eyes settled on the bloodstains on his stolen uniform.

Bellamy grimaced as he glanced down, wondering if she was thinking about the Chancellor. Bellamy hoped he'd survived—he had enough blood on his hands already. But it probably didn't matter one way or another. Whoever the Council sent down with the next group would most certainly be authorized to execute Bellamy on the spot, regardless of the fact that the Chancellor's injury had been an accident. As soon as Octavia was well enough to move, she and Bellamy would be out of there. They'd hike for a few days, put some distance between themselves and the group, and eventually find somewhere to settle down. He hadn't spent months poring over those ancient survival guides he'd discovered on B deck for nothing. He'd be ready for whatever was waiting for them in those woods. It couldn't be worse than what was going to come hurtling down from the sky.

"How long until she'll be able to walk on it?"

Clarke turned back to Bellamy. "It's a pretty bad sprain, so I'd say a few days until she can walk, a week or two until it's fully healed."

"But possibly sooner?"

She tilted her head to the side and gave him a small smile

that, for a moment, made him forget that he was marooned on a potentially toxic planet with ninety-nine juvenile delinquents. "What's the rush?"

But before he had time to respond, someone called Clarke's name and she was gone.

Bellamy took a deep breath. To his surprise, the simple act cleared his head, leaving him more awake and alert. It'd probably turn out to be toxic, but every time he inhaled, he sensed something unnamable but intriguing, like a mysterious girl who wouldn't meet your eyes but passed closely enough for you to catch a whiff of her perfume.

He took a few steps closer to the trees, anxious for a better look but unwilling to stray too far from Octavia. They didn't look like any species he recognized, but then again, the only Earth botany book he'd been able to find had been about plants native to Africa, and he thought he'd heard Wells say they were on the East Coast of what had once been the United States.

A twig snapped next to him. Bellamy whipped around and saw a girl with a long, narrow face and stringy hair. "Can I help you?"

"Wells says everyone who's not hurt should collect wood."

A thread of irritation coiled around Bellamy's stomach, and he gave the girl a tight smile. "I don't think Wells is in any position to be giving orders, so if it's all right with you, I'm going to worry about myself, okay?" She shifted uneasily for a moment before shooting a nervous glance over her shoulder. "Off you go," Bellamy said, motioning her forward with his hands. He watched her scurry off with satisfaction.

He craned his neck and stared up at the sky, his eyes drinking in nothing but emptiness in all directions. It didn't matter where they were. Any spot on this planet was going to be infinitely better than the world they'd left behind.

For the first time in his life, he was free.

CHAPTER 8

Glass

Glass spent the rest of the night on Luke's couch, grateful that Camille didn't ask why she refused to sleep in Carter's old room. They'd decided that it was best for Glass to stay hidden in Luke's flat until the shift change at 0600, when there would be fewer guards on patrol.

She'd tossed and turned all night. Every time she rolled over, the bracelet dug into her skin, a painful reminder that while she was in danger, Wells was hundreds of kilometers away, fighting to survive on a planet that hadn't been able to support life for centuries. It'd always been his dream to see Earth, but not like this. Not when it might still be toxic. Not after seeing his father shot right in front of him.

As she lay staring at the ceiling, she couldn't keep her ears from searching for sounds in the darkness. The faintest murmur from the other side of Luke's door was enough to turn her stomach. The silence was even worse.

Just as the circadian lights began to creep under the front door, Luke's bedroom door opened, and both he and Camille staggered out wearily. Clearly, neither of them had slept much either. Luke was already dressed in off-duty civilian clothes, but Camille wore only one of Luke's old undershirts, the hem of which skimmed the tops of her slender thighs. Glass blushed and looked away.

"Good morning." The formality in Luke's voice made Glass wince. The last time Luke had said those words to her, the two of them had been in his bed, and he'd whispered them in her ear.

"Good morning," she managed, shoving the memory out of her head.

"We need to get that bracelet off." Luke gestured toward her wrist.

Glass nodded and rose from the couch, shifting uneasily as Camille looked back and forth between her and Luke. Finally, she crossed her arms and turned to him. "Are you sure this is a good idea? What if someone sees you?"

Luke's expression darkened. "We talked about this." He spoke quietly, but Glass heard the note of frustration in his voice. "If we don't help her, they're going to *kill* her. It's the right thing to do."

The right thing to do, Glass thought. That was all she meant to him anymore, a life he didn't want on his conscience.

"Better her than you," Camille said, her voice trembling.

Luke leaned over and kissed the top of her head. "It's going to be fine. I'll take her back to Phoenix and then come straight home."

Camille sighed and tossed Glass a shirt and a pair of pants. "Here," she said. "I know it's not up to your Phoenix standards, but you'll look a bit more believable in this. You aren't going to pass for a sanitation worker with that hair." She gave Luke's arm a squeeze and then slipped back into his bedroom, leaving Glass and Luke alone.

Glass stood holding the clothes awkwardly in her arms, and for a moment, they just stared at each other. The last time she'd seen Luke, she'd have thought nothing of changing in front of him. "Should I . . ." She trailed off, gesturing toward Carter's room.

"Oh," Luke said, reddening slightly. "No, I'll just . . . I'll be right back." He retreated to his bedroom. Glass changed as quickly as she could, trying to ignore the whispers that escaped through the door, stinging her skin like pinpricks.

When Luke returned, Glass was dressed in a pair of loose gray pants that barely clung to her hips and a rough blue

T-shirt that chafed her skin. Luke surveyed her critically. "Something's still off," he said. "You don't look like a prisoner, but you definitely don't look like a Waldenite."

Glass began to smooth the sides of her wrinkled trousers self-consciously, wondering whether Luke preferred being with a girl who looked at home in these clothes. "It's not that," he said. "It's your hair. Girls don't wear it that long here."

"Why?" she asked, realizing with a small measure of guilt that she'd never even noticed.

Luke had turned and began rummaging through a small storage bin against the wall. "Probably because it'd be too hard to take care of. We don't get the same water allotment on Walden that you do on Phoenix." He turned around with a look of triumph on his face and produced an ancient-looking stained cap.

Glass gave him a weak smile. "Thanks." She took the hat from Luke, their hands brushing, and placed it on her head.

"I don't think we're quite there yet," he said, surveying her with a frown. He stepped toward her and removed the hat with one hand, and with his other, reached over her shoulder to gather her hair, gently twisting it into a knot on top of her head. "There," he said in satisfaction, placing the cap on top.

The silence stretched between them. Slowly, Luke reached up and tucked a few stray strands behind Glass's ear. His rough fingers lingered on her neck, and he looked into her eyes, unblinking.

"Ready?" Glass asked, breaking the spell as she stepped to the side.

"Yes. Let's go." Luke stepped back stiffly and led her out into the hallway.

There weren't as many circadian lights on Walden as there were on Phoenix, so although it was technically dawn, the corridors were mostly dark. Glass couldn't tell where Luke was leading her, and she clenched her hands to keep herself from reaching for his.

Finally, Luke stopped in front of the faint outline of a door. He dug into his pocket, producing something Glass couldn't see and holding it up to the scanner. The door beeped and slid open. Glass's insides twisted as she realized that wherever Luke took her, he'd leave a trail of log-ins and access codes. She couldn't bear to think what would happen when the Council figured out that he'd helped an escaped criminal.

But there was no other option. After she said one last good-bye to her mother, she'd wait for the guards to find her. She wouldn't try to see Luke again. She couldn't ask him to risk his safety for her. Not after what she'd done.

A faint light flickered wearily to life, casting a dirty, yellowish glow over machinery Glass didn't recognize. "Where are we?" she asked, her voice echoing strangely.

"One of the old workshops. This is where they used to

repair the Earthmade equipment, before it was all replaced. I came here for some of my training."

Glass started to ask why the guards would train here, but bit back the question. She always forgot that Luke had already started his mechanical apprenticeship when he was accepted into the engineering corps of the guards. He rarely spoke about that part of his life. Looking back, Glass was ashamed that she hadn't tried harder to learn about Luke's world; it was no wonder he'd turned to Camille.

Luke stood next to an enormous machine, pushing different buttons, his brow furrowed in concentration. "What is *that*?" Glass asked when it started to hum ominously.

"A laser cutter," Luke said without glancing up.

Glass hugged her wrist protectively to her chest. "No way."

Luke gave Glass a look that was equal parts amusement and irritation. "No arguing. The sooner we get that thing off of you, the better your chances of hiding."

"Can't we just figure out how to unlock it?"

Luke shook his head. "It has to be cut off." When she didn't move, he held out his hand with a sigh. "Come here, Glass," he said, beckoning her over.

Glass's feet locked into the floor. Although she'd spent the last six months imagining Luke calling to her, she'd never thought that a piece of deadly machinery would be involved. Luke raised an eyebrow. "Glass?"

Glass took a tentative step forward. It wasn't like she had anything to lose. Better to have Luke slice her wrist off than a medic inject poison into her vein.

Luke tapped a flat surface in the middle of the machine. "Just put your hand here." He flipped a switch and the whole machine began to vibrate.

Glass trembled as her skin made contact with the cold metal.

"It'll be okay," Luke said. "I promise. Just hold still."

Glass nodded, too afraid to speak. The humming continued and was soon accompanied by a high-pitched screech.

Luke made a few more adjustments, then came to stand next to her. "Ready?"

She swallowed nervously. "Yes."

Luke placed his left hand over her arm, and with his right, started to move another lever toward her. To her horror, she saw that it was emitting a thin red line of light that pulsed with dangerous energy.

She started to shake, but Luke gripped her arm tighter. "It's okay," he murmured. "Just stay still."

The light was getting closer. Glass could feel the heat on her skin. Luke's face tensed with concentration, his eyes fixed on Glass's wrist as he moved the laser steadily along.

Glass closed her eyes, bracing herself for the searing pain, the screaming of her nerves as they lost contact with her hand.

"Perfect." Luke's voice cut through her terror. Glass looked down and saw the bracelet had been split into two neat pieces, freeing her wrist.

She sighed, her breath ragged. "Thank you."

"You're welcome." He smiled at her, his hand still clutching her arm.

Neither of them spoke as they slipped out of the workshop and began to wind their way back up toward the skybridge.

"What's wrong?" Luke whispered as he guided Glass around a corner and up another flight of stairs, narrower and darker than anything on Phoenix.

"Nothing."

In the past, Luke would've reached over, taken her chin in his hand, and looked her in the eye until she giggled. *You're a terrible liar, Rapunzel*, he'd say, a reference to the fairytale about the girl whose hair grew a foot anytime she fibbed. But this time, Glass's lie evaporated into the air.

"So how have you been?" she asked finally, when she couldn't bear the weight of the silence any longer.

Luke glanced over his shoulder and raised an eyebrow. "Oh, you know, apart from being dumped by the girl I loved and then having my best friend executed for a bullshit infraction, I'd say not too bad."

Glass cringed as his words landed in her chest. She'd never heard that kind of bitterness in Luke's voice before.

"But at least I had Camille. . . ."

Glass nodded, but as she stole a glance at Luke's familiar profile, shards of indignation gathered, sharp and dangerous, in her mind. What did he think she had done to be Confined? Why wasn't he more curious or surprised? Did he think she was such a terrible person that she would have committed an infraction?

Luke stopped abruptly, causing Glass to stumble into him. "Sorry," she muttered, scrambling to regain her balance.

"Does your mother know what happened?" Luke asked, turning to face her.

"No," Glass said. "I mean, she knew I was Confined, but she can't have known about the Earth mission." The Chancellor had made it clear that the operation was top secret. Their parents wouldn't be informed until it was certain their children had survived the journey—or until the Council was sure they'd never return.

"It's good that you're going to see her."

Glass said nothing. She knew he was thinking of his own mother, who'd died when he was only twelve, which was why he'd ended up living with his then-eighteen-year-old neighbor Carter.

"Yeah," Glass said in a shaky voice. She'd been desperate to see her mother, but even without the bracelet, it wouldn't take the guards long to find her. What was more important?

Saying good-bye? Or sparing her mother the pain of seeing her daughter being dragged away toward certain death? "We should keep going."

They crossed the bridge in silence as Glass drank in the sight of the twinkling stars. She hadn't realized how much she loved the view from the skybridge until she'd been locked in a tiny, windowless cell. She stole a glance at Luke, not sure whether to be hurt or relieved that he didn't turn to look at her.

"You should go back," Glass said as they reached the Phoenix checkpoint, which was, as Luke had promised, free of guards. "I'll be okay."

Luke's jaw tightened and he gave her a bitter smile. "You're an escaped convict, and I'm *still* not good enough to meet your mother."

"That's not what I meant," she said, thinking of the scan trail he'd already left behind. "It's not safe for you to help me. I can't let you risk your life. You've already done so much."

Luke took a breath as if to say something, then nodded. "Okay, then."

She forced what she hoped was a smile, holding back tears. "Thank you for everything."

Luke's face softened slightly. "Good luck, Glass." He started to lean in, and Glass couldn't help tipping her head up, out of habit—but then he stepped back, wrenching his eyes from her with an almost physical force. Without a word, Luke turned and moved soundlessly back the way they'd come. Glass watched him go, her lips aching for the good-bye kiss they'd never feel again.

When she reached the entrance to her flat, Glass raised her fist and tapped lightly. The door opened and Glass's mother, Sonja, peered around it. A symphony of emotions played across her face in an instant—surprise, joy, confusion, and fear.

"Glass?" she gasped, reaching for her daughter, as if she wasn't sure she was really there. Glass leaned gratefully into her mother's hug, drinking in the smell of her perfume. "I thought I'd never see you again." She gave Glass one more squeeze before pulling her inside and closing the door. Sonja stepped back and stared at her daughter. "I was just counting down the days." Her voice faded into a whisper. "You turn eighteen in three weeks."

Glass grabbed her mother's clammy hand and led her to the couch. "They were going to send us to Earth," Glass told her. "A hundred of us." She took a deep breath. "I was supposed to be one of them."

"Earth?" Sonja repeated slowly, holding the word almost at a distance, as if trying to get a better look. "Oh my god."

"There was an altercation at the launch. The Chancellor . . ." Glass's head swam as she recalled the scene from the launch deck. She sent up a silent prayer that Wells was okay down there on Earth, that he was with Clarke and didn't have to grieve alone. "In the chaos, I was able to get away," Glass continued. The details weren't important right now. "I just came to say I love you."

Her mother's eyes widened. "So that's how the Chancellor was shot. Oh, Glass," she whispered, wrapping her arms around her daughter.

The thud of footsteps echoed out in the hallway, and Glass flinched. She looked warily at the door before turning back to face her mother. "I can't stay long," she said, rising shakily to her feet.

"Wait!" Sonja jumped up and clutched Glass's arm, pulling her back to the couch. Her fingers tightened around her wrist. "The Chancellor is on life support, which means that Vice Chancellor Rhodes is in charge. You shouldn't go yet." She paused. "He has a very different approach to . . . governing. There's a chance that he'll pardon you. He can be convinced." Sonja stood and gave Glass a smile that did little to illuminate her glistening eyes. "Just wait here."

"Do you have to go?" Glass asked, her voice small. She couldn't bear to say another good-bye. Not when every good-bye could be forever.

Her mother bent down and kissed Glass's forehead. "I won't be long."

She watched Sonja apply a hurried layer of lipstick and slip out into the still-empty corridor, then pulled her knees into her chest and hugged them tightly, as if trying to keep everything inside her from spilling out.

Glass wasn't sure how long she slept, but curled up on the cushions that still remembered the shape of her body, it seemed possible that the past six months had been a nightmare. That she hadn't actually been imprisoned in a cell that contained nothing besides two metal cots, a silent, seething Arcadian cell mate, and the ghosts of sobs that remained long after her tears dried up.

When she opened her eyes her mother was sitting next to her on the couch, stroking Glass's matted hair. "It's all taken care of," she said softly. "You've been pardoned."

Glass rolled over to look up at her mother's face. "How?" she asked, the surprise shocking her out of her sleep, chasing away the images of Luke that lingered on her eyelids when she first woke up. "Why?"

"People are growing restless," her mother explained. "None of the convicted juveniles have made it past their retrials in the last year, and it makes the justice system look anything but just. You're going to be the exception—the proof that the system's still working how it's supposed to, that those who can contribute to society are given the chance to return to it. It took a little convincing, but eventually Vice Chancellor Rhodes saw my side of things," her mother finished, sinking back into the couch, looking exhausted but relieved.

"Mom—I can't—I don't—thank you." Glass didn't know what else to say. She smiled as she pushed herself up into a seated position and rested her head against her mother's shoulder. She was free? She almost couldn't comprehend the meaning of the word.

"You don't need to thank me, sweetheart. I'd do anything for you." Sonja pushed a piece of Glass's hair behind her ear and smiled. "Just remember, you're not to tell anyone about the Earth mission—I mean it."

"But what happened to the others? Is Wells okay? Can you find out?"

Sonja shook her head. "As far as you're concerned, there was no mission. What's important is that you're safe now. You have a second chance," her mother murmured. "Just promise me you won't do anything foolish."

"I promise," Glass said finally, shaking her head in disbelief. "I promise."

CHAPTER 9

Clarke

Clarke slipped through the flap of the designated infirmary tent and stepped into the clearing. Even without the luxury of windows, she sensed that it was dawn. The sky erupted with color, and the pungent air stimulated sensors in her brain Clarke had never realized existed. She wished she could share the experience with the two people who had made her yearn to see Earth in the first place. But Clarke would never have that chance.

Her parents were gone.

"Good morning."

Clarke stiffened. It was almost unfathomable that Wells's voice had once been her favorite sound in the universe. He was the reason her parents were dead, their bodies floating through the depths of space, moving farther and farther from everything they'd known and loved. In a moment of weakness, Clarke had confided a secret that wasn't hers to share. And even though he'd sworn not to tell a soul, Wells hadn't even waited twenty-four hours before skipping off to his father, so desperate to be the perfect son, Phoenix's golden child, that he betrayed the girl he'd pretended to love.

She turned to face Wells. There was nothing to keep her from lunging at him, but she wanted to avoid any confrontation that would prolong the exposure.

As she strode past him, Wells grabbed her arm. "Hold on a second, I just wanted to—"

Clarke spun around and wrenched herself free. "Don't *touch* me," she hissed.

Wells took a step back, his eyes wide. "I'm sorry," he said. His voice was steady, but she could see the hurt on his face. Clarke had always been able to tell what Wells was feeling. He was a terrible liar, which was how she'd known, in that brief moment, that his promise to keep her secret had been sincere. But something had changed his mind, and it was Clarke's parents who had paid the price.

Wells didn't move. "I just wanted to make sure you were doing okay," he said quietly. "We're going to finish sorting through the wreckage today. Is there anything in particular you need for your patients?"

"Yes. A sterile operating room, IVs, a full-body scanner, *real* doctors . . ."

"You're doing an incredible job."

"I'd be doing even better if I'd spent the past six months training at the hospital instead of in Confinement." This time, Wells had braced for the barb, and his face remained impassive.

The sky was growing brighter, filling the clearing with an almost golden light that made everything look like it'd been polished overnight. The grass seemed greener, glistening with tiny drops of water. Purple blossoms began unfurling from what had seemed like an unremarkable shrub. The long, tapered petals stretched toward the sun, twisting in the air as if dancing to music only they could hear.

Wells seemed to read her mind. "If you hadn't been Confined, you'd never have come here," he said quietly.

She whipped her head back to face him. "You think I should be grateful for what you did? I've seen kids *die*, kids who never wanted to come here but had to because some little shit like you turned them in just to feel important."

"That's not what I meant." Wells sighed and met her gaze straight on. "I'm so sorry, Clarke. I can't tell you how sorry. But I didn't do it to *feel important*." He started to step forward, but then seemed to think better of it and shifted his weight back. "You were suffering, and I wanted to help. I couldn't bear it, seeing you like that. I just wanted to help make the pain go away."

The tenderness in his voice made Clarke's stomach twist. "They killed my parents," she said quietly, imagining the scene as she had so many times before. Her mother bracing for the prick of a needle, her body systematically shutting down until those final dreadful moments when only her brain was left. Had they been offered the customary last meal? Clarke's heart twinged as she imagined her father's lifeless body in a release capsule, his fingers stained red from the berries he'd eaten alone. "That kind of pain never goes away."

For a moment, they just stared at each other, the silence taking on a physical weight. But then Wells broke eye contact and turned his head up toward the trees above them. There were faintly musical sounds coming from the leaves.

"Do you hear that?" Wells whispered without looking at her.

The song was both haunting and joyful, the first few notes an elegy for the fading stars. Yet just when Clarke was sure her heart would break with the bittersweet loveliness, the melody soared, trumpeting the arrival of the dawn.

Birds. Real birds. She couldn't see them, but she knew they were there. She wondered if the first colonists had heard birds singing as they'd boarded the final ship. Would the music have been a song of farewell? Or had the creatures already joined their voices together in a requiem for the dying Earth?

"It's incredible," Wells said, turning to look at her with a smile she recognized from long ago. Clarke shivered. It was like seeing a ghost—a specter of the boy to whom she'd been foolish enough to give her heart.

Clarke couldn't suppress a smile as she watched Wells shift from side to side outside her front door. He always got nervous about kissing her in public, but it had gotten worse since he'd started officer training. The idea of making out with his girlfriend while in uniform seemed to make him uncomfortable, which was unfortunate because the sight of him in his uniform made her want to kiss him even more than usual.

"I'll see you tomorrow." Clarke turned to press her thumb to the scanner.

"Wait," Wells said, glancing over his shoulder before grabbing hold of her arm.

Clarke sighed. "Wells," she started as she tried to wiggle out of his grasp. "I need to go."

He grinned as he tightened his grip. "Are your parents home?"

"Yes." She inclined her head toward the door. "I'm late for dinner."

Wells stared at her expectantly. He much preferred eating with her family to sitting across from his father in silence, but she couldn't invite him to join them. Not tonight.

Wells cocked his head to the side. "I won't make a face this time, no matter what your father added to the protein paste. I've been practicing." His face broke into a comically bright smile as he nodded emphatically. "Wow. This is delicious!"

Clarke pressed her lips together for a moment before responding. "I just need to have a private conversation with them."

Wells's face grew serious. "What's going on?" He released her arm and brought his hand to her cheek. "Is everything okay?"

"It's fine." She stepped to the side and tilted her head so her eyes wouldn't betray her by sending distress signals from behind the lies. She needed to confront her parents about their experiments, and she couldn't put it off any longer.

"Okay, then," he said slowly. "See you tomorrow?"

Instead of kissing her on the cheek, Wells surprised Clarke by wrapping his arms around her waist and pulling her close. His lips pressed against hers, and for a moment, she forgot about everything except the warmth of his body. But by the time she'd closed the door, the tingle of Wells's touch on her skin had been replaced by a prickle of dread.

Her parents were sitting on the couch. Their heads turned to her. "Clarke." Her mother rose to her feet, smiling. "Was that Wells with you outside? Does he want to join us for din—"

"No," Clarke said, more sharply than she'd meant to. "Can you sit down? I need to talk to you." She crossed the room and settled on a chair facing her parents, trembling as two violent forces waged war for control of her body: burning fury and desperate hope. She needed her parents to admit what they'd done to justify her anger, but she also prayed they'd have a good excuse. "I figured out the password," she said simply. "I've been in the lab."

Her mother's eyes widened as she sank back onto the couch. Then she took a deep breath, and for a moment, Clarke hoped she'd try to explain, that she had the words to make it all better. But then she whispered the phrase Clarke had been dreading. "I'm sorry."

Her father took his wife's hand, his eyes on Clarke. "I'm sorry you had to see that," he said quietly. "I know it's . . . shocking. But they don't feel any pain. We make sure of that."

"How could you?" The question felt flimsy, incapable of supporting the weight of her accusation, but she couldn't think of anything else to ask. "You're experimenting on people. On *children*." Saying it aloud made her stomach churn. Bile crept up her throat.

Her mother closed her eyes. "We didn't have a choice," she said softly. "We've spent years trying to test radiation levels in other ways—you know that. When we reported back to the Vice Chancellor there was no way to gather conclusive evidence without human studies, we thought he understood it was a dead end. But then he insisted that we . . ." Her voice cracked. Clarke didn't need her to finish the sentence. "We had no choice," she repeated desperately.

"We always have a choice," Clarke said, trembling. "You could have said no. I would have let them *kill* me before I agreed to that."

"But he didn't threaten to kill us." Her father's voice was infuriatingly quiet.

"Then what the hell are you doing this for?" Clarke asked shrilly.

"He said he would kill *you*."

The birdsong trailed off, leaving a charged silence in its wake, as if the music had seeped into the stillness, imbuing the air with melody. "Wow," Wells said softly. "That was amazing." He was still facing the trees, but he'd extended his arm toward her, as if reaching through time to hold the hand of the girl who used to love him.

The spell was broken. Clarke stiffened and, without a word, headed back toward the infirmary.

It was dark inside the tent. Clarke almost tripped as she stepped in, making a mental note to change the bandages on one boy's leg, fix the sloppy stitches she'd given the girl with the gash on her thigh. She'd finally found a container with real bandages and surgical thread, but there wasn't going to be much more she could do if they didn't find the actual medicine chest. It hadn't turned up in the wreckage, most likely thrown from the dropship during the crash and destroyed.

Thalia was lying on one of the cots. She was still asleep, and the newest bandage seemed to be holding up. Clarke had already changed the wrappings three times since she'd found Thalia after the crash, blood pouring out of an ugly gash in her side.

The memory of stitching up the wound made Clarke's stomach churn, and she hoped that her friend remembered even less. Thalia had passed out from the pain and had been fading in and out of consciousness ever since. Clarke knelt down and brushed a strand of damp hair back from her friend's brow.

"Hi," she whispered as Thalia's eyes fluttered open. "How are you feeling?"

The injured girl forced a smile that seemed to drain the energy from the rest of her body. "I'm just great," Thalia said, but then winced, the pain flashing in her eyes.

"You used to be a much better liar."

"I never *lied.*" Her voice was hoarse but still full of mock indignation. "I just told the guard that I had a neck problem and needed an extra pillow."

"And then convinced him that black-market whiskey would keep you from singing in your 'sleep,'" Clarke added with a smile.

"Yeah. . . . It's too bad Lise wasn't willing to play along."

"Or that you can't carry a tune to save your life."

"That's what made it so great!" Thalia protested. "The night guard would've done anything to shut me up at that point."

Clarke shook her head with a smile. "And you say that Phoenix girls are lunatics." She gestured toward the thin blanket draped over Thalia. "May I?"

Thalia nodded, and Clarke pulled it back, trying to keep her face neutral as she unwrapped the bandage. The skin around the wound was red and swollen, and pus was forming in the gaps between the stitches. The wound itself wasn't the problem, Clarke knew. While it looked bad, it was the kind of injury they wouldn't bat an eye at in the medical center. The infection was the real threat.

"That bad?" Thalia asked quietly.

"Nah, you look great," Clarke said, the lie falling smoothly from her lips. Her eyes slid involuntarily toward the empty cot where a boy who died the day before had spent his final hours.

"That wasn't your fault," Thalia said quietly.

"I know." Clarke sighed. "I just wished he hadn't been alone."

"He wasn't. Wells was here."

"What?" Clarke asked, confused.

"He came to check on him a few times. I think the first time he came into the tent, he was looking for you, but once he saw how badly that boy was hurt . . ."

"Really?" Clarke asked, not quite sure whether to trust the observations of a girl who'd spent most of the past day unconscious.

"It was definitely him," another voice called. Clarke looked over and saw Octavia sitting up, a playful smile on her face. "It's not every day Wells Jaha comes and sits by your bed."

Clarke looked at her in disbelief. "How do you even know Wells?"

"He visited the care center with his father a few years ago. The girls were talking about it for weeks. He's kind of a supernova."

Clarke smiled at the Walden slang as Octavia continued. "I asked him if he remembered me. He said he did, but he's too much of a gentleman to say no." Octavia gave an exaggerated sigh and placed the back of her hand against her forehead. "Alas. My one chance at love."

"Hey, what about me?" A boy Clarke had thought was asleep shot Octavia an injured look, and she blew him a kiss.

Clarke just shook her head and turned back to Thalia,

her eyes traveling from her friend's face back to the infected wound.

"That's not a good sign, is it?" Thalia asked quietly, fatigue beginning to tug at the ragged edges of her voice.

"It could be worse."

"Your lying skills are slipping as well. What's going on?" She managed to raise an eyebrow. "Is love making you soft?"

Clarke stiffened and snatched her hand back from Thalia's blanket. "Are your injuries making you delirious?" She glanced over her shoulder and was relieved to see Octavia absorbed in conversation with the Arcadian boy. "You *know* what he did to me." She paused as her stomach churned with revulsion. "What he did to my *parents*."

"Of course I know." Thalia looked at Clarke with a mixture of frustration and pity. "But I also know what he risked to come here." She smiled. "He loves you, Clarke. The kind of love most people spend their whole lives looking for."

Clarke sighed. "Well, I hope, for your sake, that you never find it."

CHAPTER 10

Bellamy

It was crazy how much their surroundings could change throughout the day. In the mornings, everything felt crisp and new. Even the air had a sharpness to it. Yet in the afternoon, the light mellowed and the colors softened. That's what Bellamy liked best about Earth so far—the unexpectedness. Like a girl who kept you guessing. He'd always been drawn to the ones he couldn't quite figure out.

Laughter rose up from the far side of the clearing. Bellamy turned to see two girls perched on a low tree branch, giggling as they swatted at the boy attempting to climb up and join them. Nearby, a bunch of Walden boys were playing a game of keep-away with an Arcadian girl's shoe, the owner of which was laughing as she skidded barefoot across the grass. For a moment, he felt a twinge of regret that Octavia still wasn't well enough to join in—she'd had so little fun in her life. But then again, it was probably best that she didn't form any real attachments. As soon as her ankle healed, she and Bellamy would be off for good.

Bellamy tore open a crumpled nutrition pack, squeezed half the contents into his mouth, then slipped the carefully folded wrapper back into his pocket. After sorting through the remainder of the wreckage, they'd discovered what they'd all feared: The few weeks' worth of nutrition packets they'd found when they first landed was all they'd been sent with. Either the Council had assumed the hundred would figure out how to live off the land after a month . . . or they didn't plan on them surviving that long.

Graham had strong-armed most people into handing over any packs they'd salvaged and had supposedly put an Arcadian named Asher in charge of distributing them, but there was already a fledgling black market; people were trading nutrition packs for blankets and taking on extra water shifts in exchange for reserved spots inside the crowded tents. Wells had spent the day trying to get everyone to agree to a more formal system, and while some people had seemed interested, it hadn't taken Graham long to shut him down.

Bellamy turned as the laughter at the short end of the clearing gave way to shouts.

"Give that to me!" one of the Waldenites cried, trying to wrench something away from another. As Bellamy hurried over, he realized it was an ax. The first boy was holding the handle with both hands and was trying to swing it out of reach while the second boy attempted to grab on to the blade.

Others began to descend on the boys, but instead of pulling them apart, they darted between the trees, scooping items into their arms. Tools were scattered on the ground—more axes, knives, even spears. Bellamy smiled as his eyes landed on a bow and arrow.

Just this morning, he'd found animal prints—goddamn real tracks, leading into the trees. His discovery had caused a huge commotion. At one point, there'd been at least three dozen people gathered around, all making intelligent, helpful observations like *It's probably not a bird* and *It looks like it has four legs*. Finally, Bellamy had been the one to point out that they were hooves, not paws, which meant that it was probably an herbivore, and therefore something they could conceivably catch and eat. He'd just been waiting for something to hunt with, and now, in his first stroke of good luck on Earth, he had it. Hopefully he and Octavia would be long gone before the nutrition packets ran out, but he wasn't taking any chances.

"Hold it, everyone," a voice rang out over the crowd. Bellamy glanced up as Wells reached the tree line. "We can't just let random people carry weapons. We need to sort and organize these, and *then* decide who should have them."

A flurry of snorts and defiant glares rose up from the crowd.

"That guy took the Chancellor hostage," Wells went on, pointing at Bellamy, who'd already swung the bow and arrows over his shoulder. "Who knows what else he's capable of. You want someone like *him* walking around carrying a deadly weapon?" Wells raised his chin. "We should at least put it to a vote."

Bellamy couldn't help but laugh. Who the hell did this kid think he was, anyway? He reached down, picked a knife up off the ground, and began walking toward Wells.

Wells stood his ground, and Bellamy wondered if he was trying not to flinch, or if maybe Wells was less of a pushover than Bellamy had thought. Just when it seemed like he might stab Wells in the chest, Bellamy flipped the weapon so that the handle faced Wells, and pushed it into his hand.

"Breaking news, pretty boy." Bellamy winked. "We're all criminals here."

But before he had time to respond, Graham sauntered over. As he looked from Wells to Bellamy, a wry smile flickered across his face.

"I agree with the right honorable mini-Chancellor," Graham said. "We should lock up the weapons."

Bellamy took a step back. "What? And put you in charge of those as well?" He ran his finger along the bow. "No way. I'm ready to hunt."

Graham snorted. "And what exactly did you hunt back on Walden except for girls with low standards and even lower self-esteem?"

Bellamy stiffened but didn't say anything. It was a waste of time to rise to Graham's bait, but he could feel his fingers clenching.

"Or maybe you don't even have to chase after them," Graham continued. "I suppose that's the benefit to having a sister."

With a sickening crunch, Bellamy's fist sank into Graham's jaw. Graham staggered back a few steps, too stunned to raise his arms before Bellamy landed another punch. Then he righted himself and struck Bellamy with a powerful, well-aimed shot to the chin. Bellamy lunged forward with a growl, using his whole body weight to send Graham flying backward. He landed on the grass with a heavy thud, but just when Bellamy was about to deliver a swift kick, Graham rolled to the side and knocked Bellamy's legs out from under him.

Bellamy thrashed around, trying to sit up in time to gain leverage over his opponent, but it was too late. Graham had him pinned to the ground and was holding something just above his face, something that glinted in the sun. A knife.

"That's *enough*," Wells shouted. He grabbed Graham by the collar and flung him off Bellamy, who rolled over onto his side, wheezing.

"What the hell?" Graham bellowed, scrambling to his feet.

Bellamy winced as he rose onto his knees and then slowly stood up and walked over to pick up the bow. He shot a quick glance at Graham, who was too busy glaring at Wells to notice.

"Just because the Chancellor used to tuck you into bed doesn't mean you're automatically in charge," Graham spat. "I don't care what Daddy told you before we left."

"I have no interest in being in *charge*. I just want to make sure we don't *die*."

Graham exchanged a glance with Asher. "If that's your concern, then I suggest you mind your own business." He reached down and scooped up the knife. "We wouldn't want there to be any accidents."

"That's not how we're going to do things here," Wells said, holding his ground.

"Yeah?" Graham raised his eyebrows. "And what makes you think you have any say over that?"

"Because I'm not an idiot. But if you're anxious to become the first thug to try to kill someone on Earth in centuries, be my guest."

Bellamy exhaled as he crossed the clearing toward the area where he'd seen the animal tracks. He didn't need to get pulled into a pissing contest, not when there was food to find. He swung the bow over his shoulder and stepped into the woods.

As he'd learned at a young age, if you wanted to get something done, you had to do it yourself.

Bellamy had been eight years old during the first visit.

His mother hadn't been home, but she'd told him exactly what to do. The guards rarely inspected their unit. Many of them had grown up nearby, and while the recruits liked showing off their uniforms and hassling their former rivals, investigating their neighbors' flats felt like crossing the line. But it was obvious the officer in charge of this regiment wasn't a local. It wasn't just his snooty accent. It was the way he'd looked around their tiny flat with a mixture of surprise and disgust, like he couldn't imagine human beings living there.

He'd come in without knocking while Bellamy had been trying to clean the breakfast dishes. They only had running water a few hours a day, generally while his mother was working in the solar fields. Bellamy was so startled, he dropped the cup he was cleaning and watched in horror as it bounced on the floor and rolled toward the closet.

The officer's eyes darted back and forth as he read something off his cornea slip. "Bellamy Blake?" he said in his weird Phoenix accent that made it sound like his mouth was full of nutrition paste. Bellamy nodded slowly. "Is your mother home?"

"No," he said, working hard to keep his voice steady, just like he'd practiced.

Another guard stepped through the door. After a nod from the officer, he began asking questions in a dull, flat tone that suggested he'd given the same speech a dozen times already that day.

"Do you have more than three meals' worth of food in your residence?" he droned. Bellamy shook his head. "Do you have an energy source other than . . ."

Bellamy's heart was beating so loudly, it seemed to drown out the guard's voice. Although his mother had drilled him countless times, practicing any number of scenarios, he never imagined the way the officer's eyes would move around their flat. When his eyes landed on the dropped cup then moved to the closet, Bellamy thought his chest was going to explode.

"Are you going to answer his question?"

Bellamy looked up and saw both men staring at him. The officer was scowling impatiently, and the other guard just looked bored.

Bellamy started to apologize, but his "Sorry" came out like a wheeze.

"Do you have any permanent residents other than the two people registered for this unit?"

Bellamy took a deep breath. "No," he said, forcing the word out. He finally remembered to affect the annoyed expression his mother had him practice in the mirror.

The officer raised one eyebrow. "So sorry to have wasted your time," he said with mock cordiality. With a final glance around the flat, he strode out, followed by the guard, who slammed the door shut behind him.

Bellamy sank to his knees, too terrified to answer the question rattling through his mind: What would have happened if they'd looked in the closet?

CHAPTER 11

Glass

As she trailed behind Cora and Huxley on their way to the Exchange, Glass found herself wishing that her mother had waited a few more days before spreading the news of her pardon. At first, she'd been overjoyed to see her friends. When they'd walked through her door that morning, all three girls had burst into sobs. But now, watching Cora and Huxley exchange knowing smiles as they passed a boy Glass didn't recognize, she felt more alone than she ever had in her cell.

"I bet you have a ton of points saved up," Huxley said as she wrapped her arm around Glass. "I'm jealous."

"All I have is what my mother transferred to me this

morning." Glass gave her a weak smile. "The rest were eliminated after my arrest."

Huxley shuddered dramatically. "I still can't believe it." She lowered her voice. "You never did tell us why you were Confined."

"She doesn't want to talk about that," Cora said as she glanced nervously over her shoulder.

No, you *don't want to talk about that*, Glass thought as they turned onto the main B deck corridor, a long, wide passage bordered by panoramic windows on one side and benches tucked between artificial plants on the other. It was midday, and most of the benches were occupied by women her mother's age talking and sipping sunflower root tea. Technically, you were supposed to use ration points at the tea stand, but Glass couldn't remember the last time she'd been asked to scan her thumb. It was just one of the many small luxuries of life on Phoenix that she'd never given a second thought until she started spending time with Luke.

As the girls strode down the corridor, Glass could feel nearly every pair of eyes turn to her. Her stomach twisted as she wondered what had been more shocking—the fact that she'd been Confined or the fact that she'd been pardoned. She held her head up high and tried to look confident as she walked past. Glass was supposed to be an example of the Colony's sense of justice, and she would have to keep face as though her life depended on it. Because this time, it did.

"Do you think there's any chance Clarke will get pardoned too?" Huxley asked as Cora shot her a warning look. "Did you guys ever like, hang out, while you were in Confinement?"

"Oh my god, Huxley, will you give it a rest?" Cora said, touching Glass's arm in a supportive gesture. "Sorry," she said. "It's just that, when Clarke was sentenced just after you, nobody could believe it: two Phoenix girls in a few months? And then when you came back, there were all these rumors. . . ."

"It's fine," Glass said, forcing a smile to signal that she was okay talking about it. "Clarke got put into solitary pretty quickly, so I didn't see her much. And I don't know whether she'll be pardoned," she lied, remembering her mom's imperative that she not talk about the Earth mission. "I'm not sure when she turns eighteen—my case was reevaluated since it's almost my birthday."

"Oh, right, your birthday!" Huxley squealed, clapping her hands. "I forgot it's coming up. We'll have to find you something at the Exchange."

Cora nodded, seeming overjoyed to have found their way back to such an acceptable topic, as the girls approached their destination.

The Phoenix Exchange was in a large hall at the end of

B deck. In addition to panoramic windows, it held an enormous chandelier that had supposedly been evacuated from the Paris Opera house hours before the first bomb fell on Western Europe. Whenever Glass heard the tale, she felt a twinge of sadness for the people who might've been saved instead, but she couldn't deny that the chandelier was breathtaking. Dancing with reflected light from the ceiling and the windows, it looked like a small cluster of stars, a miniature galaxy spinning and shimmering overhead.

Huxley let go of Glass's arm and dashed over to a display of ribbons, oblivious to the nearby group of girls who'd fallen silent at Glass's arrival. Glass blushed and hurried after Cora, whose eyes were trained on a textile booth near the back wall.

She stood awkwardly next to Cora while her friend rummaged through the fabric, quickly reducing the orderly stack into a messy pile while the Walden woman behind the table gave her a tight smile. "Look at all this crap," Cora muttered as she flung a piece of burlap and a few strips of fleece to the side.

"What are you looking for?" Glass asked, running her finger along a tiny scrap of pale-pink silk. It was beautiful, even with the rust marks and water stains along the edges, but it would be impossible to find enough matching pieces for a small evening bag, let alone a dress.

"I've spent a million years collecting scraps of blue satin, and I finally have enough for the slip, but I need to layer something over it so it doesn't look too patchworky." Cora wrinkled her nose as she examined a large piece of clear vinyl. "How much is this?"

"Six," the Walden woman said.

"You're not serious." Cora rolled her eyes at Glass. "It's a *shower curtain*."

"It's Earthmade."

Cora snickered. "Authenticated by who?"

"How about this?" Glass asked, holding up a piece of blue netting. It looked like it had once been part of a storage bag, but no one would be able to tell once it was applied to the dress.

"Oooh," Cora cooed, snatching it out of Glass's hand. "I like it." She held it against her body to check the length, then smiled up at Glass. "Good thing your time in Confinement didn't affect your fashion sense." Glass stiffened but said nothing. "So, what are you going to wear?"

"To what?"

"To the viewing party," she said, enunciating her syllables as one might do with a small child. "For the comet?"

"Sorry." Glass shrugged. Apparently, spending six months in Confinement was no excuse for failing to keep up with the Phoenix social calendar.

"Your mother didn't tell you about it when you got back?" Cora continued, holding the netting around her waist like a petticoat. "There's a comet on track to pass right by the ship—the closest any has come since the Colony was founded."

"And there's a viewing party?"

Cora nodded. "On the observation deck. They've been making all sorts of exceptions so there can be food, drinks, music, everything. I'm going with Vikram." She grinned, but then her face fell. "I'm sure he won't mind if you come along. He knows there are, well, extenuating circumstances." She gave Glass a sympathetic smile and turned back to the Walden woman. "How much?"

"Nine."

Suddenly, Glass's head began to pound. She murmured an excuse to Cora, who was still negotiating with the shop-keeper, and wandered off to look at the display of jewelry on a nearby table. She brushed her fingers absently along her bare throat. She'd always worn a necklace chip, the device some girls on Phoenix chose as an alternative to earbuds or cornea slips. It was fashionable to have the chip embedded in a piece of jewelry, if you were lucky enough to have a relic in the family or managed to find something at the Exchange.

Her eyes traveled over the glittering assemblage and a glint of gold caught her eye—an oval locket on a delicate chain. Glass inhaled sharply as a wave of pain crashed over her, filling every inch of her body with a throbbing mix of grief and sorrow. She knew she should turn away and keep walking, but she couldn't help it.

Glass reached out a trembling arm and picked up the necklace. The outline blurred as tears filled her eyes. She ran her finger carefully over the carving in the back, knowing without having to look that it was an ornate cursive *G*.

"Are you sure you don't mind spending your birthday on Walden?" Luke asked, leaning his head back next to hers on the couch. The look of concern on his face was so sincere, it almost made her laugh.

"How many times do I have to tell you?" Glass swung her legs up so they were lying across Luke's. "There's nowhere else I'd rather be."

"But didn't your mom want to throw you some fancy party?"

Glass rested her head on her shoulder. "Yes, but what's the point if you can't be there?"

"I don't want you giving up your whole life just because I can't be a part of it." Luke ran his fingers down Glass's arm, suddenly serious. "Do you ever wish we hadn't stopped you that night?"

As a member of the prestigious mechanical engineering unit, Luke wasn't normally assigned to checkpoint duty, but he'd been called in one evening when Glass had been hurrying back from studying with Wells.

"Are you kidding?" She raised her head to kiss his cheek. The taste of his skin was enough to make her whole body tingle, and she moved her lips down, tracing the line of his jaw up to his ear. "Breaking curfew that night was the best decision I've ever made," she whispered, smiling as he shuddered slightly.

The curfew wasn't strictly enforced on Phoenix, but she'd been stopped by a pair of guards. One of them had given Glass a hard time, forcing her to provide a thumb scan and then asking hostile questions. Eventually, the other guard had stepped in and insisted on escorting Glass the rest of the way.

"Walking you home was the best decision I ever made," he murmured. "Although it was torture trying to keep myself from kissing you that night."

"Well, then, we'd better make up for lost time now," Glass teased, moving her lips back to his. Her kisses grew more urgent as he placed his hand on the back of her head and wove his fingers through her hair. Glass shifted until she was sitting mostly in Luke's lap, feeling his other arm move down to her waist to keep her from falling.

"I love you," he whispered in her ear. No matter how many times she heard the words, they never ceased to make her shiver.

She pulled away just long enough to breathe, "I love you too," then kissed him again, running her hand lightly down his side and then resting her fingers on the sliver of skin between his shirt and his belt.

"We should take a break," Luke said, gently pushing her hand to the side. Over the past few weeks, it'd become increasingly difficult to keep things from progressing too far.

"I don't want to." Glass gave him a coy smile and returned her lips to his ear. "And it's *my* birthday."

Luke laughed, then groaned as he rose to his feet with Glass in his arms.

"Put me down!" Glass giggled, kicking her feet in the air. "What are you doing?"

Luke took a few steps forward. "Taking you to the Exchange. I'm trading you in for a girl who won't try so hard to get me in trouble."

"*Hey.*" She huffed with mock indignation, then started pounding her fists into his chest. "Put me down!"

He turned away from the door. "Are you going to behave yourself?"

"What? It's not *my* fault you're too hot to keep my hands off of."

"Glass," he warned.

"Fine. Yes, I promise."

"Good." He walked back to the couch and laid her gently back down. "Because it'd be a shame if I couldn't give you your present."

"What is it?" Glass asked, pushing herself up into a seated position.

"A chastity belt," Luke said gravely. "For me. I found it at the Exchange. It cost a fortune, but it's worth it to protect—"

Glass smacked him in the chest. Luke laughed and wrapped his arms around her. "Sorry," he said with a grin. He reached into his pocket then paused. "It's not wrapped or anything."

"That's okay."

He pulled something out of his pocket and extended his arm toward her. A gold locket glittered on his palm.

"Luke, it's beautiful," Glass whispered, reaching out to take the locket. Her eyes widened as her fingers ran along its delicate edges. "This is Earthmade." She looked up at him in surprise.

He nodded. "Yes, at least, it's supposed to be, according to the records." He picked it up out of her hand. "May I?"

Glass nodded, and Luke stepped behind her to fasten the clasp. She shivered at the touch of his hand on her neck as he brushed her hair to the side. She could only imagine how much something like this cost—Luke must have used his entire savings on it. Even as a guard, he didn't have many ration points to spare. "I love it," Glass said, running her finger along the chain as she turned to face him.

His smile lit up his whole face. "I'm so glad." Luke ran his hand down her neck and turned the locket over, revealing a *G* etched into the gold.

"Did you do that?" Glass asked.

Luke nodded. "Even in a thousand years, I want people to

know that it belonged to you." He pressed his finger against the locket, pushing the metal against her skin. "Now you just have to fill it with your own memories."

Glass smiled. "I know what memory I want to start with." She looked up, expecting to see Luke roll his eyes, but his face was serious. Their eyes met, and for a long moment, the flat was silent except for the sound of their beating hearts.

"Are you sure?" Luke asked, his brow furrowing slightly as he ran a finger along the inside of her arm.

"More sure than I've been of anything in my life."

Luke took Glass's hand, and a current of electricity shot through her. He squeezed his fingers around hers and, without a word, led her toward his bedroom.

Of course he'd traded it, Glass told herself. It'd be ridiculous to keep such a valuable item, especially after she'd broken his heart. Yet the thought of her discarded necklace languishing alone in the Exchange unleashed a pang of grief that threatened to rip her heart in two. A prickle on the back of her neck pulled Glass from her thoughts. She braced herself, expecting to see another vague acquaintance staring at her with open suspicion. But when she turned around, her eyes landed on someone else entirely.

Luke.

He stared at her just long enough for Glass to blush, then

broke away as his eyes flitted toward the table. An odd expression crossed his face as his gaze landed on the necklace. "I'm surprised no one's snatched it up yet," he said quietly. "It's so beautiful." His arm dropped back to his side, and he turned around to give her a small, sad smile. "But then again, the beautiful ones can hurt you the most."

"Luke," Glass began, "I—" But then she noticed a familiar figure behind Luke. Camille stood behind the counter of the paper texts stall, her eyes fixed on Glass.

Luke glanced over his shoulder and then turned back to Glass. "Camille's covering for her father. He's been sick."

"I'm sorry," Glass said. But before she had time to say anything else, she was distracted by the sound of raised voices.

Glass turned and saw Cora shouting at the Walden woman. "If you refuse to charge me a reasonable price, then I'll have no choice but to report you for fraud." The woman paled and said something Glass couldn't hear, but apparently, it was to Cora's liking, because she smiled and held her thumb up to be scanned.

Glass grimaced, embarrassed by her friend's behavior. "Sorry—I should go."

"Don't," Luke pleaded, touching her arm. "I've been worried about you." He lowered his voice. "What are you doing here? Is it safe?"

The concern in his voice filled some of the smaller cracks

in her battered heart, but not enough to make the pain go away. "It's safe. I was pardoned, actually," Glass said, trying hard to keep her voice steady.

"Pardoned?" His eyes widened. "Wow. I never thought . . . That's incredible." He paused, as if unsure how to go on. "You know, you never told me why you were Confined in the first place."

Glass cast her eyes toward the ground, fighting an overwhelming urge to tell Luke the truth. *He deserves to be happy*, she reminded herself firmly. *He's not yours anymore.*

"It doesn't matter," she said finally. "I just want to put it all behind me."

Luke stared at her, and for a moment Glass wondered if he could see straight through her. "Well, take care of yourself," he said finally.

Glass nodded. "I will." She knew she was doing the right thing, for once. She just wished it didn't hurt so much.

CHAPTER 12

Clarke

Clarke sat in the dark infirmary tent, watching nervously as Thalia tossed and turned in her sleep, restless from the fever that set in as the infection grew worse.

"What do you think she's dreaming about?"

Clarke turned and saw Octavia sitting up, staring at Thalia wide-eyed.

"I'm not sure," Clarke lied. From the expression on Thalia's face, Clarke could tell she was thinking about her father again. She'd been Confined for trying to steal medicine after the Council had weighed against treating him; with limited medical supplies, they'd deemed his prospects too grim to be worth the resources. Thalia still didn't know what happened to him—whether he'd succumbed to his disease after her arrest, or whether he was still clinging to life, praying that he'd get to see his daughter again someday.

Thalia moaned and curled into a ball, reminding Clarke of Lilly on one of her bad nights, when Clarke would sneak into the lab so her friend wouldn't have to be alone. Although no one was keeping Clarke from helping Thalia, she felt just as frantic, just as helpless. Unless they found the medicine that had been flung from the dropship, there was nothing she could do to ease her suffering.

The flap flew open, flooding the tent with light and cool, pungent air, and Bellamy tumbled in. He had a bow slung over his shoulder, and his eyes were bright. "Good afternoon, ladies," he said with a grin as he strode over to Octavia's cot. He stooped down to ruffle her hair, which was still secured with a neatly tied red ribbon. He was close enough that Clarke couldn't help but notice the faint smell of sweat clinging to his skin, blending with another scent she couldn't identify but that made her think of trees.

"How's the ankle?" he asked Octavia, making an exaggerated show of squinting and examining it from all angles.

She flexed it gingerly. "Much better." She turned to Clarke. "Am I ready to leave yet?"

Clarke hesitated. Octavia's ankle was still fragile, and there was no way of making an effective brace. If she put too much pressure on it, she'd sprain it all over again, or worse.

Octavia sighed, then stuck her bottom lip out in a pleading expression. "Please? I didn't come all the way to Earth to sit in a *tent*."

"*You* didn't have a choice," Bellamy said. "But *I* certainly didn't risk my ass coming here just to watch you get gangrene."

"How do you know about gangrene?" Clarke asked, surprised. No one would ever have developed that kind of infection back on the Colony, and she doubted many other people read ancient medical texts for fun.

"You disappoint me, Doctor." He raised an eyebrow. "I didn't take you for one of those."

"One of those what?"

"One of those Phoenicians who assume all Waldenites are illiterate."

Octavia rolled her eyes as she turned to Bellamy. "Not *everything* is an insult, you know."

Bellamy opened his mouth, but then thought better of it and folded his lips into a smirk. "You better watch it, or I'll leave without you." He adjusted the bow on his shoulder.

"Don't leave me," she said, suddenly serious. "You know how I feel about being trapped inside."

A strange expression flashed across Bellamy's face, and Clarke wondered what he was thinking about. Finally, he smiled. "Okay. I'll take you outside, but just for a little bit. I want to try hunting again before it gets dark." He turned to Clarke. "That is, if the doctor says it's okay."

Clarke nodded. "Just be careful." She gave him a quizzical look. "Do you really think you'll be able to *hunt*?" No one had seen a mammal yet, let alone tried to kill one.

"Someone has to. Our nutrition packs won't last a week at the rate they're going."

She gave him a small smile. "Well, best of luck." Clarke walked over to Octavia's cot and helped Bellamy lift her to her feet.

"I'm fine," Octavia said, balancing on one foot as she clutched Bellamy's arm. She hopped forward, pulling him toward the flap. "Let's go!"

Bellamy twisted to look back over his shoulder. "Oh, by the way, Clarke, I found some debris from the crash when I was out in the woods. Any interest in checking it out tomorrow?"

Clarke inhaled as her heart sped up. "You think it could be the missing supplies?" She took a step forward. "Let's go now."

Bellamy shook his head. "It was too far away. We wouldn't make it back before dark. We'll go tomorrow."

She glanced at Thalia, whose face was still contorted in pain. "Okay. First thing in the morning."

"Let's wait until the afternoon. I'll be hunting in the

morning. That's when the animals are out looking for water." Clarke suppressed the urge to ask him where he'd learned that, although she couldn't quite mask the surprise on her face. "Until tomorrow, then?" Bellamy asked, and Clarke nodded. "Great." He grinned. "It's a date."

She watched them lumber out of the tent, then went back over to Thalia. Her friend's eyes fluttered open. "Hi," she said weakly.

"How are you feeling?" Clarke asked, moving to check Thalia's vital signs.

"Great," she croaked. "Just about ready to join Bellamy on his next hunting expedition."

Clarke smiled. "I thought you were sleeping."

"I was. Off and on."

"I'm just going to take a quick look, okay?" Clarke asked, and Thalia nodded. Clarke pushed the blanket aside and lifted Thalia's shirt. Streaks of red radiated out from the oozing wound, suggesting that the infection was making its way into her bloodstream.

"Does it hurt?"

"No," Thalia said hollowly. They both knew she wasn't getting any better.

"Can you believe they're really siblings?" Clarke asked, purposefully changing the subject as she replaced Thalia's blanket.

"Yeah, it's crazy to think about." Thalia's voice grew slightly stronger.

"What's crazy is pulling a stunt like that on the launch deck," Clarke said. "But it was really brave. They would've killed him if they'd caught him." She paused. "They'll kill him when they come down."

"He's done a lot to keep her safe," Thalia agreed, turning her face away from Clarke in an attempt to hide a grimace as a new wave of pain washed over her. "He really loves you, you know."

"Who? *Bellamy?*" Clarke asked, startled.

"No. Wells. He came to *Earth* for you, Clarke."

She pressed her lips together. "I didn't ask him to."

"We've all done things we're not proud of," Thalia said, her voice quiet.

Clarke shuddered and closed her eyes. "I'm not asking anyone for forgiveness."

"That's not what I mean, and you know it." Thalia paused to catch her breath. The effort it took to speak was wearing her out.

"You need to rest," Clarke said, reaching over to pull the blanket up over her friend's shoulders. "We can talk about this tomorrow."

"*No*!" Thalia exclaimed. "Clarke, what happened wasn't your fault."

“Of course it was my fault.” Clarke refused to meet her friend’s gaze. Thalia was the only one who knew what Clarke had really done, and Clarke couldn’t bear to face that right now, to see the memory reflected in her friend’s dark, expressive eyes. “And what does it have to do with Wells anyway?”

Thalia closed her eyes and sighed, ignoring the question. “You need to let yourself be happy. Or else, what’s the point of anything?”

Clarke opened her mouth to launch a retort, but the words disappeared as she watched Thalia lean over, suddenly coughing. “It’ll be okay,” Clarke whispered, running her hand through her friend’s sweat-dampened hair. “You’ll be okay.”

This time, the words weren’t a prayer but a declaration. Clarke refused to let Thalia die, and nothing was going to stop her. She wouldn’t let her best friend join the chorus of ghosts in her head.

CHAPTER 13

Wells

Wells looked up at the star-filled sky. He never imagined how homesick it would make him to stare at the familiar scene from hundreds of kilometers away. It was unsettling to see the moon so tiny and featureless, like waking up to find that your family's faces had been erased.

Sitting at the campfire around him, the others were grumbling. They'd been on Earth less than a week, and already their rations were dwindling. The fact that they had no medicine was troubling, but right now the bigger concern was the food supply. Either the Colony miscalculated their provisions, or Graham and his friends had been hoarding more than he'd realized. Either way, the effects were already beginning to show. It wasn't just the hollows forming under their cheekbones—there was a hunger in their eyes that terrified Wells. He could never let himself forget that they'd all been Confined for a reason, that everyone surrounding him had done something to endanger the Colony.

Wells most of all.

Just then, Clarke emerged from the infirmary tent and walked toward the campfire, her eyes skimming the circle as she searched for a spot. There was an empty space next to Wells, but her gaze skipped right over him. She sat beside Octavia, who was perched on a log, her injured leg stretched out in front of her.

Wells sighed as he turned to look around the clearing, the flames flickering on the dark forms of the three tents they'd finally built—the infirmary, a structure to hold supplies, and Wells's personal favorite, a ditch for collecting water, in case it ever rained. At least their camp wasn't turning out to be a complete failure. His father would be impressed when he joined them on Earth.

If he joined them. It was becoming harder and harder to convince himself that his father was fine, that the bullet wound was only superficial. His chest tightened painfully as he thought of his father clinging to life in a hospital bed, or worse, his body floating somewhere through space. His father's words still rang in his ears: *If anyone can make this mission a success, it's you.* After a lifetime of urging Wells to work harder and do better, he wondered if the Chancellor might have given his last order to his son.

A strange noise came from the trees. Wells sat up straighter, all his senses on the alert. There was a crackling sound, followed by a rustling. The murmurs by the fire turned to gasps as a strange shape materialized out of the shadows, part human, part animal, like something from the ancient myths.

Wells leapt to his feet. But then the creature moved past the tree line and into the light.

Bellamy stood with an animal carcass draped over his shoulders, a trail of blood in his wake.

A deer. Wells's eyes traveled over the lifeless animal, taking in its soft brown fur, spindly legs, delicately tapered ears. As Bellamy moved toward them, the deer's head swayed back and forth from its limp neck—but it never made a full arc, because each time it swung back, it knocked against something else.

It was another head, swinging from another slender neck. *The deer had two heads.*

Wells froze as everyone around the fire scrambled to their feet, some of them inching forward for a better look, others backing up in terror. "Is it safe?" one girl asked.

"It's safe." Clarke's voice came from the shadows, and then

she stepped into the light. "The radiation might have mutated the genetic material hundreds of years ago, but there wouldn't be any trace of it now."

Everyone fell silent as Clarke stretched out her hand to stroke the creature's fur. Standing in a pool of moonlight, she never looked so beautiful.

Clarke turned to Bellamy with a smile that made Wells's stomach twist. "We're not going to starve." Then she said something Wells couldn't hear, and Bellamy nodded.

Wells exhaled, willing his resentment to drain away. He took another deep breath before walking toward Bellamy and Clarke. She stiffened as he approached, but Wells forced himself to keep his eyes on Bellamy. "Thank you," Wells said. "This will feed a lot of people."

Bellamy stared at him questioningly as he shifted his weight from one foot to the other.

"I mean it," Wells said. "Thanks."

Finally, Bellamy nodded. Wells went back to his place by the fire, leaving Bellamy and Clarke to talk quietly, their heads bowed together.

The observation deck was completely empty. Staring out into the immeasurably vast sea of stars, Wells could easily imagine that they were the only two living things in the entire universe. He tightened his arm around Clarke. She pressed her head against his chest and exhaled, sinking closer to him as the air left her body. As if she was happy to let him breathe for them both.

"How'd it go today?" she murmured.

"Fine," Wells said, not sure why he was bothering to lie when Clarke was pressed against his chest. She could read his heartbeat like it was Morse code.

"What happened?" she asked, concern flickering in her large green eyes.

His officer training entailed periodic trips to Walden and Arcadia to monitor the guards. Today, he'd observed them seize a woman who'd gotten pregnant with an unregistered child. There'd be no chance at lenience. She would be Confined until she gave birth, the child would be placed in the Council's care, and the mother would be executed. The law was harsh but necessary. The ship could only support a certain number of lives, and allowing anyone to disrupt the delicate balance would jeopardize the entire race. But the look of panic in the woman's eyes as the guards had dragged her away was burned into Wells's brain.

Surprisingly, it'd been his father who helped Wells make sense of what he'd seen. That night at dinner, he'd sensed something was wrong, and Wells had told him about the incident, trying to sound soldierly and detached. But his father had seen through the act and, in a rare gesture, put his hand over Wells's across the table. "What we do isn't easy," he'd told his son, "but it's crucial.

We can't afford to let our feelings keep us from doing our duty—keeping the human race alive."

"Let me guess," Clarke said, interrupting his thoughts. "You arrested some criminal mastermind for stealing books from the library."

"Nope." He swept a piece of hair behind her ear. "She's still at large. They're forming a special task force as we speak."

She smiled, and the flecks of gold in her eyes seemed to sparkle. He couldn't imagine a prettier color.

Wells turned his attention back to the enormous window. Tonight, the clouds covering Earth didn't remind him of a shroud—they were merely a blanket. The planet hadn't died, it'd only slipped into an enchanted sleep until the time came for it to welcome humanity home.

"What are you thinking about?" Clarke asked. "Is it your mom?"

"No," he said slowly. "Not really." Wells reached out and absentmindedly wrapped a lock of Clarke's hair around his finger, then let it fall back to her shoulder. "Though I guess, in a way, I'm always thinking about her." It was hard to believe that she was really gone.

"I just want to make sure she's proud of me, wherever she is," Wells continued, a chill passing over him as he glanced toward the stars.

Clarke squeezed his hand, transferring her warmth to him.

"Of course she's proud of you. Any mother would be proud of a son like you."

Wells turned back to Clarke with a grin. "Just mothers?"

"I imagine you're a hit with grandparents, too." She nodded gravely, but then giggled when Wells playfully smacked her shoulder.

"There's someone else I want to make proud."

Clarke raised an eyebrow. "She'd better watch her back," she said, reaching out to wrap her hands behind Wells's head. "Because I'm not very good at sharing."

Wells grinned as he leaned forward and closed his eyes, brushing his lips against hers for a teasing kiss before moving down to her neck. "Neither am I," he whispered into her ear, feeling her shiver as his breath tickled her skin. She pulled him closer, her touch melting away the tension until he forgot about his day, forgot that he'd have to repeat it all tomorrow and the day after that. All that mattered was the girl in his arms.

The smell of the roasting deer was foreign and intoxicating. There was no meat on the Colony, not even on Phoenix. All the livestock had been eliminated in the middle of the first century.

"How do we know when it's done?" an Arcadian girl named Darcy asked Wells.

"When the outside starts to crisp and the inside turns pink," Bellamy called without turning his head.

Graham snorted, but Wells nodded. "I think you're right."

After the meat cooled, they chopped it into smaller pieces and began passing it around the fire. Wells carried some to the other side of the circle, distributing it to the crowd.

He handed a piece to Octavia, who held it in front of her as she looked up at Wells. "Have you tried it yet?"

Wells shook his head. "Not yet."

"Well, *that's* not fair." She raised her eyebrows. "What if it turns out to be disgusting?"

He glanced around the circle. "Everyone else seems to be okay with it."

Octavia pursed her lips together. "I'm not like everyone else." She looked at him for a moment, as if waiting for him to speak, then smiled and pushed her piece toward him. "Here, you take the first bite and tell me what you think."

"I'm okay, thanks," Wells said. "I want to make sure everyone else—"

"Come on." She giggled as she tried to slip it into his mouth. "Take a bite."

Wells snuck a quick glance around the circle to make sure Clarke hadn't been watching. She wasn't—she was caught up in conversation with Bellamy.

Wells turned back to Octavia. "Okay," he said, taking the

piece of meat from her hands. She looked disappointed not to feed it to him, but Wells didn't care. He took a bite. The outside was tough, but as his teeth sank in, the meat released a flood of flavor unlike anything Wells had tasted before, simultaneously salty and smoky and faintly sweet. He chewed some more and then swallowed, bracing for his stomach to reject the alien substance. But all he felt was warmth.

The kids who'd eaten first had risen from the fire and begun milling around the clearing, and for a few minutes, the soft hum of their conversation merged with the crackling of the flames. But then the sound of confused murmurs began to rise to the surface, making the skin on the back of Wells's neck prickle. He rose to his feet and walked over to where a group was standing near the tree line.

"What's going on?" he asked.

"*Look*." One of the girls pointed to something in the trees.

"What?" Wells squinted into the darkness.

"There," another girl said. "Did you see it?"

For a moment, Wells thought they were playing a trick on him, but then something caught his eye. A flash of light, so brief that he might have imagined it. There was another flash a few feet away, then another, this one a little higher up. He took a step toward the edge of the clearing, which was now ablaze with glowing lights, as if invisible hands had decorated it for a party. His eyes landed on the closest orb, a ball of light hanging from the lowest branch of a nearby tree.

There was something moving inside. A creature. It was some sort of insect, with a tiny body and disproportionately large, delicate wings. The word fluttered to Wells's lips. *Butterfly.*

Some of the others had followed him into the forest and were now staring in wonder alongside him. "Clarke," he whispered into the darkness. She needed to see this. He tore his eyes away and spun around, ready to go run and find her. But she was already there.

Clarke stood a few feet away, utterly transfixed. A soft glow lit up her face, and the tense, worried expression that had clung to her features since the crash had fallen away.

"Hey," Wells said softly, not wanting to disrupt the stillness. He expected Clarke to scowl at him, or silence him, or walk away. But she didn't move. She stood right where she was, staring up at the luminous butterflies.

Wells didn't dare move or say another word. The girl he thought he'd lost was still in there, somewhere, and in that instant, he knew: He could make her love him again.

CHAPTER 14

Bellamy

Bellamy didn't know why the ancient humans even bothered doing drugs. What was the point of shooting junk into your veins when walking through the forest had the same effect? Something happened each time he crossed the tree line. As he moved away from the camp in the early morning sunlight, setting out on another hunting expedition, he began taking deeper breaths. His heart pounded with strong, slow, steady beats, his organs marching in time to a pulse in the ground. It was like someone had hacked into his brain and cranked up his senses to a setting Bellamy hadn't known existed.

But the best part was the quiet. The ship had never been completely silent. There was always a low hum of background noise: the drone of the generators, the buzz of the lights, the echo of footsteps in the hallway. It had freaked him out the first time he entered the forest, not having anything to drown out his thoughts. But the more time he spent here, the quieter his mind became.

Bellamy scanned the ground, his eyes skipping over the rocks and damp patches as they searched for clues. There were no tracks to follow as there'd been yesterday, but something told Bellamy to turn right, and go deeper into the forest where the trees grew thicker, covering the ground with strange shadows. That's where he would go if he were an animal.

He reached behind his shoulder to grab one of the arrows from the sling he'd constructed. Although it was terrible to watch them die, his aim had vastly improved over the past few days, so he knew the animals didn't suffer much. He'd never forget the pain and fear in the first deer's eyes as it staggered across the ground. Yet shooting an animal was less of a crime than a lot of the crap the other kids had done to end up here. While he might be cutting the creature's life short, Bellamy knew that it had lived every moment of that life completely free.

The hundred prisoners might have been promised their freedom, but Bellamy knew he wouldn't be afforded the same privilege, not after what he'd done to the Chancellor. If he was still around when the next ship landed, the first person off it would probably shoot him on the spot.

Bellamy was done with all of it—the punishments, the stations, the system. He was through following other people's rules. He was sick of having to fight to survive. Living in the forest wouldn't be easy, but at least he and Octavia would be free.

Holding his arms out for balance, he half shuffled, half skidded down the slope, trying his best to not make any noise that could scare an animal away. He landed at the bottom with a thud, mud squelching under his tattered boots. Bellamy winced as water sloshed through the gap above the soles. It would be uncomfortable walking back to camp with wet socks, something he'd learned the hard way. He wasn't sure why that wasn't mentioned in any of the books he read. What was the point of knowing how to build a snare out of vines, or which plants to use to treat burns, if you couldn't walk?

Bellamy laid his socks over a branch to dry, then dipped his feet into the stream. It was already hotter out than it had been when he left camp, and the cold water felt incredible on his skin. He rolled his pants up to his knees and waded in farther, grinning like a complete doofus as the water swirled around his calves. It was one of his favorite things about Earth, how mundane stuff like washing your feet suddenly felt like a huge deal.

The trees weren't as dense by the stream, and the sun shone brighter. Bellamy's face and arms suddenly felt unbearably hot. He pulled off his T-shirt, crumpled it into a ball, and tossed it onto the grass before reaching down to scoop water into his hands and splash it over his face. He smiled, still blown away by the revelation that water could have a *taste*. They'd always made crude jokes about the ship's recycled water supply, how you were basically drinking your great-grandfather's piss. Yet now he realized that the centuries of filtration and purification had stripped the liquid until it was no more than a collection of hydrogen and oxygen molecules. He reached down and cupped another handful. If he'd had to describe it, he would say it tasted like a combination of Earth and sky—and then he'd punch whoever laughed at him for it.

A crack sounded from inside the woods. Bellamy spun around so quickly, he lost his balance and fell backward with a splash. He quickly scrambled to his feet, rocks and mud shifting beneath his bare toes as he turned to look for the source of the sound.

"Sorry, I didn't mean to scare you."

Bellamy pushed his hair back and saw Clarke standing on the grass. It was startling to see someone else in the woods, which he'd come to think of as belonging exclusively to him. But the flash of irritation he was expecting never came. "You couldn't wait till afternoon?" he asked, making his way back to the bank.

Clarke blushed. "We need that medicine," she said as she looked away from his bare chest. She was so tough most of the time, it was easy to forget that she grew up in a world of fancy concerts and lecture parties. Bellamy grinned as he shook his head, sending droplets of water flying.

"*Hey*," she shouted, jumping backward as she tried to flick the water off. "We haven't tested this stream yet. That could be toxic."

"Since when did our badass surgeon become such a priss?" He sat down in a sunny patch of grass and patted the spot next to him in invitation.

"A *priss*?" Clarke lowered herself to the ground with a huff. "You could barely hold the knife last night, your hand was shaking so badly."

"Hey, I *killed* the deer. I think I did more than my fair share. Besides"—he paused as he lay back on the grass—"you're the one who's trained to cut things open."

"I'm not, really."

Bellamy brought his hands behind his head and tilted his face toward the sun, exhaling as the warmth seeped into his skin. It was almost as nice as being in bed with a girl. Maybe even better, because the sun would never ask him what he was thinking. "Sorry to insult you," he said, stretching out the words as a relaxed heaviness settled in his limbs. "I know you're a doctor, not a butcher."

"No, I mean I was Confined before I finished my apprenticeship."

The note of sorrow in her voice reverberated strangely in Bellamy's gut. He gave her a weak smile. "Well, you're doing a great job for a quack."

She stared at him, and for a second, he worried he'd offended her. But then she nodded and stood up. "You're right," she said. "Which is why we need to find that medicine. Come on."

Bellamy rose to his feet with a groan, slipped into his shoes and socks, then slung his shirt over his shoulder.

"I'd recommend putting your shirt back on."

"Why? Are you worried you won't be able to control yourself? Because if you're concerned about my virtue, I have to tell you, I'm not—"

"I meant"—she cut him off with a small smile—"there are some poisonous plants out here that could make that pretty back of yours erupt with pus-filled boils."

He shrugged. "For all I know, that might be your thing, doctor girl. I'll take my chances."

She laughed for what Bellamy was pretty sure was her first time on Earth. He felt a surprising flicker of pride that he'd been the one to make it happen.

"Okay," he said lightly, pulling his shirt over his head and smiling to himself when he caught Clarke's eyes on his stomach. "The wreckage was farther west. Let's go." He started walking up the slope, then turned to look at Clarke. "The direction the sun sets in."

She ran a few steps to catch up to him. "You taught yourself all of this?"

"I guess. There aren't a lot of lectures on Earth's geography on Walden." The statement didn't carry the bitterness it might have, had it been directed at Wells or Graham. "I'd always been interested in that stuff, and then when I found out they were planning on sending Octavia to Earth . . ." He paused, not sure how much it was safe to share. But Clarke was looking at him expectantly, her green eyes full of curiosity and something else he couldn't quite identify. "I figured, the more I knew, the better equipped I'd be to keep her safe."

They reached the top of the slope, but instead of heading back toward camp, Bellamy led them deeper into the woods. The trees grew so close together that their leaves blocked most of the sun. What little light made it through dappled the ground in golden pools. Bellamy smiled as he saw Clarke taking care to step around them, like a little kid trying to avoid the lines crossing the skybridge.

"This is how I imagined Sherwood Forest," she said, her

voice full of reverence. "I almost expect to see Robin Hood pop out from behind a tree."

"Robin Hood?"

"You know." She stopped to look at him. "The exiled prince who stole medicine to give to the orphans?" Bellamy stared at her blankly. "With the enchanted bow and arrows? You kind of remind me of him, now that I think about it," she added, smiling.

Bellamy ran his hand along a vine-covered branch that shimmered slightly in the dim light. "We don't get a lot of story time on Walden," he said stiffly. But then his voice softened. "There aren't many books, so I used to make up fairy tales for Octavia when she was little. Her favorite was about an enchanted trash can." He snorted. "It was the best I could do."

Clarke smiled. "It was brave, what you did for her," she said.

"Yeah, well, I'd say the same thing about you, but I have a feeling you're not exactly here by choice."

She held up her wrist, which, like all the others', was still encased in the monitor bracelet. "What gave it away?"

"I'm sure he deserved it," Bellamy said with a grin. But instead of laughing, Clarke turned away. He'd meant it as a joke, but he should have known that he couldn't be so glib with her—with anyone who was here, really. They were all hiding something. Bellamy most of all.

"Hey, I'm sorry," he said. He apologized so rarely, the word felt strange in his mouth. "We'll find the medicine chest. What's in it, anyway?"

"Everything. Sterile bandages, painkillers, antibiotics . . . things that could make all the difference to . . ." She paused for a moment. "To the injured people."

Bellamy knew she was thinking about the one girl she was always watching over, her friend.

"You really care about her, don't you?" He held out his hand to help her over a moss-covered log blocking their path.

"She's my best friend," Clarke said, taking his hand. "The only person on Earth who knows the real me."

She shot an embarrassed smile at Bellamy, but he nodded. "I know what you mean." Octavia was the only person in the world who truly knew him. There was no one else he really cared about ever seeing again.

But then he glanced over at Clarke, who was leaning over to breathe in the scent of a bright-pink flower, the sun catching the gold strands in her hair, and suddenly he wasn't so sure.

CHAPTER 15

Clarke

Bellamy led Clarke down a steep hill bordered by slender trees whose branches wove together to form a sort of archway. The silence felt ancient, as if even the wind hadn't dared to disturb the solitude of the trees for centuries.

"I'm not sure I ever thanked you for what you did for Octavia," Bellamy said, breaking the spell.

"Does this count as a thank-you?" Clarke teased.

"I think it's the closest you're going to get." He shot her a sidelong look. "I'm not the best at stuff like that."

Clarke opened her mouth, but before she could launch a retort, she stumbled over a rock. "Whoa there," Bellamy said with a laugh, grabbing Clarke's hand to steady her. "And apparently, you're not the best at stuff like *walking*."

"This isn't walking. This is *hiking*—something no human has done for hundreds of years, so give me a break."

"It's okay. It's all about division of labor. You keep us alive, and I'll keep you on two feet." He gave her a playful squeeze, and Clarke felt her face flush. She hadn't realized she was still clutching his hand.

"Thanks," she said, letting her arm fall to her side.

Bellamy paused as they reached the point where the ground flattened out again. "This way," he said, gesturing to the left. "So, how did you end up becoming a doctor?"

Clarke's eyebrows knit in confusion. "I wanted to. Didn't you choose to . . ." She trailed off, realizing, to her embarrassment, that she had no idea what Bellamy had done back on the ship. Clearly he hadn't been a guard.

He stared at her, as if trying to determine whether or not she was joking. "It doesn't work that way on Walden," he said slowly, stepping deeper into the green-tinged shade. "If you've got a great record and you get lucky, you can become a guard. Otherwise you just do whatever job your parents had."

Clarke tried to keep the surprise from registering on her face. Of course she knew only certain jobs were available to Waldenites, but she hadn't realized they had no choice at all. "So what were you?"

"I was . . ." He pressed his lips together. "You know what? It doesn't matter what I did back there."

"I'm sorry," Clarke said quickly. "I didn't mean that—"

"It's fine," Bellamy cut her off, taking a step forward. They continued walking, although now, the silence had an edge to it.

"Hold on," Bellamy whispered, reaching out a hand to block her path. In one fluid motion, he pulled out one of the arrows tucked into his sling and raised his bow. His eyes fixed on a spot where the trees were so dense, it was almost impossible to distinguish the shrubs from the shadows. Then she saw it—a flash of motion, a glint of light reflected in an eye. Clarke held her breath as an animal emerged, small and brown with long, tapered ears that flicked back and forth. A rabbit.

She watched the creature spring forward, its tail almost twice as long as its body, twitching curiously. *Aren't rabbits supposed to have little, fluffy tails?* she wondered. But before she could remember her old notes from Biology of Earth class, Clarke saw Bellamy's elbow draw back, chasing every thought out of her head.

Her gasp caught in her throat as Bellamy's arrow shot forward, landing with a terrible thwack right in the creature's chest. For a second, Clarke wondered if she could save it—run over, remove the arrow, and stitch it back up.

Bellamy grabbed her arm, squeezing it just hard enough to convey both assurance and warning. That rabbit was going to help keep them alive, Clarke knew. It would give Thalia a little strength. She tried to close her eyes, but they remained locked on the animal.

"It's okay," Bellamy said quietly. "I got it through the heart. He won't suffer for long." He was right. The rabbit stopped twitching and slowly fell to the forest floor, then went still. Bellamy turned to her. "Sorry. I know it's not easy to watch someone suffer."

A chill passed over her that had nothing to do with the dead rabbit. "Someone?"

"Some*thing*." He corrected himself with a shrug. "Anything."

Clarke watched Bellamy jog over to the rabbit, extract the arrow, and swing the creature over his shoulder. "Let's go this way," he said, inclining his head.

The tension seemed to have drained away, Bellamy's mood visibly bolstered by his successful kill. "So, what's the story with you and Wells?" he asked, shifting the rabbit over to his other shoulder.

Clarke braced for a rush of indignation at his nosiness, but it never came. "We dated for a little bit, a while ago, but it didn't work out."

Bellamy snickered. "Yeah, well, that part was obvious."

He paused, waiting for Clarke to continue. "So," he prodded, "what happened?"

"He did something unforgivable."

Instead of making a joke or using the opportunity to make a jab at Wells, Bellamy grew serious. "I don't think anything's unforgivable," he said quietly. "Not if it's done for the right reasons."

Clarke didn't say anything, but couldn't help wondering whether he was talking about what Octavia had done to be Confined, or something else.

Bellamy glanced up, as if the treetops had caught his attention, then looked back at Clarke. "I'm not saying he didn't do something terrible, whatever it was. All I mean is that I sort of understand where he's coming from." He reached out to run his finger along the bright-yellow moss spiraling up the trunk of a tree. "Wells and I are the only two people who *chose* to be here, who came for a reason."

Clarke started to reply, but realized that she wasn't sure what to say. They were so different on the surface—Wells, whose belief in structure and authority had resulted in her parents' execution, and Bellamy, the hotheaded Waldenite who'd held the Chancellor at gunpoint. But they were both willing to do anything to get what they wanted. To protect the people they cared about.

"Maybe you're right," she said quietly, surprised by his insight.

Bellamy paused, then increased his stride, suddenly excited by whatever he saw. "It was up here," he said, pulling her up another shallow slope into a clearing. The grass was dotted with white flowers, except for a spot about halfway down that was burned black. Pieces of the dropship lay scattered about like bones. Clarke broke into a run.

She heard Bellamy call her name but didn't bother to look back. She stumbled forward, hope blooming in her chest. "Come on, come on, come *on*," she muttered to herself as she began rummaging through the wreckage with a manic frenzy.

Then she saw them. The metal boxes that had once been white but were now discolored by the dirt and flames. She grabbed the closest one and held it up, her heart pounding so fast it became difficult to breathe. Clarke fumbled with the misshapen clasp. It wouldn't open. The heat had welded the hinges shut. Frantically, she shook the box, praying that the medicine had survived.

The sound of pill bottles rattling around inside was the sweetest thing she had ever heard.

"Is that it?" Bellamy asked, skidding to a breathless stop next to her.

"Can you open this?" Clarke shoved the box at his chest.

He held it up, squinting at the clasp. "Let me see." He removed a knife from his pocket, and with a few quick movements, pried the chest open.

Exhilaration fizzed through Clarke's body. Before she realized what she was doing, she had thrown her arms around Bellamy. He joined in her laughter as he staggered backward, and wrapped his arms around her waist, lifting her up and spinning her through the air. The colors of the clearing swirled, green and gold and blue all blurring until there was nothing in the world but Bellamy's smile, lighting up his eyes.

Finally, he set her down gently on the ground. But he didn't loosen his hold. Instead, he pulled her even closer, and before Clarke had time to catch her breath, his lips were on hers.

A voice in the back of her brain told her to stop, but it was overpowered by the smell of his skin and the pressure of his touch.

Clarke felt like she was melting into his arms, losing herself in the kiss.

He tasted like joy, and joy tasted better on Earth.

CHAPTER 16

Glass

"I don't know," Sonja said slowly, squinting at her daughter in the dim light of the bedroom. "What if we take the skirt off that one and combine it with the green bodice?"

Glass forced herself to take a deep, calming breath. She'd been trying on gowns for two hours, and they were no closer to picking one for the comet viewing party than when they'd started. "Whatever you think, Mom," she said, hoping her smile didn't look as strained as it felt.

"I'm not sure." Glass's mother sighed. "It'll be hard to have it ready in time, but we'll just have to do our best."

Glass reminded herself that her mother was only trying to help. She saw the comet viewing party as the perfect moment for Glass to reenter Phoenix society, armed with the official pardon and dressed to perfection. Glass knew the Vice Chancellor would be there, and that it was essential to play her part; she'd gotten back her life in exchange for giving him a better image, which was a more than fair trade-off. Still, Glass felt anxious about making herself the center of attention.

"Or maybe we should go back to the tulle?" Her mother gestured to the pile of discarded gowns. "Just put it back on and we can—" She was cut off by the beep of a message alert from the kitchen.

"I'll get it," Glass said quickly, hurrying from the room before her mother had time to protest. It wouldn't be for her, of course. Her friends only contacted each other via chips; message screens were generally reserved for pointless updates from sanitation, or slightly more ominous alerts from the Council. But it would at least provide a brief respite from dress talk. Glass projected the message queue in the air in front of her. Her breath caught in her chest as she saw the blinking name at the top. It was from Luke.

Dear Miss Sorenson,

Security recovered a missing item of yours near the solar fields. It will be held at the checkpoint until 1600 today.

She had to read it several times before the message sank in. She and Luke had created this system long ago, before she got her chip, in case her mother ever snooped through her messages. He wanted her to meet him by the solar fields that afternoon.

"Glass?" Sonja called from the other room. "What was it?"

She deleted the message quickly. "Just a reminder about the comet viewing, as if we could forget!" She glanced at the clock and sighed. It was only 1015. The next few hours were going to pass more slowly than they had in Confinement.

"Oh," Glass's mother gasped when Glass stepped back into the bedroom. "Maybe this is the one after all. You look beautiful."

Glass turned hesitantly toward the mirror. She saw what her mother meant. But it wasn't the dress. Her cheeks were flushed, her eyes bright with anticipation.

She looked like a girl in love.

At 1540, Glass climbed the endless flight of stairs up to the solar fields that covered the top of Walden. The plants themselves were off-limits to everyone except scientists and gatherers, but there was a small, enclosed deck overlooking the fields. It must've been designed for supervising the workers but had fallen out of use and was almost always empty.

When she reached the top, Glass moved to the edge of the

platform and sat down against the railing, her legs dangling over the side. She felt her body relax as her eyes traveled over the rows of plants stretching their leaves toward the solar panels. The far side of the field was bordered by an enormous window that made it look as though the crops were growing right out of the stars. She and Luke used to meet here all the time. It was safer than him sneaking onto Phoenix, or having Glass wander through his residential unit.

"Hey."

Glass turned to see Luke standing stiffly behind her. She started to get to her feet, but he shook his head. "Can I join you?" She nodded and moved her legs to the side to make room, and he lowered himself to the ground. "Thanks for coming," he said awkwardly. "Your mom didn't suspect anything, did she?"

"It's fine. She was too busy trying to solve a dress crisis."

Luke surprised Glass with a smile, then cleared his throat. "Glass, I . . . I haven't been able to stop thinking about what happened," he said, and her whole body tensed. She kept her eyes trained carefully on the ground. "I mean, what someone like you could possibly be Confined for. But then I remembered—a few months after we broke up, I heard a rumor about a girl on Phoenix who was arrested for . . ." His voice broke as he trailed off. Glass turned back to face him and saw that his eyes were glistening. "The timing made sense. But I never believed it could be you." Luke stared straight ahead, as if looking at something far in the distance. "I told myself that you'd never keep something like that a secret from me. I needed to believe that you trusted me more than that."

Glass bit her lip, trying to hold back the flood of words welling up in her throat. She so desperately wanted to tell him, but what good would come from admitting the truth? Better to let him think she was just a silly, spoiled Phoenix girl who'd broken his heart. He was happy with Camille right now—and he deserved to be happy.

But then Luke reached over and cupped her chin in his hand, and all her thoughts faded away.

Glass woke up smiling. Although it'd been a few weeks since the night she and Luke had spent together, she couldn't stop thinking about it. But just as she began to replay the events in her head, a wave of nausea rolled over her.

She tumbled out of bed and staggered through the hallway to the bathroom, grateful that the lights were working, probably thanks to her mother's new "friend," the head of the Resource Board.

Glass sank to the cold floor of the bathroom and quickly shut the door behind her, her brain battling with her stomach. She forced herself to breathe, trying to keep quiet. The last thing she needed was for her mother to drag her off to the medical center.

Her stomach won out, and Glass leaned over the toilet just in time. She gagged, tears stinging her eyes, then slumped back against the wall. There was no way she'd be able to meet Wells for lunch, although she felt terrible standing him up again. She'd been spending all her time with Luke, and hadn't been much of a friend to Wells lately. She missed him. He never seemed to resent her flakiness, which somehow made her feel worse. Especially after everything that had happened with his mother, and now Clarke was apparently acting strange . . . She really needed to catch up with him.

"Glass?" her mother called out from the other side of the door. "What's going on in there?"

"Nothing," Glass said, trying to keep her voice light.

"Are you ill?"

Glass groaned softly. Their new flat had no privacy. She missed their old, spacious flat with the windows full of stars. She still didn't understand why they'd had to downgrade just because her father had made the unusual and mortifying decision to sever his marriage contract and move out.

"I'm coming in," her mother's voice called from the other side of the door. Glass hastily wiped her mouth and tried to rise to her feet but slid back down as another wave of nausea sent her stomach into revolt. The door opened and Glass saw her mother, dressed for an evening out despite the fact that it wasn't even noon. But before she had a chance to ask where she was going—or where she was coming *from*—her mother's eyes widened, and she visibly paled under her generously applied blush. "What's going on?"

"Nothing," Glass said, try to shake the haze from her mind long enough to come up with an explanation that would get her mother to leave her alone. Stomach viruses were rare on Phoenix, and anyone who seemed vaguely contagious was required to spend the duration of their illness in quarantine. "I'm fine."

"Were you"—Sonja looked behind her and lowered her voice, which was ridiculous considering they were the only two people in the flat—"throwing up?"

"Yes, but I'm fine. I think I just—"

"Oh my god," her mother said, closing her eyes.

"I'm not sick, I promise. I don't need to be quarantined. I've just been nauseous the past few mornings, but it goes away by the afternoon."

When her mother opened her eyes, she didn't look any less worried. The room started to spin, and Sonja's voice grew faint, as if she were speaking from somewhere far away. Glass could barely make out her question, something about how long it'd been since her last—

Suddenly, Glass's confusion hardened into a ball of dread. She looked up at Sonja and saw the terrifying realization reflected in her mother's eyes.

"Glass." Sonja's voice was hoarse. "You're pregnant."

Staring at Luke's face, full of sympathy and understanding, Glass felt her last bit of self-control shatter. "I'm sorry." Her breath caught in her throat as she tried to stifle a sob. "I should've told you, I just—I didn't see any reason for both of us to die."

"Oh, Glass." Luke reached out and wrapped his arms tight around her. She nestled gratefully into his familiar embrace, her tears spilling onto the jacket of his guard uniform. "I can't believe it," he murmured. "I can't believe you did this all on your own. I knew you were brave, but I never thought . . . What happened?" he asked finally, and Glass knew what he meant. Who he was referring to.

"He—" She swallowed as she struggled to breathe. It felt like her heart was about to break apart, unable to contain both the grief and relief pouring into her chest. Finally, she just shook her head. There were no words.

"Oh my god," he whispered, grabbing her hand and lacing his fingers between hers, squeezing it tight. "I'm so sorry." He sighed. "Why didn't you tell me any of this the night you escaped? I had no idea." He closed his eyes as if to shut out the memory.

"You were with Camille. I knew she was a good friend of yours, and I figured . . . you'd finally found someone who made you happy." Glass smiled and wiped away the tears that were still running down her face. "You deserved it, after everything I put you through."

Luke reached out to brush a strand of hair behind her ear. “There’s only one person in the universe who can make me happy, and she’s sitting right here with me.” He stared at her, as if drinking her in. “From the moment I saw you again, I knew it wasn’t Camille—she’s a great friend, always will be, but that’s all she is to me now, and I’ve told her that. I love you, Glass. I never stopped loving you. And I never will.”

He leaned forward and brushed his lips against hers, lightly at first, as if giving their mouths a chance to become reacquainted. For a moment it felt like their first kiss all over again. But a moment was all it took.

He pressed against Glass, her lips parting as his mouth sank into hers. She was vaguely aware of his hand tangling in her hair, then slipping down her back, pulling her closer to him as he wrapped his other arm around her waist.

Finally, Glass shifted back and let her lips break away from his. “I love you,” she whispered, needing desperately to say it. *I love you I love you I love you* throbbed through her body as Luke smiled and pulled her back to him.

CHAPTER 17

Wells

It was nearly noon, and Clarke had been gone for hours. One of the Arcadian girls had seen her head into the woods earlier that morning, and it had taken all of Wells's self-control to keep from running after her. The thought of her venturing off on her own made his stomach feel like a punching bag for his imagination. But he had to accept that, of all the people in camp, Clarke knew how to take care of herself. He also knew how important it was to find the missing medicine. Just yesterday, they'd dug another grave.

He wandered toward the de facto cemetery that had cropped up on the far side of the clearing. Over the past few days, Wells had arranged for wooden markers to be placed at the head of each mound, something he remembered from old photographs. He'd wanted to carve the names onto the crosses, but he only knew the names of three of the five kids sleeping beneath the soil, and it didn't seem right to leave the others blank.

He shuddered and turned back to the graves. The concept of burying the dead had initially struck him as repulsive, but there hadn't seemed to be any alternative. The thought of burning the bodies was even worse. But although the normal practice of releasing corpses into space was certainly tidier, there was something reassuring about gathering the dead together. Even in death, they'd never be alone.

It was also strangely comforting to have a place to visit, to say the things you couldn't say to people you could see. Someone, possibly a Walden girl he'd seen flitting near the trees, had gathered fallen branches and rested them along the wooden markers. In the evening, the pods still glowed to life, casting a soft light over the cemetery that gave it an almost unearthly beauty. It would have been nice to have somewhere on the ship where it wouldn't have seemed strange to talk to his mother.

Wells glanced up at the darkening sky. He had no idea if the Colony lost contact with the dropship when it crashed, but he hoped that the monitors in the bracelets were still transmitting data about their blood composition and heart rates. They must have collected enough information to prove that Earth was safe, and would surely begin sending groups of citizens down soon. For a moment he dared to let himself hope that his father and Glass would be among them.

"What are you doing over here?"

Wells turned and saw Octavia moving toward him slowly. Her ankle was healing quickly; her limp was starting to look like a saunter.

"I don't know. Paying my respects, I suppose." He gestured toward the graves. "But I was just leaving," he added quickly as he watched her toss her dark hair over her shoulder. "It's my turn to go for water."

"I'll go with you." Octavia smiled, and Wells looked away uncomfortably. The long lashes that made her look so innocent when she was sleeping in the infirmary tent now lent a feral gleam to her enormous blue eyes.

"Are you sure that's a good idea with your ankle? It's a long walk."

"I'm *fine*," she said, her voice full of playful exasperation as she fell into stride next to him. "Though you're very sweet to be concerned. You know," she went on, increasing her pace to catch up with Wells, who hadn't noticed he'd lengthened his step, "it's ridiculous that everyone hangs on to Graham's every word. You know so much more than he does."

Wells grabbed one of the empty jugs next to the supply

tent and turned toward the forest. They'd discovered a stream not far from camp, and everyone strong enough to carry a full container took turns going for water. At least, they were *supposed* to take turns. He hadn't seen Graham go for days.

Octavia paused as Wells stepped across the tree line. "Are you coming?" he asked, throwing a glance over his shoulder.

She tilted her head back, her eyes widening as she scanned the shadowy outlines of the trees in the fading light. "I'm coming." Her voice grew quiet as she darted to Wells's side. "I haven't been in the woods yet."

Wells softened. Even he, who'd spent most of his life dreaming about coming to Earth, found it frightening at times—the vastness, the unfamiliar sounds, the sense that anything could be hiding beyond the light of the campfire. And he'd had time to prepare. He could only imagine what it was like for the others, who were snatched from their cells and shoved onto the dropship before they had time to process what was going on, that they were being sent to a foreign planet that had never been more to them than an empty word.

"Careful," he said, pointing at a tangle of roots hidden by a mass of purple leaves. "The ground gets pretty uneven here."

Wells took Octavia's small hand and helped her climb over a fallen tree. It was strange to think that something without a pulse could die, but the soggy, peeling bark was decidedly corpse-like.

"So is it true?" Octavia asked as they began walking down the slope that led to the stream. "Did you really get yourself Confined so you could come with Clarke?"

"I suppose it is."

She sighed wistfully. "That's the most romantic thing I've ever heard."

Wells gave her a wry smile. "Trust me, it's not."

"What do you mean?" Octavia asked, cocking her head to one side. In the shadows of the forest, she looked almost childlike again.

Wells glanced away, suddenly unable to look her in the eye. He wondered grimly what Octavia would say if she knew the truth.

He wasn't the brave knight who'd come to rescue the princess. He was the reason she'd been locked away in the dungeon.

Wells glanced at his collar chip for the fourteenth time since he'd sat down two minutes earlier. The message Clarke had sent him earlier that day had sounded anxious, and she'd been acting strange for the past few weeks. Wells had barely seen her, and the few times he managed to track her down, she'd been practically twitching with nervous energy.

He couldn't help but worry that she was about to break up with him. The only thing that kept the anxiety from burning a hole through his stomach was the knowledge that she probably wouldn't have chosen the library to dump him. It'd be cruel to tarnish the spot they both loved best. Clarke wouldn't do that to him.

He heard footsteps and rose to his feet as the overhead lights flickered back on. Wells had been still for so long that the library had forgotten his presence, the dim safety lights on the floor providing the only light. Clarke approached, still wearing her scrubs, which normally made him smile—he loved that she didn't spend hours stressing over her appearance, like most girls on Phoenix—but the blue top and pants fell too loosely from her frame, and there were dark circles under her eyes.

"Hey," he said, stepping forward to kiss her lightly in greeting. She didn't move away, but she didn't kiss him back. "Are you okay?" he asked, even though he knew full well that she wasn't.

"Wells," she said, her voice breaking. She blinked back tears. His eyes widened in alarm. Clarke never cried.

"Hey," he murmured, putting his arm around her to lead her to the couch. Her legs seemed to buckle beneath her. "It'll be okay, I promise. Just tell me what's going on."

She stared at him, and he could see her urge to confide in him battling her fear. "I need you to promise me that you won't say anything about this to anyone."

He nodded. "Of course."

"I'm serious. This isn't gossip. This is real, life-or-death."

Wells squeezed her hand. "Clarke, you know you can tell me anything."

"I found out . . ." She took a breath, closed her eyes for a moment, and then started again. "You know about my parents' radiation research." He nodded. Her parents were in charge of a massive ongoing study meant to determine when, if ever, it would be safe for humans to return to Earth. Whenever his father had spoken of an Earth mission, Wells had thought of it as a distant possibility, more of a hope than a real plan. Still, he knew how important the Griffins' work was to the Chancellor and to the whole Colony. "They're doing human trials," Clarke said softly. A chill traveled down Wells's spine, but he said nothing, just tightened his grasp on her hand. "They're experimenting on children," Clarke finally said, her voice barely a whisper.

Her voice was hollow, as if the thought had been circulating for so long, it no longer held any meaning. "What children?" he asked, his brain racing to understand.

"Unregistereds," Clarke said, her tear-filled eyes flashing with sudden anger. "Children from the care center whose parents were executed for violating the population laws." He could hear the unspoken accusation. *People your father killed.*

"They're so young. . . ." Clarke's voice trailed off. She sank back and seemed to shrink, as if the truth had taken some part of her with it.

Wells slid his arm behind her, but instead of recoiling as she'd done every day over the past few weeks, she leaned into him and rested her head against his chest. "They're all so sick." He could feel her tears seeping through his shirt. "Some of them have already died."

"I'm so sorry, Clarke," he murmured as he searched for something to say, anything to make her pain go away. "I'm sure your parents are doing their best to make sure it's . . ." He paused. There weren't any words that could make it better. He had to do something, to put a stop to it before the guilt and horror destroyed her. "What can I do?" he asked, his voice becoming firm.

She bolted upright and stared at him, a different kind of terror filling her eyes. "Nothing," she said with a resolve that took him by surprise. "You have to promise me that you'll do *nothing*. My parents made me swear not to tell anyone. They didn't want to do this, Wells. It wasn't their choice. Vice Chancellor Rhodes is *making* them. He threatened them." She grabbed Wells's hands. "Promise me you won't say anything. I just . . ." She bit her lip. "I just couldn't keep it from you anymore. I had to tell someone."

"I promise," he said, though his skin was growing warm with fury. The slimy bastard had no right to go around the Chancellor like that. He thought of his father, the man who had an unflinching sense of right and wrong. His father never would have approved human trials. He could put a stop to it immediately.

Clarke stared at him, searching his eyes, and then gave him a small, trembling smile that vanished almost as quickly as it had appeared. "Thank you."

She returned her head to Wells's chest, and he wrapped his arm around her. "I love you," he whispered.

An hour later, after he'd walked Clarke home, Wells headed back along the observation deck alone. He needed to *do* something. If something didn't change soon, the guilt would destroy her, and he refused to stand by and watch.

Wells had never broken a promise before. It was something his father had impressed upon him from an early age—a leader never goes back on his word. But then he thought of Clarke's tears, and knew he didn't have a choice.

He turned around and began walking toward his father's office.

They filled the water jug at the stream and started to make their way back to the camp. After giving enough one-word answers, Wells had gotten Octavia to stop asking about Clarke, but now she was walking along sullenly, and he felt guilty. She was a sweet girl, and he knew she meant well. How had she wound up here?

"So," Wells said, breaking the silence, "what could you have possibly done to end up in Confinement?"

Octavia looked at him in surprise. "Haven't you heard my brother talking about it?" She gave him a tight smile. "He loves telling people about how I was caught stealing food for the younger kids in the care center—the little ones who are always bullied into giving up their rations—and how the monsters on the Council Confined me without batting an eye."

Something in Octavia's voice gave him pause. "Is that really how it happened?"

"Does it matter?" she asked with a weariness that suddenly made her seem older than fourteen. "We're all going to think what we want about each other. If that's the story Bellamy needs to believe, then I'm not going to stop him."

Wells stopped to rearrange the heavy water jug. Somehow, they'd ended up in a different part of the woods. The trees grew even closer together here, and he could see far enough ahead to tell how far they'd strayed.

"Are we lost?" Octavia glanced from side to side, and even in the dim light he could see the panic flash across her face.

"We'll be fine. I just need to—" He stopped as a sound shuddered through the air.

"What was that?" Octavia asked. "Are we—"

Wells cut her off with a shush and took a step forward. It sounded like a twig snapping, which meant that something was moving just behind the trees. He kicked himself for not bringing a weapon. It would've been nice to bring back his own kill, to show that Bellamy wasn't the only one who could learn how to hunt. The sound came again, and Wells's frustration turned to fear. Forget catching dinner—if he wasn't careful, he and Octavia might become dinner themselves.

He was about to grab her hand and run away when something caught his eye. A glint of reddish gold. Wells lowered the water jug and took a few steps forward. "Stay here," he whispered.

Just ahead, he could see an open space beyond the trees. Some kind of clearing. He was about to shout the name hovering on his lips when he froze, skidding to a stop.

Clarke was standing in the grass, locked in an embrace with none other than *Bellamy*. As she brought her lips up to the Waldenite, fury tore through Wells. Heat shot up through his chest to settle in his racing heart.

Somehow, he managed to wrench his eyes away and stagger back into the trees before a wave of nausea sent his head spinning. He grabbed on to a branch for balance, gasping as he tried to force air into his lungs. The girl he'd risked his life to protect wasn't just kissing someone else—she was kissing the hothead who may have gotten his father killed.

"Whoa." Octavia's voice came from beside him. "Their walk looks a lot more fun than ours."

But Wells had already turned and begun walking in the other direction. He was vaguely aware of Octavia scampering after him, asking something about a medicine chest, but her voice was drowned out by the pulsing of blood in his head. He didn't care whether they'd found the missing medicine. There was no drug strong enough to repair a broken heart.

CHAPTER 18

Clarke

By the time Clarke and Bellamy returned to camp with the medicine, darkness had fallen. She'd only been in the woods for a few hours, but as they stepped through the tree line into the clearing, it felt like she'd left a lifetime ago.

They'd spent most of the walk back in silence, but every time Clarke's arm accidentally brushed against Bellamy's, electricity seemed to dance across her skin. She'd been mortified after their kiss, and had spent the next five minutes stammering an apology while he grinned. Eventually, he cut her off with a laugh and told her not to worry about it. "I know you're not the type of girl to make out with random guys in the woods," he'd said with a mischievous grin, "but maybe you should be."

But as they approached the clearing, all thoughts of the kiss were pushed aside by the shadowy outline of the infirmary tent. Clarke took off with the medicine tucked under her arm.

The tent was empty except for a delirious, feverish Thalia, and to Clarke's surprise, Octavia, who was just settling back in her old cot. "The other tent is just so *small*," Octavia was saying, but Clarke couldn't do more than nod.

She flung the medicine chest onto the floor, filled a syringe, and plunged the needle into Thalia's arm. Then Clarke turned back to the box, searching for painkillers. She quickly gave Thalia a dose and smiled as her friend's face relaxed in sleep.

Clarke knelt next to Thalia for a few more minutes, breathing a deep sigh of relief at her steady pulse. For a moment, she looked down at the bracelet on her wrist and wondered if, somewhere up in the sky, someone was monitoring her own heart rate. Dr. Lahiri, perhaps, or another of the Colony's top doctors, reading the hundred's vital signs like the day's news. Surely they had seen that five people had died already. . . . She wondered if they'd chalk the deaths up to radiation poisoning and rethink their colonization efforts, or if they'd be smart enough to realize they'd been killed because of the rough landing. She wasn't sure which scenario she preferred. She certainly wasn't ready for the Council to extend its jurisdiction to Earth. And yet her mother and father had devoted their lives to helping humanity return home. A permanent settlement would mean, in a way, that her parents had succeeded too. That they hadn't died for nothing.

Finally, she scooped the medicine back into the chest and placed it in the corner of the tent. Tomorrow, she'd find a place to lock it up, but for now, Clarke felt like she could finally rest. If someone was indeed monitoring their body count up in space, she was going to make damn sure they didn't drop below ninety-five.

She took a few shaky steps and collapsed on her cot without even bothering to take off her shoes.

"Is she going to be okay?" Octavia asked. Her voice sounded far away.

Clarke murmured yes. She could barely open her eyelids.

"What other medicine was in there?"

"Everything," Clarke said. Or at least, she tried to say it. By the time the word reached her lips, exhaustion had numbed her brain. The last thing she remembered was hearing Octavia rise from her cot before falling into a deep, dreamless sleep.

When Clarke awoke the next morning, Octavia was gone, and bright light was streaming in through the tent flap.

Thalia lay on her side, still asleep. Clarke rose with a

groan, her muscles stiff from their hike yesterday. But it was a good kind of pain; she'd walked through a forest that hadn't been seen by a single human being in three hundred years. Her stomach squirmed as she thought about another distinction she'd inadvertently earned—the first girl to kiss a boy on Earth since the Cataclysm.

Clarke smiled as she hurried over to Thalia. She couldn't wait until she was well enough to hear all about it. She pressed the back of her hand against her friend's forehead and was relieved to feel that it was cooler than it had been last night. She gently pulled back the blanket to look at Thalia's stomach. Her skin still showed signs of an infection, but it hadn't spread any farther. As long as Thalia had a full course of antibiotics, she'd make a full recovery.

It was hard to know exactly, but based on the strength of the light, she guessed that at least eight hours had passed since Thalia's last dose. She turned and walked over to the corner where she'd stashed the medicine chest, frowning slightly as she realized it was open. Clarke crouched down and inhaled sharply, blinking to make sure her eyes weren't playing tricks on her.

The chest was empty.

All the antibiotics, the painkillers, even the syringes—they were all gone. "No," Clarke whispered. There was nothing. "No," she said again, scrambling to her feet. She ran over to the nearest cot and started to throw the bedding aside, then did the same with her own.

Her eyes landed on Octavia's cot, and her panic momentarily hardened into suspicion. She hurried over and began rummaging through the pile of blankets. "Come on," she muttered to herself, but her hands came up empty.

"*No.*" She kicked the ground. The medicine wasn't in the tent, that much was clear. But whoever had taken it couldn't have gone far. There were fewer than a hundred human beings on the planet, and Clarke wasn't going to rest until she found the thief who was jeopardizing Thalia's life. She probably wouldn't have to look very far.

After a quick search of the flat to make sure her parents weren't home, Clarke hurried to the lab and entered the code. She kept expecting her parents to change the password, but either they didn't know how often she visited the kids, or they didn't want to stop her. Perhaps they liked knowing that Clarke was keeping them company.

As she made her way toward Lilly, Clarke smiled at the others, though her chest tightened when she saw how few were awake. Most were growing sicker, and there were more empty beds than there'd been the last time.

She tried to force this thought out of her head as she approached Lilly, but as her eyes locked on her friend, her hands began to tremble.

Lilly was dying. Her eyes barely fluttered open when Clarke whispered her name, and even when her lips moved, she didn't have the strength to turn the shapes into words.

There were more flaky red patches on her skin, although fewer of them were bleeding, as Lilly no longer had the energy to scratch them. Clarke sat there, fighting a wave of nausea as she watched the irregular rise and fall of her friend's chest. The worst part was that she knew this was only the beginning. The other subjects had lingered on for weeks, their symptoms growing increasingly gruesome as the radiation poisoning progressed through their bodies.

For a moment, Clarke imagined carrying Lilly to the medical center, where they could at least put her on high-intensity pain medication even if it was too late to save her. But that would be tantamount to asking the Vice Chancellor to execute her parents. Then he'd just find someone else to finish what her mother and father had started. All Clarke hoped was that their research proved conclusive so that the experiments could stop, so that these test subjects wouldn't have suffered in vain.

Lilly's translucent eyelids fluttered open. "Hey, Clarke," she croaked, the beginnings of a smile flickering on her face before a new wave of pain washed them away.

Clarke reached over and grasped Lilly's hand, giving it a gentle squeeze. "Hey," she whispered. "How are you feeling?"

"Fine," Lilly lied, wincing as she struggled to sit up.

"It's okay." Clarke placed a hand on her shoulder. "You don't need to sit."

"No, I want to." The girl's voice was strained.

Clarke gently helped her sit, then adjusted the pillows behind her. She suppressed a shudder as her fingers brushed against Lilly's back. She could feel every vertebra poking out from her sallow skin.

"How did you like the Dickens anthology?" Clarke asked, glancing under Lilly's bed, where they kept the books Clarke had stolen from the library.

"I only read the first story, the one about Oliver Twist." Lilly gave Clarke a weak smile. "My vision is . . ." She trailed off. They both knew that once the subjects had trouble seeing, the end wasn't far. "But I didn't like it, anyway. It reminded me too much of the care center."

Clarke hadn't asked any questions about Lilly's life before this. She'd gotten the sense that Lilly didn't want to talk about it. "Was it really that bad?" she said carefully.

Lilly shrugged. "We all looked out for one another. We didn't have anyone else. Well, except this one girl. She had a *brother*, a real-life older brother." She looked down, suddenly blushing. "He was . . . nice. He used to bring her things—extra food, pieces of ribbon . . ."

"Really?" Clarke asked, pretending to believe the comment

about a girl with a brother as she brushed a lock of hair off Lilly's damp forehead. Even this far along in her sickness, Lilly had a flair for the dramatic.

"He sounds nice," Clarke said vaguely as her eyes flitted toward the bald patches on Lilly's head, which were becoming difficult to ignore.

"Anyway," Lilly said, her voice strained, "I want to hear about your birthday. What are you going to wear?"

Clarke had almost forgotten that her birthday was next week. She didn't feel much like celebrating. "Oh, you know, my best scrubs," she said lightly. "I'd rather hang out here with you than go to some silly party, anyway."

"Oh, Clarke," Lilly groaned in mock exasperation. "You have to do *something*. You're starting to be seriously boring. Besides, I want to hear about your birthday dress." She winced suddenly, doubling over in pain.

"Are you okay?" Clarke asked, her hand on Lilly's fragile arm.

"It hurts," Lilly gasped.

"Can I get you anything? Do you want some water?"

Lilly opened her eyes, which were now pleading. "You can make it stop, Clarke." She was cut off by a groan. "Please make it stop. It's only a matter of time. . . ."

Clarke turned her head to the side so Lilly wouldn't see her tears. "It'll be okay," she whispered, forcing a fake smile. "I promise."

Lilly whimpered before falling silent again, then leaned back and closed her eyes.

Clarke pulled the blankets up over her friend's chest, trying to ignore the demon that was clawing its way to the front of her mind. She knew what Lilly was asking for. And it wouldn't be difficult. She was so frail at this point, it would take just a few well-combined painkillers to ease her into a coma. She'd slip away painlessly.

What am I thinking? Clarke asked herself, drawing back in horror. The blood on her parents' hands had spread to her own. This whole nightmare had infected her, turned her into a monster. Or maybe it wasn't her parents' fault. Maybe she'd always had this darkness inside of her, waiting to rise to the surface.

Just as she was about to leave, Lilly spoke again. "Please," she begged. "If you love me, please." Her voice was quiet but contained an edge of desperation that terrified Clarke. "Just make it all stop."

Bellamy was chopping wood on the far side of the clearing. Although the morning was cool, his T-shirt was already soaked through with sweat. Clarke tried not to notice how it clung to his muscular chest. When he saw her running toward him, he lowered his ax to the ground and turned to face her with a grin.

"Well, hello there," he said as she came to a stop and

paused to catch her breath. "Couldn't stay away, could you?" He stepped forward and placed his hand on her waist, but Clarke swatted his arm away.

"Where's your sister?" she asked. "I can't find her anywhere."

"Why?" Urgency shoved the playfulness out of his voice. "What's wrong?"

"The medicine we found is missing." Clarke took a deep breath, bracing herself for her next words. "And I think Octavia took it."

"*What?*" His eyes narrowed.

"She was the only other person in the tent last night, and she seemed really fixated on the drugs—"

"*No,*" Bellamy snapped, cutting her off. "Of all the criminals on this goddamn planet, you think *my sister* is the thief?" He stared at her, his eyes burning with anger. But when he spoke again, his voice was quiet. "I thought you were different. But I was wrong. You're just another stupid Phoenix bitch who thinks she knows better than everyone else."

He kicked the handle of the ax, then pushed past her without another word.

For a moment, Clarke stood rooted to the ground, too stunned by Bellamy's words to move. But then she felt something inside her tear, and suddenly she was running toward the trees, staggering into the shade of the forest canopy. Her throat raw, she slumped onto the ground, wrapping her arms around her knees to keep the anguish from flowing out of her chest.

Alone in the shadows, Clarke did something else on Earth for the first time. She cried.

CHAPTER 19

Bellamy

Bellamy paused to adjust the bird that he'd slung over his shoulder. The confrontation with Clarke had left him so agitated that he'd grabbed his bow and stormed off into the woods without a second thought. Only after shooting this bird near the stream had he started to calm down. It was a good kill—his first bird, much harder than animals on the ground—and its feathers would be perfect for the new arrows he'd been working on, to take with them when he and Octavia headed out on their own. As he stepped back into camp, he realized that he hadn't seen Octavia since early that morning, and felt a twinge of concern. He should have checked on her before he left.

The fire was already built up, and a dozen faces turned to look at Bellamy as he approached. But no one was smiling. He shifted the bird over to his other shoulder to give them a better view of his kill. Why the hell were they staring at him like that?

An angry shout pulled his attention to a group at the far end of the clearing, near the wreckage of the dropship. They were clustered in a circle around something on the ground. He inhaled sharply as the shape on the ground moved.

Then he saw her, and his confusion erupted into a rage unlike anything he'd ever felt.

It was *Octavia*.

He threw the bird on the ground and broke into a run.

"Out of my way," Bellamy shouted as he forced his way inside the circle.

Octavia was on the ground, tears streaming down her cheeks. Graham and a few of the Arcadians stood over her, a deranged gleam in their eyes.

"*Get away from her*," Bellamy bellowed as he charged forward. But before he could reach Octavia, an arm hooked around his neck, nearly crushing his windpipe. Bellamy wheezed and looked around frantically. Wells was standing in front of him, his expression cold and firm. "What the *hell?*" Bellamy sputtered. "Get out of my way."

When Wells didn't move, Bellamy gritted his teeth and

lunged at him, but someone else had a hold on his collar and jerked him back. "Get off of me!" Bellamy spat, shooting his elbow back with enough force to make whoever was behind him grunt and let go.

Octavia was still on the ground, her eyes wide with terror as she looked from Bellamy to Graham, who was standing over her. "You better tell me what's going on, *right now*," Bellamy said through clenched teeth.

"I heard you and Clarke talking about the missing medicine earlier," Wells said with infuriating calmness. "No one besides Octavia knew about it. She must have taken it."

"I didn't take *anything*." Octavia sobbed. She wiped her face with the back of her hand and sniffed. "They've all gone crazy." She rose shakily to her feet and started to take a step toward Bellamy.

"You're not going anywhere," Graham snapped, grabbing Octavia's wrist and wrenching her back.

"Let *go* of her!" Bellamy bellowed. He dove for Graham, but Wells stepped in front of him, and someone else wrenched his arm behind his back. "Get off of me!" Bellamy thrashed wildly as he tried to wrench himself free, but there were too many sets of hands holding him down, locking him in place.

"Look," Bellamy continued, trying in vain to keep his voice steady, "she's been injured ever since we landed. Do you really think she was up to stealing medicine and dragging it off somewhere outside of camp?"

"She was up to following me into the woods yesterday," Wells answered calmly. "We walked pretty far together."

Bellamy thrashed against the arms holding him, unable to quell his rage as the implication of Wells's words sank in. If he so much as laid a hand on his sister . . .

"Just take it easy," Wells said. He nodded at a Walden boy, who stepped forward with a coil of rope.

"Then tell that creep to take his disgusting hands off my sister," Bellamy spat.

Clarke suddenly appeared, pushing her way through the crowd. "What's going on?" she asked, her eyes wide when they landed on Octavia. "Are you okay?" Octavia shook her head, tears streaming down her face.

"We just need Octavia to tell us where the medicine is," Wells said calmly, "and then we'll get this all sorted out."

"I *don't have it.*" Octavia's voice had grown ragged.

"We know you're lying," Graham hissed. Octavia yelped as he tightened his hold on her wrist, and Bellamy struggled against the hands that held him. "You're only making things worse."

"So what are you going to do?" Bellamy spat at Wells. "Keep us both tied up?"

"Exactly," Wells said, his jaw tightening. "We'll keep

Octavia locked up until she tells us where she hid the medicine, or we find evidence pointing to another suspect."

"Lock her up?" Bellamy made a show of looking around the clearing. "And how do you propose to do that?"

Clarke stepped forward, a tense look on her face. "I spend most of the day in the infirmary tent, anyway," she said curtly. "Octavia can stay there. I'll keep an eye on her and make sure she doesn't sneak off."

"Are you serious?" Graham snorted. "She stole the medicine from under your nose, and your plan is to *keep an eye on her*?"

Clarke turned to Graham with a scowl. "If that's not good enough for you, Graham, you can post a guard outside the door."

"This is ridiculous." Bellamy's whole body was beginning to shake as his anger smoldered into exhaustion. "Look at her," he said weakly. "She's obviously not a danger to anyone. Just untie her and I promise I won't let her out of my sight." He scanned the crowd that had assembled around them, scouring the audience for a sympathetic face. Surely someone else saw that this whole thing was complete bullshit. But no one was willing to meet his eyes.

"You're all insane." His mouth curled into a snarl as he turned back to face Graham. "You set her up. *You* stole those meds."

Graham snickered and shot a look at Asher. "I told you he was going to say that."

The sky was growing dark, the clouds weaving into a blanket of gray. Bellamy took a deep breath. "Fine. Believe whatever you want. Just untie Octavia and let us go. We'll leave camp for good. We won't even take any of your precious supplies." He glanced at his sister, but she didn't look happy at the idea; her features seemed frozen in shock. "You'll never have to think about us again."

A fleeting look of pain crossed Clarke's face before she retreated behind her mask of steely resolve. *She'll get over it*, Bellamy thought bitterly. She'd find someone else to go traipsing through the woods with her.

"I don't think so," Graham said, sneering. "Not until we get back the meds. We can't let anyone else die just because your little sister's a drug addict."

The accusation made every nerve in Bellamy's body sizzle until his fingers itched to close around Graham's neck.

"Enough," Clarke said, shaking her head at Graham and raising a hand. "I want the medicine back more than anyone, but you're not helping."

"Fine," Bellamy snapped. "But *I'm* taking her into the tent. And *no one* is going to put their hands on her again."

He wrenched free from his captors and strode over to Octavia, grabbing her hand as he locked eyes with Graham.

"You're going to regret this," Bellamy said in a low, dangerous voice. He wrapped his arm around his trembling sister and led her toward the infirmary tent, a grim determination overtaking him.

He'd do whatever it took to protect her. He always had.

It was the third guard visit in the last few months. They had been coming more often that year, and Octavia was getting bigger. Bellamy tried not to think about what would happen next time, but even he knew they wouldn't be able to hide her forever.

"I can't believe they looked in the closet," his mother said hoarsely, staring at Octavia, whom Bellamy had carried to the couch. "Thank god she didn't cry."

Bellamy looked over at his toddler sister. Everything about her was miniaturized, from her tiny sock-clad feet to her impossibly small fingers. Everything except her round cheeks and enormous eyes, which always glistened with tears she never seemed to shed. Was it normal for a two-year-old to be so quiet? Did she somehow know what would happen if someone found her?

Bellamy walked over and sat down next to Octavia, who turned her head to stare at him with her deep-blue eyes. He reached forward to touch one of her dark, glossy curls. She looked just like that doll head he'd found while scavenging for relics in the storage room. He'd thought about taking it home to Octavia, but decided the ration points he'd get for it at the Exchange were more important. He also hadn't been sure whether it was right to give a baby a disembodied doll's head, no matter how pretty it was.

He grinned as Octavia grabbed his finger with her tiny fist. "Hey, give that back," he said, pretending to wince. She smiled but didn't giggle. He couldn't remember ever hearing her laugh.

"It was too close," his mother was muttering to herself as she paced back and forth. "Too close . . . too close . . . too close."

"Mom. Are you okay?" Bellamy asked, feeling his panic return. She walked over to the sink, which was still spilling over with dishes despite the fact that this morning had been their water hour. He hadn't been able to finish before the guards came. It would be another five days before they'd have the chance to wash them again.

There was a faint crash down the hallway, followed by a peal of laughter. His mother gasped and looked around the flat. "Get her back in the closet."

Bellamy put his arm in front of Octavia. "It's fine," he said. "The guards were just here. They're not going to be back for a while."

His mother took a step forward. Her eyes were wide and full of terror. "Get her out of here!"

"*No*," Bellamy said, sliding off the couch and standing in front of Octavia. "That wasn't even the guards. It was just someone messing around. She doesn't need to go back in yet."

Octavia whimpered but fell silent as their mother fixed her with a wild-eyed stare.

"Oh no, oh no, oh no," their mother was muttering, running her hands distractedly through her already disheveled hair. She leaned back against the wall and slid down to the floor, landing with a sharp thud.

Bellamy glanced at Octavia, then walked slowly over to his mother, kneeling carefully beside her. "Mom?" A new kind of fear welled up inside him, different from what he'd felt during the inspection. This fear was cold and seemed to be creeping out from his stomach, turning his blood to ice.

"You don't understand," she said faintly, staring at something just behind Bellamy's head. "They're going to kill me. They're going to take you and they're going to kill me."

"Take me where?" Bellamy asked, his voice quivering.

"You can't have both," she whispered, her eyes growing even larger. "You can't have both." She blinked and refocused her gaze on Bellamy. "You can't have a mother and a sister."

CHAPTER 20

Glass

Glass swept up the final flight of stairs and turned into her corridor. She wasn't worried about being stopped by the guards for violating curfew. She felt like she was floating, her steps featherlight as she skimmed silently down the hallway. She raised her hand to her lips, where the memory of Luke's kiss still lingered, and smiled.

It was a little after three in the morning; the ship was empty, the lights in the hallway a dim glow. Tearing herself away from Luke made her ache with an almost physical pain, but she knew better than to risk getting caught by her mother. If she fell asleep quickly enough, she might be able to trick her mind into thinking that she was still with Luke, his warm, sleeping form curled up next to her.

She pressed her thumb against the key panel on the door and slipped inside.

"Hello, Glass." Her mother's voice came from the sofa.

Glass gasped and started stammering. "Hi, I was . . . I . . ." She fumbled for words, trying to come up with a plausible reason for why she'd been out in the middle of the night. But she couldn't lie; not anymore, not about this.

They stood in silence for a long moment, and although she couldn't make out the expression on her mother's face, Glass could feel her confusion and anger radiating through the darkness. "You were with *him*, weren't you?" Sonja finally asked.

"Yes," Glass said, relieved to be telling the truth at last. "Mom, I love him."

Her mother took a step forward, and Glass realized that she was still wearing a black evening dress, the outline of faded lipstick on her mouth, dying traces of her perfume in the air.

"Where were *you* tonight?" Glass asked wearily. It was like last year all over again. Ever since her father had left them, her mother had barely been around, staying out all hours of the night and sometimes sleeping through the day. Now Glass didn't have the energy to be embarrassed, or even angry, about her mother's behavior. All she could feel was a faint pang of sadness.

Sonja's lips twisted into a gruesome approximation of a smile. "You have no idea what I've done to protect you" was all she said. "You need to stay away from that boy."

"That *boy*?" Glass cringed. "I know you think he's just—"

"That's *enough*," her mother snapped. "Don't you realize how lucky you are to even be here? I'm not going to let you die for some Walden trash who seduces Phoenix girls and then abandons them."

"He's not like that!" Glass exclaimed, her voice growing shrill. "You don't even know him."

"He doesn't care about you. You were ready to *die* to save him. While you were in Confinement he'd probably forgotten all about you."

Glass winced. It was true that Luke had started seeing Camille while Glass was in Confinement. But she couldn't blame him, not after the cruel things she'd said when she broke up with him in a desperate attempt to keep him safe.

"Glass." Sonja's voice quivered with the strain of trying to remain calm. "I'm sorry to be harsh. But with the Chancellor still on life support, you need to be careful. If he wakes up and has any reason, any reason at all, to revoke your pardon, he will." She sighed. "I can't let you risk your life again. Have you already forgotten what happened last time?"

But of course Glass hadn't forgotten. The memory of it was as permanent as the scars from the bracelet on her skin, something she would carry with her the rest of her life.

And her mother didn't even know the whole truth.

Glass ignored the guards' strange looks as she passed the checkpoint and began crossing the skybridge toward Walden. Let them think she was off to buy drugs if they wanted. No punishment they gave her could possibly hurt more than what she was about to do.

It was late afternoon, and the corridors were thankfully empty. Luke would be back from his morning shift by now, but Carter would still be at the distribution center, where he worked sorting nutrition packets. Glass knew it was foolish—Carter hated her, and he would hate her even more once he found out that she had broken Luke's heart—but she couldn't bear to break up with Luke with Carter in the other room.

She paused at the door, absently bringing her hand to her stomach. She had to do it now. She'd already put this off so many times. She'd muster the courage to break up with him, then hesitate as the terrible words rose to her mouth. *Next time*, she always promised herself. *I just need to see him one more time.*

But now her stomach was growing noticeably rounder. Even on half rations, it was getting harder and harder for Glass to disguise her weight gain under the shapeless dresses that prompted snickers from Cora. Soon she would start to show. And once she did, there would be questions. The Council would demand to know who the father was. If she was still in touch with Luke, he would find out, and volunteer himself in some misguided attempt to save her that would only end in both of their deaths.

You're saving his life, Glass told herself as she knocked on the door, realizing that this was the last time she would ever stand in this spot. The last time she'd see Luke smile at her like she was the only girl in the universe. Her own words of encouragement sounded hollow to her ears.

But when the door opened, it wasn't Luke standing there. It was Carter, wearing nothing but a pair of plain work pants.

"He's not here," he growled, his eyes narrowing as he took in her flushed cheeks.

"Oh, sorry," Glass said, taking an involuntary step back. "I'll come back later."

But Carter surprised her by reaching out and grabbing her arm, his hand clamping painfully over her wrist.

"What's the hurry?" he asked with a sudden grin that made her stomach churn. "Come on in and wait. I'm sure he just got held up."

Glass winced, rubbing her wrist, as she followed Carter inside. She'd forgotten how tall he was.

"Did you not have work today?" she asked in her most polite

voice, perching on the edge of the couch where she and Luke usually sat. Her heart cramped as she realized she'd never be able to curl up against his shoulder again, or run her fingers through his curls as he lay with his head in her lap.

"I wasn't in the mood," Carter said with a careless shrug.

"Oh," Glass said, biting back a criticism. If Carter wasn't careful, he'd get demoted yet again, and the only position below the distribution center was sanitation duty. "I'm sorry," she added, because she wasn't sure what else to say.

"No, you're not," Carter said, taking a pull of an unmarked bottle. Glass wrinkled her nose. Black-market whiskey. "You're just like all the other assholes on Phoenix. All you care about is yourself."

"You know what, I should be going," Glass said, moving quickly across the living space toward the door. "Tell Luke I'll see him later."

"Hold it," Carter called. Glass ignored him and grabbed the handle without turning around, but before she could open the door, Carter reached over her shoulder and leaned forward to slam it shut.

"Let me go," Glass ordered, turning to face him.

Carter's grin widened, sending chills down Glass's spine. "What's the problem?" he asked, reaching down to rub his hands over her arms. "We both know how much you like slumming it down on Walden. Don't pretend to be all choosy."

"What are you talking about?" Glass spat, wincing as she tried unsuccessfully to break his grip.

He frowned, digging his fingers painfully into her arms. "You think you're being so rebellious, sneaking around with Luke. But I've known plenty of Phoenix girls like you. You're all the same." Still holding one of her arms, he reached his other hand around and started to fumble with the waistband of her pants.

"Stop," Glass said, trying to push him away, horror spreading rapidly through her veins. Then, more loudly, "Stop it! Let me *go*!"

"It's okay," Carter murmured, yanking her closer to him and wrenching her arms above her head. Glass tried to move away, but he weighed more than twice what she did and she couldn't wriggle free. She thrashed around wildly, trying to jab her knee into his stomach, but she was trapped.

"Don't worry," Carter said, filling her ear with his sour breath. "Luke won't mind. He owes me this, after all I've done for him. Besides, we share *everything*."

Glass opened her mouth to scream, but Carter had pushed himself up against her chest, and there was no air in her lungs. Black spots danced before her vision, and she felt herself losing consciousness.

Then the door opened, and Carter jumped back so quickly, Glass lost her balance and fell to the floor.

"Glass?" Luke asked, stepping inside. "Are you okay? What's going on?"

Glass tried to catch her breath, but before she had time to answer, Carter called out from the couch, where he was already reclined in an attitude of calculated carelessness, "Your girlfriend was just showing me the latest Phoenix dance move." He snorted. "I think she needs a little more practice."

Luke tried to catch Glass's gaze, but she looked away. Her heart thumped wildly with fear-fueled adrenaline and rage.

"Sorry I was late—I got caught up talking to Bekah and Ali," Luke said as he reached down to help her up, naming two of his friends from the engineering corps who had always been nice to Glass. "Hey, what's wrong?" he asked quietly when she didn't take his hand.

After what had just happened, all she wanted to do was throw herself into Luke's arms, to allow the warmth of his body to convince hers that everything was okay. But she'd come here for a reason. She couldn't let him comfort her.

"Are you okay? Should we go talk in my room?"

Glass glanced over at Carter, summoning her anger and hatred for him to the surface, letting it boil her blood. She stood up.

"I'm not going into your room," she said, forcing an edge into her voice she didn't recognize. "Ever again."

"What? What's wrong?" Luke asked. He gently pulled on her

hand but she snatched it away. "Glass?" The confusion in his voice was enough to make her heart throb.

"It's over," she said, shocked at the coldness in her own voice. A strange numbness spread through her, as if her nerves were shutting down to protect her from the grief that would surely destroy her. "Did you really think it was going to last?"

"Glass." Luke's voice was low and strained. "I'm not sure what you're talking about, but could we continue this conversation in my room?" He reached out to place his hand on her arm, and she recoiled from his touch.

"*No.*" She pretended to shudder in horror, looking away so that he couldn't see the tears in her eyes. "I can't believe I let you take me in there in the first place."

Luke fell silent, and Glass couldn't help glancing back at him. He was staring at her, his eyes full of hurt. He had always worried that he wasn't good enough for Glass—that he was keeping her from a better life on Phoenix. And now here she was, using the same fears she had once dismissed to turn Luke against her. "Is that really how you feel?" he asked finally. "I thought we—Glass, I love you," he said helplessly.

"I never loved you." She forced the words out of her mouth with such intensity, they seemed to tear out her very soul. "Don't you see? This was all just a *game* to me, seeing how long I could go on before I got caught. But I'm done now. I'm bored."

Luke reached up to take her chin, turning her face up so that their eyes met. She could feel him searching her for some sign that the real Glass was hidden deep inside. "You don't mean that." His voice cracked. "I don't know what's going on, but this isn't you. Glass, talk to me. Please."

For a brief moment, Glass wavered. She could tell him the truth. Of course he would understand; he would forgive all the terrible things she'd just said. She would lean her head on his shoulder and pretend that everything would be okay. They could face this together.

But then she thought of Luke being executed—the lethal injection shutting down his body before it was released into the cold emptiness of space.

The only way to save Luke's heart was to break it.

"You don't even *know* me," she said, jerking away from his touch, the pain of her grief slicing sharp and hot through her chest. "Here," she finished, blinking back tears as she reached behind her neck to unhook the clasp of her locket. "I don't want this anymore."

As she dropped it into Luke's hand he stared at her wordlessly, shock and hurt etched in sharp lines across his face.

She was only vaguely aware of running out of the door and slamming it shut, and then she was racing down the hall, concentrating on the thud of her steps across the skybridge. Left, right, left, right. *Just get home*, Glass told herself. *Just get home, and then you can cry.*

But the moment she turned the corner, she staggered and slid to the floor, both hands clutching her stomach. "I'm sorry," Glass whispered softly, uncertain whether she was speaking to the baby, or Luke, or her own bruised and damaged heart.

CHAPTER 21

Clarke

The tension in the infirmary tent was so thick, Clarke could practically feel it pressing against her chest when she breathed.

She hovered wordlessly at Thalia's side, trying in vain to battle the infection that had already claimed her kidneys and seemed hell-bent on taking her liver next, seething in silent fury at Octavia's selfishness. How could she sit there, watching Thalia slip in and out of consciousness, and not return the stolen medicine?

But then she glanced over to the corner, where Octavia lay curled up. The sight of her round cheeks and thick lashes made her look painfully young, and Clarke's anger was replaced by doubt and guilt. Maybe Octavia hadn't done it. But if not, who had?

Her eyes lowered to the bracelet that encased her wrist. If Thalia could just hold on until the next wave of colonists arrived, she'd be okay. But there was no knowing when that would be. The Council would wait until they had conclusive data on the radiation levels, regardless of what was happening on Earth.

Thalia's death, she knew, would matter as little to the Council as Lilly's had. Orphans and criminals didn't count.

As she watched Thalia's labored breathing, Clarke felt a surge of white-hot fury. She refused to sit here and just wait for her friend to die. Hadn't humans cured illnesses for millennia before the discovery of penicillin? There had to be *something* in the woods that fought infection. She tried to remember what little she'd learned about plants in Biology of Earth class. Who knew if those plants were even around anymore—everything seemed to have evolved strangely after the Cataclysm. But she had to at least try.

"I'll be back," she whispered to her sleeping friend. Without a word to the Arcadian boy standing guard outside, Clarke hurried out of the infirmary and began to walk toward the trees, not bothering to grab anything from the supply tent lest she attract any unwanted attention. But she didn't manage to go more than ten meters without a familiar voice scratching at her eardrums.

"Where are you going?" Wells asked as he fell in step next to her.

"Looking for medicinal plants." She was too tired to lie to Wells, and it didn't matter anyway; he always saw through her lies. Somehow, the self-righteousness that blinded him to the most glaring truths didn't prevent him from reading the secrets in her eyes.

"I'll come with you."

"I'm fine on my own, thanks," Clarke said, increasing her pace, as if that could possibly deter the boy who'd traveled across the solar system to be with her. "You stay here in case they need someone to lead an angry mob."

"You're right. Things got a little out of hand last night," he said with a frown. "I didn't mean for anything bad to happen to Octavia. I only wanted to help. I know you need that medicine for Thalia."

"You *only wanted to help*. I've heard that one before." Clarke whipped around to face Wells. She didn't have the time or the energy to deal with his need for redemption right now. "Guess what, Wells. Someone ended up Confined this time too."

Wells stopped in his tracks, and Clarke jerked her head away, unable to look at the hurt in his eyes. But she refused to let him make her feel guilty. Nothing she could say to him could begin to approximate the pain he'd caused her.

Clarke stared straight ahead as she strode into the trees, still half expecting to hear the thud of footsteps behind her. But this time there was only silence.

By the time she reached the creek, the fury Clarke had carried into the woods had been replaced by despair. The scientist in her was mortified by her own naïveté. It was foolish to think that she would somehow recognize a plant from a class she'd taken six years ago, let alone that it would even look the same after all this time. But she refused to turn back, restrained partly by her own stubborn pride and partly by a desire to avoid Wells for as long as possible.

It was too chilly to wade through the water, so she climbed up the slope and walked along the ridge to cross over to the other side. This was the farthest she'd ever been from camp, and it felt different out here; the air even *tasted* somehow different than it did closer to the clearing. She closed her eyes, hoping that it would help her identify the strange swirl of scents that she had no words to describe. It was like trying to recall a memory that hadn't been hers to begin with.

The ground was flatter here than she'd seen elsewhere in the woods. Up ahead, the gap between the trees grew even wider, and the trees themselves seemed to part into straight lines on either side, as if they could sense Clarke's presence and had stood aside to let her pass.

Clarke started to pull a star-shaped leaf from a tree, then froze as a glint of light caught her eye. Something nestled in between two enormous trees was reflecting the fading sunlight.

She took another step forward, her heart racing.

It was a window.

Clarke began walking toward it slowly, feeling as though she were moving through one of her own dreams. The window was framed by two trees, which must have grown out of the ruins of the structure, whatever it had been. But the glass wasn't clear. As she got closer, she saw that the window was actually made from different pieces of colored glass that had been arranged to create an image, although there were too many cracks to tell what it had once been.

She reached forward and gently brushed her finger against the glass, shivering as the cold seeped into her fingers. It was like touching a corpse. For a moment, she found herself wishing Wells was with her. No matter how angry she was with him, she'd never deprive him of the chance to see one of the ruins he'd spent his whole life dreaming about.

She turned and walked around one of the large trees. There was another window, but this one had been smashed, sharp fragments of glass glittering on the ground. Clarke stepped forward and crouched down to peer inside. The jagged opening was almost large enough to crawl through. The sun was only beginning to set, and the orange rays seemed to shine right into the opening, revealing what looked like a wooden floor. Every instinct in Clarke's brain was shouting at her to keep away, but she couldn't bring herself to stop.

Taking care not to let her skin touch the glass, Clarke reached her arm through the opening of the window and brushed her hand against the wood. Nothing happened. She clenched her fingers into a fist and rapped on it, coughing as a cloud of dust rose into the air. It felt solid. She paused, considering. The building had survived this long. Surely the floor would be able to hold her weight.

Carefully, she slid one leg through the opening, then the other. She held her breath, but nothing happened.

When she looked up and around her, Clarke sucked in her breath.

The walls soared on all sides, converging in a point many meters above her head, higher than even the roof above the solar fields. It wasn't as dark as she'd expected. There were windows along the other wall that she hadn't been able to see. These were made of clear glass, but they weren't broken. Beams of sunlight shone through, illuminating millions of dust particles dancing through the air.

Clark rose slowly to her feet. There was a railing up ahead that ran parallel to the floor at about waist height. She took a few hesitant steps toward it and gasped, startling herself again as the sound echoed far above her head.

She was standing on a balcony overlooking an enormous open space. It was almost completely dark, probably because most of the building was now underground, but she could just make out the outline of benches. She didn't dare venture any closer to the edge for a better look, but as her eyes adjusted to the darkness, more shapes sharpened into focus.

Bodies.

At first she thought she'd only imagined it, that her mind was using the shadows to play tricks on her. She closed her eyes and willed herself not to be such a fool. But when she turned back, the shapes were the same.

Two skeletons were draped over one of the benches, and another, smaller one lay at their feet. Although there was no knowing whether the bones had been disturbed, from what she could tell, these people had died huddled together. Had they been trying to keep warm as the skies darkened and nuclear winter set in? How many people had been left at that point?

Clarke took another small step forward, but this time, the wood creaked dangerously. She froze and started to inch her way back. But a loud crack sang out through the silence, and with a sudden lurch, the floor fell out from underneath her.

She waved her hands wildly, grabbing hold of the balcony

edge as the railing and floor tumbled through the air. Her legs dangled over a vast, open space as the pieces landed with a thud on the stone far below.

She screamed, a loud, wordless cry that rose up toward the ceiling and then faded away, joining the ghosts of whatever other screams still lingered in the dust. Her fingers started to slide.

"*Help!*" Using every ounce of strength in her body, she tried to pull herself up, her arms shaking with the effort, but her grip was failing. She started to scream again, but there was no more air left in her lungs, and the word died on her lips before she realized it had been Wells's name.

CHAPTER 22

Wells

Wells broke into a sprint as Clarke's scream ignited every nerve in his body. It had been difficult following Clarke through the woods, especially since he had to keep his distance—she would have been furious if she'd spotted him. But now he was flying over the grass and could barely feel his boots hitting the ground. He had just reached the stained-glass window when a second, louder scream filled the air.

"Clarke!" he yelled, sticking his head through the gap in the broken glass. It was dark inside the ruin, but there was no time to take out his flashbeam. Up ahead, he could just make out fingers clinging to a ledge. Wells ducked inside, landing with a thud on a wooden platform, and then slid forward on his stomach, reaching over the edge to wrap one hand around Clarke's wrist while he grabbed on to the stone wall for leverage. "I've got you," he said.

But he spoke too soon. One of her hands disappeared, and he was now supporting her entire weight. He could feel himself slipping toward the edge. "*Clarke!*" he screamed again. "Hold on!"

With a grunt, he managed to pull himself up into a sitting position, then pressed one foot against the wall. His hand was sweating, and he could feel himself losing his grip. "*Wells*," she shrieked. Her voice echoed through the cavernous space, making it sound like there were a hundred Clarkes in peril.

He gritted his teeth and pulled, gasping with relief and exhaustion when Clarke's other hand regained its hold. "You're almost there. Come on."

She placed her elbows on the wooden platform, and he reached over to grab her upper arm, heaving the rest of her body up over the ledge. They collapsed into a heap against the stone wall.

Clarke was sobbing as she struggled to catch her breath. "It's okay," Wells said, wrapping his arm around her. "You're okay." He waited for her to recoil from his touch, but instead, she buried herself in his arms. Wells tightened his hold.

"What are you doing here?" she asked from inside his embrace, her voice muffled. "I thought . . . I hoped . . ."

"I followed you—I was worried," Wells spoke into her hair. "I could never let anything happen to you. No matter what." He spoke without thinking, but as the words left his lips he knew that they were true. Even if she kissed someone else—even if she wanted to be with someone else—he would always be there for her.

Clarke didn't say anything, but she stayed in his arms.

Wells held her there, terrified to say anything else and end this moment too soon, his relief expanding into joy. Maybe he had a chance to win her back. Maybe, here in the ruins of the old world, they could start something new.

CHAPTER 23

Bellamy

He'd start with letting the bastards starve. Then, maybe when they were all so weak with hunger that they had to *crawl* over to him and beg for forgiveness, then he'd consider going out to hunt. But they'd have to make do with a squirrel or something else small—no way was he killing another deer for them.

Bellamy had spent the night unable to sleep, watching the infirmary tent in order to make damn sure no one got anywhere *near* his sister. Now that it was morning, he'd resorted to pacing around the perimeter of the camp. He had too much energy to sit still.

Bellamy stepped over the tree line, feeling his body relax slightly as the shadows washed over him. Over the past few weeks, he'd discovered that he enjoyed the company of trees more than people. He shivered as a breeze swept across the back of his neck, and looked up. The patches of sky visible through the branches were beginning to turn gray, and the air suddenly felt different—almost damp. He lowered his head and kept walking. Perhaps Earth had had enough of their bullshit already and was initiating a second nuclear winter.

He turned and began drifting in the direction of the stream, where there were usually animal tracks to follow. But then a flash of movement in a tree a few meters away caught his attention, and he paused.

Something bright red was waving in the wind. It might've been a leaf, except there wasn't anything else close to that shade nearby. Bellamy squinted, then took a few steps forward, feeling a strange prickle on the back of his neck. It was Octavia's hair ribbon. It made absolutely no sense—she hadn't been out in the woods for days—but he'd recognize it anywhere. There were some things you could never forget.

The halls were dark as Bellamy scurried up the stairs to their flat. It had been worth staying out after curfew, as long as he didn't get caught. He'd broken through an old air shaft, too small for anyone but a child to crawl through, into an abandoned storage room he'd heard about on C deck. It was full of all kinds of treasures:

a brimmed hat topped with a funny-looking bird; a box that said EIGHT MINUTE ABS on it, whatever that meant; and a red ribbon he'd found wrapped around the handle of a strange wheeled bag. Bellamy had traded his other discoveries in exchange for ration points, but he'd kept the ribbon, even though it would have fed them for a month. He wanted to give it to Octavia.

He pressed his thumb to the scanner and carefully opened the door, then froze. Someone was moving inside. His mother was normally asleep by now. He took a silent step forward, just enough to hear better, and felt himself relax as a familiar sound filled his ears. His mother was singing Octavia's favorite lullaby, something she used to do all the time, sitting on the floor and singing through the door of the closet until Octavia fell asleep. Bellamy sighed with relief. It didn't sound like she was in the mood to scream at him, or worse, have one of her endless crying fits that made Bellamy want to hide in the closet with his sister.

Bellamy smiled as he crept into the main room and saw his mother kneeling on the floor. "Hush, little baby, don't you cry, mama's gonna buy you a star in the sky. And if that star can't carry a tune, mama's going buy you a piece of the moon." Another sound drifted through the darkness, a faint wheeze. Was the ventilation system acting up again? He took a step forward. "And if the moon ever loses its shine, mama's gonna buy you—"

Bellamy heard the sound again, although this time, it sounded more like a gasp.

"Mom?" He took another step. She was crouched over something on the floor. "*Mom,*" he bellowed, lunging forward.

His mother had her hands around Octavia's neck, and even in the darkness, Bellamy could see that his sister's face was blue. He knocked his mother to the side and scooped Octavia into his arms. For one heart-stopping second, he was sure she was dead, but then she twitched and started coughing. Bellamy exhaled, and his heart began thumping wildly.

"We were just playing a game," his mother said faintly. "She couldn't sleep. So we were playing a game. . . ."

Bellamy held Octavia close, making soothing noises, staring at the wall as a strange feeling came over him. He wasn't sure what his mother had been doing, but he was sure she was going to try again.

Bellamy rose onto the balls of his feet and stretched his arm toward the ribbon. His fingers wrapped around the familiar satin, but as he tried to pull it down, he realized the ornament wasn't just caught on the branch—it had been tied there.

Had someone found the ribbon and tied it to the tree for safekeeping? But why wouldn't they just have brought it back to camp? He absentmindedly ran his hand down the branch, letting the rough bark dig into his skin as he traced a line from the branch down to the trunk. But then he froze. His fingers were hovering on the edge of a dip in the trunk, where a chunk of wood had been scooped out. There was something sticking out—a bird's nest, maybe?

Bellamy grabbed on to the edge and pulled, watching in horror as the medicine he and Clarke had discovered came tumbling out. The pills, syringes, bottles—all of it was scattered in the grass by his feet. His brain raced for an explanation, anything to staunch the panic welling up in his chest.

He sank to the grass with a groan and closed his eyes.

It was true. Octavia *had* taken the medicine. She'd hidden it in the tree and used her hair ribbon as a marker so she could find it again. But he couldn't think why she'd done it. Had she worried about what would happen if one of them had gotten sick? Maybe she'd been planning to take the supplies with them when they set out on their own.

But then Graham's words rang in his ears. *We can't let anyone else die just because your little sister's a drug addict.*

The boy assigned to stand guard outside the infirmary tent had fallen asleep. He barely managed to scramble to his feet and mumble a quick "Hey, you can't go in there" before Bellamy burst through the flap. He jerked his head around, confirming that it was empty except for Clarke's sleeping sick friend, then strode over to where Octavia was sitting cross-legged on her cot, braiding her hair.

"What the hell do you think you're doing?" he hissed.

"What are you talking about?" Her voice was a mixture of boredom and irritation, as if he were pestering her about schoolwork like he always used to when checking up on her in the care center.

Bellamy threw the hair ribbon down on her cot, wincing as he saw horror rush to Octavia's face. "I didn't . . . ," she stammered. "It wasn't . . ."

"Cut the bullshit, O," he snapped. "Now you can finish braiding your goddamn hair while a girl is dying in front of you."

Octavia's eyes darted to Thalia, then shifted down. "I didn't think she was really that sick," she said softly. "Clarke had already given her medicine. By the time I realized she needed more, it was too late. I can't confess now. You saw how they were. I didn't know what they'd do to me." When she looked up again, her deep-blue eyes were filled with tears. "Even you hate me now, and you're my brother."

Bellamy sighed and sat down next to his sister. "I don't hate you." He grabbed her hand and gave it a squeeze. "I just don't understand. Why'd you do it? The truth this time, please."

Octavia fell silent, and he could feel her skin growing clammy as she began to tremble. "O?" He released her hand.

"I needed them," she said, her voice small. "I can't sleep

without them." She paused and closed her eyes. "At first, it was just at night. I kept having these terrible dreams, so the nurse at the care center gave me medicine to help me sleep, but then it got worse. There were times when I couldn't breathe, when it felt like the whole universe was closing in on me, crushing me. The nurse wouldn't give me any more medicine, even when I asked, so I started stealing pills. It was the only thing that made me feel better."

Bellamy stared at her. "*That's* what you were caught stealing?" he asked slowly, the realization overtaking him. "Not food for the younger kids in the care center. *Pills.*"

Octavia didn't say anything, just nodded, her eyes full of tears.

"O," Bellamy sighed. "Why didn't you tell me?"

"I know how much you worry about me." She took a deep breath. "I know how you want to protect me all the time. I didn't want you to feel like you'd failed."

Bellamy felt pain radiating out from a spot behind his heart. He didn't know which hurt more: that his sister was a drug addict, or that she hadn't told him the truth because he'd been so blinded by his insane need to watch over her. When he finally spoke, his voice was hoarse. "So what do we do now?" he asked. For the first time in his life, he had no idea how to help his sister. "What will happen when we give the medicine back?"

"I'll be okay. I just need to learn how to live without them. It's already easier here." She reached out and took his hand, giving him a strange, almost pleading look. "Do you wish you hadn't come here for me?"

"No," Bellamy said firmly, shaking his head. "I just need some time to process everything." He rose to his feet, then looked back at his sister. "But you need to make sure Clarke gets the medicine. *You* have to be the one to tell her. I'm serious, O."

"I know." She nodded, then turned to look at Thalia and seemed to deflate a little. "I'll do it tonight."

"Okay." Sighing, Bellamy strode out of the tent and into the clearing. When he reached the tree line, he took a deep breath, allowing the damp air to seep through his lungs into his aching chest. He tilted his head back to let the wind wash over his flushed skin. Now that the sky was unobstructed by trees, it looked even darker, almost black. Suddenly, a line of jagged light flashed across the sky, followed by a violent, resounding crack that made the earth shudder. Bellamy jumped, and screams filled the clearing. But they were quickly drowned out by another deafening boom, this one louder than the first, like the sky was about to tumble to Earth.

Then something did start to fall. Drops of liquid were cascading down his skin, dripping off his hair, and quickly seeping into his clothes. *Rain*, Bellamy realized, real rain. He tilted his face up toward the sky, and for a moment, his wonder drowned out all the rest—his anger at Graham and Wells and Clarke, his concern for his sister, the screams of the idiot kids who didn't know that rain was harmless. He closed his eyes, letting the water wash away the dirt and sweat caked on his face. For a second, he let himself imagine that the rain could wash everything away: the blood, the tears, the fact that he and Octavia had failed each other. They could have a clean start, try again.

Bellamy opened his eyes. He was being ridiculous, he knew. The rain was only water, and there was no such thing as a clean start. That was the thing about secrets—you had to carry them with you forever, no matter what the cost.

CHAPTER 24

Glass

As she walked across the skybridge, the terrible realization that her mother was right hung like a weight on Glass's heart. She couldn't risk a single misstep—not for her sake, but for Luke's. What if the Chancellor woke up and revoked her pardon, and then Luke did something stupid and admitted the truth about the pregnancy? It was like history was repeating itself, and yet she knew she'd always make the same choice. She would always choose to protect the boy she loved.

She'd been avoiding Luke for several days, though he'd been summoned for so many emergency shifts lately that she wasn't sure he'd even noticed. She'd finally arranged to meet at his flat this evening, and the thought of him greeting her with a smile made her chest ache. At least this time, there'd be no tricks, no lies. She'd simply tell him the truth, no matter how difficult. Maybe he'd seek comfort in Camille again, and then things would truly come full circle. The thought came with a knife-sharp pang, but Glass ignored it and kept walking.

As she approached the far end of the skybridge, her eyes landed on a small group gathered near the checkpoint. A few guards stood speaking in a tight circle, while a number of civilians whispered and pointed at something through the long, star-filled window that bordered the walkway. Glass suddenly recognized a few of the guards—they were Luke's team, members of the elite guard's engineering corps. The woman with graying hair who was moving her fingers rapidly through the air, manipulating a holo-diagram in front of her face, was Bekah. Next to her was Ali, a boy with dark skin and bright-green eyes fixed intently on the image Bekah was creating.

"Glass!" Ali exclaimed warmly, looking up as she approached. He jogged forward a few steps and clasped her hands in his. "It's great to see you. How are you?"

"I'm . . . good," she stammered, confused. How much did they know? Were they greeting her as Luke's ex, the snotty Phoenix girl who'd broken his heart, or as Luke's escaped-convict girlfriend? Either way, Ali was being much kinder than she deserved.

Bekah shot Glass a quick smile and then returned to her

diagrams, frowning as she rotated a complicated-looking three-dimensional blueprint. "Where's Luke?" Glass asked as she glanced from side to side. If they were still on duty, he wouldn't be home yet either.

Ali gestured out the window with a grin. "Look outside."

Glass turned slowly, every atom in her body turning to ice. She knew already what she would see. Two figures in space suits were floating outside, each tethered to the ship by a thin cord. They had tool kits strapped to their backs and were using their gloved hands to move along the skybridge.

As if in a trance, Glass moved slowly forward and pressed her face against the window. She watched in horror as the two figures nodded at each other, then disappeared under the skybridge. Luke's unit was responsible for crucial repairs, but he'd only been a junior member of the team when they were dating last year. She knew he'd been promoted, but she had no idea he would be out on spacewalks this soon.

The thought of him outside—nothing separating him from the cold emptiness of space but a laughably thin cord and a pressurized suit—made Glass feel dizzy. She grabbed on to the railing to steady herself, sending up a silent prayer to the stars to keep him safe.

She hadn't left the flat in two weeks. Not even her loosest clothes could mask the bump that had emerged with alarming suddenness. Glass wasn't sure how much longer her mother would be able to make excuses for her. She'd stopped responding to her friends' messages, and eventually, they'd stopped sending them. Everyone except for Wells, who contacted her every day without fail.

Glass pulled up her message queue to reread the note he'd sent her that morning.

I know something must be wrong, and I hope you know that I'm always here for whatever you need. But even if you don't (or can't) write back, I'm going to keep filling your queue with my stupid ramblings because, no matter what happened, you're still my best friend and I'll never stop wishing you were here.

The rest of the note went on to talk about Wells's frustrations with officer training, then ended with a few cryptic allusions to something about Clarke. Glass hoped there was nothing seriously wrong—Clarke needed to realize how good she had it. She would never find a sweeter, smarter boy on Phoenix. Although the honor of the sweetest, smartest boy in the Colony went to Luke. Luke, who was no longer in her life.

The only thing that kept Glass sane was the growing presence inside her. Placing her hand on her stomach, Glass whispered to the baby, telling him again—she felt certain, somehow, that it was a boy—how much she loved him.

There was a sudden knock at the door, and Glass hurried to stand up, to try to run into her bedroom and lock it shut. But the three guards had already burst inside.

"Glass Sorenson," one of them barked, his eyes traveling to her stomach, the bump glaringly obvious. "You are under arrest for violation of the Gaia Doctrine."

"Please just let me explain." She gasped as panic gushed through her. It felt like she was drowning. The room was spinning, and it was hard to tell which words were coming out of her mouth and which were dashing manically through her skull.

In a flash, one of the guards grabbed her arms and wrenched her wrists behind her back while another secured them with cuffs. "No," she whimpered. "Please. It was an accident." She pressed her feet into the floor, but there was no use. The guards were forcibly dragging her across the room.

And then some wild, frantic instinct took over, and Glass thrashed against the guard restraining her, kicking wildly against his shins and shoving her elbow into his throat. He tightened his grip on her shoulder as he dragged her out through the corridor and into the stairwell.

A sob wrenched up from inside her as Glass realized that she would never see Luke again, the knowledge hitting her with all the force of a hammer. Her legs suddenly gave out. The guard holding her staggered back as she slid, trying to keep her upright.

I could do it, Glass thought, taking advantage of his momentary imbalance to surge wildly forward. For a brief, shining moment, Glass felt the thrill of hope pushing through the panic. This was her chance. She would escape.

But then the guard snatched at her from behind and she lost her footing. Her shoulder smacked against the landing and, suddenly, she was falling down the sharp, narrow, dim staircase.

Everything went dark.

When Glass opened her eyes again, her whole body ached. Her knees, her shoulders, her stomach—

Her stomach. Glass tried to move her hands to feel it, but they were strapped down. No, *cuffed* down, she realized in growing horror. Of course; she was a criminal.

"Oh, sweetie, you're awake," a warm voice greeted her.

Through her blurry vision, she could just make out the shape of a figure approaching her bed. It was a nurse.

"Please," Glass croaked. "Is he okay? Can I hold him?"

The woman paused, and Glass knew even before she spoke what she would say. She could already sense it, the horrible, aching emptiness inside her.

"I'm sorry," the nurse said quietly. Glass could barely see her mouth, which gave the impression that the voice was coming from somewhere else entirely. "We couldn't save him."

Glass turned away, letting the cold metal of the handcuffs press angrily against her skin, not caring about the pain. Any feeling was better than this, this heartache that would never go away.

Finally, the two figures reappeared from underneath the skybridge. Glass exhaled loudly as she brought her hand to the window. How long had she been holding her breath?

"Are you okay?" a voice asked, and for a moment, Glass thought with horror that she was back in that hospital room with the nurse. But it was only Luke's guard friend Bekah, looking at her with concern.

Her face was wet, Glass realized. She'd been crying. She couldn't even bring herself to feel embarrassed, she was so relieved that Luke had made it back safely.

"Thanks," Glass managed, taking the handkerchief that Bekah offered, wiping away her tears. Outside, Luke was pulling himself back along the cord, placing one gloved hand over the other as he moved back toward the airlock chamber.

Around her, various onlookers started to clap and high-five one another, but Glass stayed at the window, her eyes fixed on the spot she'd last seen Luke. The thoughts that Glass had carried with her onto the skybridge seemed as distant as a long-forgotten dream. She couldn't sever their tie any more than she could cut the wire tethering him to the ship. Without Luke, life would be as empty and cold as space itself.

"Hey, you," his voice came from behind her, and Glass

spun around, throwing herself into his arms. His thermal shirt was soaked with sweat, his curls damp and dirty, but Glass didn't care.

"I was worried about you," she said, her voice muffled into his shirt.

He laughed and wrapped his arms tighter around her, planting a kiss on the top of her head. "This is a nice surprise."

Glass looked up at him, not caring that her eyes were puffy and that her nose was running. "It's fine," Luke said, exchanging an amused look with Ali before turning back to Glass. "It's all part of the job."

Her heart was still pumping too fast to speak, so she nodded, shooting an embarrassed smile at Bekah and Ali and the others. "Come on," Luke said, taking her hand and leading her down the skybridge.

As they crossed onto Walden, Glass's breathing finally returned to normal. "I can't believe you do that," she said quietly. "Aren't you terrified?"

"It's scary, but it's exhilarating, too. It's so . . . enormous out there. I know that sounds kind of stupid." He paused, but Glass shook her head. They both knew about enclosed spaces, how you could feel trapped in them, even one as vast as the ship.

"I'm just glad everything went okay," she said.

"Yeah, it did. Well, mostly." Luke's fingers loosened their grip around hers, and his voice grew slightly strained. "There was something weird going on with the airlock. Some valve must've come loose, because it was releasing oxygen out of the ship."

"But you guys fixed it, right?"

"Of course. That's what we're trained to do." He squeezed her hand.

Suddenly, Glass stopped short, turning to Luke and rising up on her toes to kiss him, right there in the middle of the crowded hallway. She didn't care anymore who saw them. No matter what happened, she thought, kissing him with an almost desperate need, she would never let anything keep them apart again.

CHAPTER 25

Bellamy

Bellamy stared into the flickering flames, the buzz of conversation around him mingling with the cracking of the logs. It had been a few hours since his confrontation with Octavia, and so far there'd been no sign of her. He hoped she'd return the medicine soon. He couldn't force her to hand it over, he knew, or their relationship would never recover. He had to show that he trusted her, and she had to do the right thing to win back that trust.

The rain had stopped, but the ground was still damp. A few scuffles had broken out over the handful of rocks that had become VIP seating around the campfire, but for the most part, everyone seemed willing to tolerate the soggy grass to sit close to the warmth of the flames. A few girls had sought out a third option and were now perched on the laps of smug-looking boys.

He scanned the circle, searching for Clarke. There was much more smoke than usual, probably because all the firewood was wet, and it took a few moments for his eyes to settle on the familiar glint of her reddish-gold hair. He squinted and realized, to his surprise, that she was sitting next to Wells. They weren't touching, or even speaking, but something had changed between them. The tension that wracked Clarke's body whenever Wells came near had disappeared, and instead of shooting wounded, furtive looks at Clarke when her head was turned, Wells was staring placidly into the fire, a content look on his face.

A shard of resentment worked its way into Bellamy's stomach. He should have known it would only be a matter of time before Clarke went running back to Wells. He should never have kissed her in the woods. He'd only ever really cared about one other girl before—and he'd gotten hurt that time too.

The clouds were thick enough to block out most of the stars, but Bellamy tilted his head back anyway, wondering how much warning they'd have before the next dropship arrived. Would they be able to see it tearing toward them—a warning flare in the sky?

But then his eyes fell on a figure moving through the darkness toward the fire: the shadowy outline of a tiny girl with her head held high. Bellamy rose to his feet as Octavia stepped into the pool of light cast by the dancing flames, sending a ripple of whispers around the circle.

"Oh, for the love of god." Bellamy heard Graham groan. "Who the hell was supposed to be watching her tonight?"

Wells shot Clarke a look, then stood to face Graham. "It's fine," he said. "She can join us."

Octavia paused, looking from Wells to Graham as the boys glared at each other. But before either of them had time to speak, she took a breath and stepped forward. "I have something to say," she said. She was trembling, but her voice was firm.

The excited whispers and confused murmurs trailed off as nearly a hundred heads turned to face Octavia. In the flickering firelight, Bellamy could see the panic creeping across her face, and felt a sudden urge to run over and hold her hand. But he forced his feet to stay rooted to the ground. He'd spent so long trying to take care of the little girl in his mind that he'd never gotten to know the person she'd become. And right now, this was something she had to do on her own.

"I did take the medicine," Octavia began. She paused to let her words sink in, then took a deep breath and continued as a rumble of *I knew it*s and *I told you so*s began to build like thunder. Octavia told the group a similar version of the story she'd told Bellamy earlier that day—how hard it'd been growing up in the care center, how her dependence on pills had turned into an addiction.

The muttering ceased as Octavia's voice cracked. "Back on the Colony, I never thought I was hurting anyone. Stealing just seemed like a way to get what I deserved. I figured everyone deserved to be able to fall asleep at night. To wake up without feeling that your nightmares had left scars inside your head." She took a deep breath and closed her eyes. When she opened them, Bellamy could see the faint shimmer of tears. "I was so selfish, so scared. But I never meant to hurt Thalia, or anyone." She turned to Clarke and swallowed the sob that seemed to be forming in her throat. "I'm so sorry. I know I don't deserve your forgiveness, but all I can ask is that you give me a chance to start over." She raised her chin and looked around the circle until she saw Bellamy, and she gave him a small smile. "Just like everyone here wants to do. I know a lot of us have done things we're not proud of, but we've been given a chance for a new beginning. I know I almost ruined it for a lot of you, but I'd like to start over—to become a better person, to help make Earth the world we want it to be."

Bellamy's heart swelled with pride. Tears were beginning to blur his vision, although if anyone called him out on it, he'd blame it on the smoke. His sister's life had been full of suffering and hardship from the very beginning. She'd made mistakes—they both had—but she'd still managed to stay brave and strong.

For a moment, no one spoke. Even the crackling of the fire faded away, as if Earth itself were holding its breath. But then Graham's voice barreled through the silence. "That's bullshit."

Bellamy bristled as a spark of anger sizzled across his chest, but he gritted his teeth. Of course Graham was going to be a bastard about it—that didn't mean the others hadn't been touched by Octavia's speech. But instead of prompting scoffs or disapproving whispers, Graham's words unleashed a tide of murmured assent that swelled quickly into shouts. He looked around the circle as he continued. "Why should we bust our asses all day, chopping wood, hauling water, doing whatever it takes to keep everyone alive, just to let some delusional drug addict walk all over us? It's like being—"

"Okay, that's enough," Bellamy said, cutting him off. He glanced at Octavia. Her bottom lip had begun to quiver as her eyes darted around the fire. "You've made your point. But there are ninety-four other people here with opinions of their own, and they don't need you to tell them what to think."

"I agree with Graham," a girl's voice called out. Bellamy turned and saw a short-haired Waldenite glaring at Octavia. "We *all* had shitty lives back on the Colony, but you don't see anyone else stealing." She narrowed her eyes. "Who knows what she'll take next time."

"Everyone just relax." Clarke had risen to her feet. "She apologized. We have to give her a second chance." Bellamy stared at her in surprise, waiting for the surge of indignation. After all, she was the one who'd accused Octavia in the first place. But as he looked at Clarke, all he felt was gratitude.

"No." Graham's voice was hard and as he looked around the circle, his eyes flashed with something other than reflected firelight. He turned to Wells, who was still standing next to Clarke. "It's just like you said. There has to be some kind of order, or else there's no way in hell we'll make it."

"So what do you recommend?" Wells asked. Graham smiled, and Bellamy felt like someone had poured ice water down his back. Fixing Graham with a glare, he hurried over to Octavia and put his arm around her.

"It'll be okay," he whispered.

"I'm sorry," Graham said, turning to Bellamy and Octavia. "But we don't have a choice. She put Thalia's life at risk. We can't take any chances. Octavia needs to die."

"What?" Bellamy sputtered. "Are you *insane*?" He jerked his head from side to side, expecting to see a sea of similarly revolted faces. But while a few people were staring at Graham in shock, a number were nodding.

Bellamy stepped protectively in front of Octavia, who was

trembling violently. He'd burn the goddamn planet to a crisp before he let anyone near his sister.

"Should we put it to a vote?" Graham raised his chin and nodded at Wells. "You're the one who was so excited to bring *democracy* back to Earth. It seems only fair."

"This is *not* what I meant," Wells snapped. His face had lost its politician's reserve, his features twisted with anger. "We're not going to vote about whether to *kill* people."

"No?" Graham raised an eyebrow. "So it's okay for your father, but not for us."

Bellamy winced and closed his eyes as he heard sounds of agreement ripple through the crowd. It was exactly what he would've said in that situation, except that Bellamy would have only meant it as a jab at Wells. He'd never *actually* propose killing someone.

"The Council doesn't execute people for fun." Wells's voice shook with fury. "Keeping humanity alive in space required extraordinary measures. Sometimes *cruel* measures." Wells paused. "But we have a chance to do better."

"So what?" Graham growled. "You're just going to give her a slap on the wrist and then make everyone pinky swear not to break the rules?" A few snickers rose up from the crowd.

"No." Wells shook his head. "You're right. There needs to be consequences." He took a deep breath. "We'll banish them from camp." His voice was firm, but when he turned to Bellamy, his eyes seemed to contain a strange mixture of anguish and relief.

"Banish?" Graham repeated. "So they can sneak back whenever they want and steal more supplies? That's bullshit."

Bellamy opened his mouth to speak, but his voice was drowned out as the buzz of voices grew louder. Finally, a girl Bellamy vaguely recognized from Walden stood up. "That sounds fair," she called out, shouting to be heard over the crowd, which grew quiet as heads turned to look at her. "As long as they promise never to come back."

Bellamy tightened his arm around Octavia, who'd gone limp. He nodded. "We'll leave at sunrise." He turned to smile at Octavia—this is what he'd planned all along. So then why did he feel more apprehension than relief?

The fire died down, and darkness settled over the camp like a blanket, muffling footsteps and muting voices as shadowy figures disappeared into tents or carried blankets toward the edges of the clearing.

Bellamy set up a makeshift cot for Octavia at the short end, near the wreckage of the dropship. They hadn't said it aloud, but they both knew neither of them wanted to sleep in a tent tonight.

Octavia curled up on her blanket and closed her eyes, though it was clear she wasn't sleeping. The trip back into the woods with Clarke to retrieve the medicine had been a tense one. No one had spoken, though Bellamy could feel Clarke's eyes boring into his back as he led the way.

Now he sat next to Octavia, his back against a tree, staring into the darkness. It was hard to wrap his mind around the fact that tomorrow, they would leave forever.

A shape moved through the shadows toward them. Wells. He had Bellamy's bow slung over his shoulder.

"Hey," Wells said quietly as Bellamy rose to his feet. "I'm sorry about what happened back there. I know banishment sounds harsh, but I wasn't sure what else to do." He sighed. "I really thought Graham was going to convince them to . . ." He trailed off as his eyes fell on Octavia. "Not that I would've let that happen, but there's only two of us and a lot of them."

Bellamy felt a smartass retort rise in his throat but swallowed it back down. Wells had done the best thing he could under the circumstances. "Thank you."

They stared at each other for a moment, then Bellamy cleared his throat. "Listen, I should probably . . ." He paused. "I'm sorry about your father." Bellamy took a deep breath and forced himself to meet Wells's eyes. "I hope he's okay."

"Thank you," Wells said quietly. "I do too." He fell silent for a moment, but when he spoke again, his voice was firm. "I know you were just trying to protect your sister. I would've done the same thing." He smiled. "I suppose I sort of did."

Wells extended his hand. "I hope you and Octavia stay safe out there."

Bellamy shook his hand and smiled ruefully. "I can't imagine anything out there worse than Graham. Keep an eye on that kid."

"Will do." Wells nodded, then turned around and headed back into the darkness.

Bellamy lowered himself to the blanket and stared out into the clearing. He could just make out the shape of the infirmary tent where Clarke would be giving Thalia the long-awaited medicine. His stomach twisted strangely as he thought back to the scene by the fire, the flames flickering over Clarke's determined face. He'd never known a girl who was so beautiful and intense at once.

Bellamy leaned back with a sigh and closed his eyes, wondering how long it would take until she stopped being the last person he thought about before he fell asleep.

CHAPTER 26

Clarke

The antibiotics were working. Although it had been less than a few hours since Clarke burst into the tent, clutching the medicine under her arm, Thalia's fever had already gone down, and she was more alert than she'd been in days.

Clarke lowered herself to perch on the edge of Thalia's cot as her friend's eyes fluttered open. "Welcome back," Clarke said with a grin. "How are you feeling?"

Thalia's eyes darted around the empty tent, then looked up to meet Clarke's. "This isn't heaven, is it?"

Clarke shook her head. "God, I hope not."

"Good. Because I always assumed there'd be boys there. Boys who didn't use water rationing as an excuse not to bathe." Thalia managed a smile. "Did anyone build the first shower on Earth while I was passed out?"

"Nope. You didn't miss much."

"Somehow, I find that hard to believe." Thalia raised her shoulders in an attempt to sit up, but settled back down with a groan. Clarke gently placed a rolled-up blanket behind her. "Thanks," she muttered and surveyed Clarke for a moment before she spoke again. "Okay, what's wrong?"

Clarke gave her a bemused smile. "Nothing! I'm just so happy you're feeling better."

"Please. You can't hide anything from me. You know I always manage to get your secrets out of you," Thalia deadpanned. "You can start by telling me where you found the medicine."

"Octavia had it," Clarke explained and quickly filled Thalia in on what had happened. "She and Bellamy are leaving tomorrow," she finished. "That's part of the deal Wells made with everyone. I know it sounds crazy, but it really felt like they were close to attacking her." She shook her head. "If Wells hadn't stepped in, I'm not sure what would've happened."

Thalia was staring at Clarke with a curious expression on her face.

"What?" Clarke asked.

"Nothing, just—this is the first time I've ever heard you

say his name without looking like you want to punch a hole through a wall."

"True," Clarke admitted with a smile. She supposed her feelings had changed—or at least, were starting to.

"So?"

Clarke began to fiddle with the pill bottles. She hadn't wanted to tell Thalia about what happened in the woods in case it made Thalia feel guilty—after all, she'd gone out looking for plants to help her and had ended up almost getting killed. "There's something else I haven't told you. It didn't seem important before, when you were so sick, but . . ." She took a breath and gave Thalia a brief account of Wells rescuing her from the ruin.

"He followed you all the way there?"

Clarke nodded. "The weird thing is, while I was hanging on that ledge, convinced I was going to die, he was the one person I was thinking about. And when he showed up, I wasn't even angry that he'd followed me. I was just relieved that he'd cared enough to go after me, despite the terrible things I've said to him."

"He loves you. Nothing you do or say can ever change that."

"I know." Clarke closed her eyes, though she was afraid of the images that she knew would emerge from the shadows. "Even when we were in Confinement and I told you I wanted to see his organs explode in space, I think there was a part of me that still loved him. And that made the pain even worse."

Thalia was looking at her with a mixture of pity and understanding. "It's time to stop punishing yourself, Clarke."

"You mean punishing him."

"No. I mean it's time to stop punishing yourself for loving him. It's not a betrayal of your parents."

Clarke stiffened. "You didn't know them. You have no idea what they'd think."

"I know they wanted what was best for you. They were willing to do something they knew was wrong in order to keep you safe." She paused. "Just like Wells."

Clarke sighed and tucked her legs up underneath her, sitting on Thalia's bed just like she used to back in their cell. "Maybe you're right. I don't know if I can fight this anymore. Hating him is exhausting."

"You should talk to him."

Clarke nodded. "I will."

"No, I mean right now." Thalia's eyes were bright with excitement. "Go talk to him."

"What? It's late."

"I'm sure he's lying wide-awake, thinking about you. . . ."

Clarke unfolded her legs, then rose to her feet. "Fine," she said, "if that's what it takes to get you to be quiet and rest."

She walked across the tent, playfully rolling her eyes at

her friend as she pulled the flap aside. She stepped into the clearing and paused, wondering if she was making a mistake.

But it was too late to turn around. Her heart was beating so fast, it seemed to have a momentum of its own, pounding a frantic message to Wells through the darkness. *I'm coming.*

CHAPTER 27

Wells

Wells stared up at the sky. He'd never felt at ease in the over-crowded tents, and after what had happened tonight, the thought of being crammed next to people who'd been ready to tear Octavia apart was unbearable. Despite the cold, he liked falling asleep looking at the same stars he'd seen from his bed at home. He loved the moments when the moon disappeared behind a cloud and it became too dark to see the outlines of the trees. The sky would seem to stretch all the way down to the ground, creating the impression they weren't on Earth at all but back up among the stars. It always gave him a small pain to open his eyes in the morning and find them gone.

Yet even the sky wasn't enough to quiet Wells's mind

tonight. He pushed himself into a seated position, wincing as he pried his blanket off the scattered rocks and branches. A rustling in a nearby tree caught his attention and he rose to his feet, craning his neck for a better look.

Wells stared in wonder as the tree, which had never boasted a single blossom since they'd landed, burst into bloom. Glimmering pink petals unfurled from pods he hadn't noticed before, like fingertips reaching out in the dark. They were beautiful. Wells rose onto his toes, stretched his arms above his head, and wrapped his fingers around a stem.

"Wells?"

He spun around and saw Clarke standing a few meters away.

"What are you doing?"

He was about to ask her the same question, but instead he walked silently toward her and slipped the flower into her hand. She stared at it, and for a moment he thought she might shove it back at him. But to his surprise and relief, she looked up at him and smiled. "Thank you."

"You're welcome." They stared at each other for a moment. "You couldn't sleep either?" he asked, and she shook her head.

Wells sat down on an exposed tree root, which was just large enough for two, and gestured for her to sit beside him.

After a moment she sank down, keeping a sliver of empty space between them. "How's Thalia doing?" he asked.

"Much better. I'm so thankful Octavia came forward." She looked down and ran her finger along the blossom. "I just can't believe they're leaving tomorrow."

There was a note of regret in her voice that made Wells's stomach clench. "I thought you'd be happy to see her go, after what she put you through."

Clarke was quiet for a moment. "Good people can make mistakes," she said slowly. She looked up, and her eyes met Wells's. "It doesn't mean you stop caring about them."

For a long moment, all they could hear was the wind rustling the leaves, the silence filling with all the words that had been left unsaid. The apologies that could never begin to convey his sorrow.

The trial of Phoenix's two most famous scientists had turned into the event of the year. There were more people gathered in the Council chamber than had ever shown up for a lecture, or any event other than the Remembrance Ceremony.

But Wells was only vaguely aware of the audience. The disgust he'd felt at their morbid curiosity—like Romans waiting for bloodshed at the Colosseum—faded away the moment his eyes landed on the girl sitting alone in the front row. He hadn't seen Clarke since the night she'd confided in him about her parents' research. Wells had told his father, who weighed the information carefully. As Wells had expected, the Chancellor had known nothing about the experiments and had immediately launched an inquiry. Yet the investigation had taken a terrible turn Wells hadn't expected, and now Clarke's parents were going to face the Council on criminal charges. Guilty and terrified, Wells had spent the past week desperate to find Clarke, but his deluge of messages had gone unanswered, and when he went to her flat, he found it sealed off by guards.

Her expression was blank as she watched the Council members take their seats. But then she turned and saw Wells. Her eyes locked with his, her gaze filled with hatred so intense that it sent bile shooting up from his stomach.

Wells shrank back into his seat in the third row. He'd only wanted his father to stop her parents' research, to put an end to Clarke's misery. He never imagined they'd end up on trial for their lives.

Two guards escorted Clarke's mother to a bench in the front. She kept her chin high as she surveyed the Council, but then her eyes settled on her daughter, and her face fell.

Clarke jumped to her feet and said something Wells couldn't hear, but it didn't matter. The sad smile on her mother's face was enough to cleave Wells's heart in two.

Another pair of guards led her father in, and the trial began.

A female member of the Council opened the proceedings by giving an overview of the investigation. According to the Griffins, she reported, they had been ordered by Vice Chancellor Rhodes to conduct human radiation trials, which Rhodes vehemently denied.

A strange numbness spread over Wells as he watched the Vice Chancellor stand, his face grave as he explained that while he'd approved their request for a new lab, he never said a word about experimenting on children.

Everyone's voices seemed very far away—the fragments of the Council members' questions and the Griffins' replies that reached his ears distorted, like sound waves from a distant galaxy. Wells heard the crowd's gasps before his brain had time to process what they were reacting to.

Then, suddenly, the Council was voting.

The first *guilty* broke through the haze that had settled over Wells. He turned to look at Clarke, who was sitting still and rigid.

"Guilty."

No. Wells thought. *No, please*.

"Guilty." The word echoed down the table until it was his father's turn. He cleared his throat, and for a brief moment, Wells believed there was a chance. That his father would figure out a way to turn the tide.

"Guilty."

"No!" Clarke's anguished shriek rose above the din of shocked whispers and satisfied murmurs. She jumped to her feet. "You can't do this. It wasn't their fault." Her face twisted with rage as she pointed at the Vice Chancellor. "*You.* You forced them to

do it, you evil, lying bastard." She took a step forward and was immediately surrounded by guards.

Vice Chancellor Rhodes gave a long sigh. "I'm afraid you're much better at experimenting on innocent children than you are at lying, Miss Griffin." He turned to Wells's father. "We know from the security log that she visited the lab on a regular basis. She *knew* about the atrocities her parents were committing and did nothing to stop it. She may have even helped."

Wells inhaled so sharply, he could feel his stomach scrape against his ribs. He waited for his father to give Rhodes one of his dismissive glares, but to Wells's horror, the Chancellor was staring gravely at Clarke. After a long moment, his jaw tightened, and he turned to face the other Council members.

"I hereby put forward a motion to try Clarke Griffin for the crime of accessory to treason."

No. His father's words sank into his skin like a paralytic, stopping his heart.

Wells could see the Council members' mouths moving, but he couldn't make out what they were saying. Every atom in his body was focused on praying to whatever forgotten god might be listening. *Let her go*, he pleaded. *I'll do anything.* It was true. He was ready to offer his life in exchange for hers.

Take me instead.

The Vice Chancellor leaned over to whisper something to Wells's father.

I don't care if it's painful.

The Chancellor's face grew even graver than it had been before.

Shove me through the release portal so my body implodes.

The person next to Wells shuddered at something the Chancellor said.

Just let her go.

He had the uncomfortable sensation of sound returning as gasps rose up from the audience. Two guards grabbed Clarke and began dragging her away.

The girl he'd do anything to protect would soon be sentenced to death. And she would have every right to die hating him.

It was all his fault.

"I'm sorry," Wells whispered, as if somehow, that could make it better.

"I know," she said, her voice soft.

Wells froze, and for a moment, he was too afraid to look at her, afraid to see the grief welling up from the wound he knew would never heal. But when he finally turned, he saw that while her eyes glistened with tears, she was smiling.

"I feel closer to them here," she said, glancing up at the trees. "They spent their lives trying to figure out how to get us home."

Wells didn't know what he could say without breaking

the spell, so instead, he leaned forward and kissed her, holding his breath until he saw her teardrop-tipped lashes flutter closed.

At first it was soft, his lips lightly brushing over her mouth, but then he felt her kiss him back, igniting every cell in his body. The familiarity of her touch, the taste of her kiss, released something in him, and he pulled her closer.

Clarke sank into Wells, her lips clinging to his lips, her skin melting into his skin, her breath mixing with his breath. The world around them faded away as Earth became nothing more than a swirl of pungent scents and damp air that made him press himself closer to her. The soft ground cradled them as they slid off the log. There was so much he needed to tell her, but his words were lost as his lips traveled across her skin, moving from her mouth to her neck.

In that moment, there was no one else. They were the only two people on Earth. Just like he'd always imagined they would be.

CHAPTER 28

Glass

Music played on Phoenix twice that year. The Council had approved the exception, and for the first time anyone could remember, the Earthmade instruments were taken from their preservation chambers and carried carefully to the observation deck for the comet viewing party.

It should have been one of the most magical nights of Glass's life. The entire population of Phoenix had flocked to the observation deck in their finery, and the elegantly dressed crowd buzzed with excitement. All around her, people were talking and laughing as they strode toward the enormous windows, clutching glasses of sparkling root wine.

Glass stood next to Huxley and Cora, who were talking

animatedly. But although Glass could see her friends' mouths moving, their words never reached her ears. Every cell in her body was focused on the musicians who were quietly taking their seats on the far side of the observation deck.

But as the musicians began to play, Glass shifted from one foot to another, growing restless, as she thought of Luke. Without him, the music that normally wrapped around her like an enchantment felt strangely empty. The melodies that once seemed to express the deepest secrets of her soul were no less beautiful now, but it made her chest ache to know that the only person she wanted to share them with was somewhere else.

Glass looked over and quickly found her mother, wearing a long gray dress and their family's gloves—kid leather, one of the only pairs left on the ship, stained with age but still infinitely precious. She was talking to someone in the Chancellor's uniform, but it wasn't the Chancellor. Glass realized with a start it was Vice Chancellor Rhodes. Though she'd only seen him a few times, she recognized his sharp nose and mocking smile.

Glass knew that she should go over, introduce herself, smile at the Vice Chancellor, and raise her glass to him in a toast. She should thank him for her freedom and look grateful and overjoyed as the crowd of well-dressed Phoenicians looked on and whispered. It's what her mother would have wanted; it's what she should have done, if she valued her life. But as Glass stared at his hateful dark eyes, she found she couldn't bring herself to move toward him.

"Here, take this. I need some air," Glass said, handing Cora her still-full glass of wine. Cora raised her eyebrows, but didn't argue—they were allotted only one glass each tonight. With a final glance to make sure that her mother wasn't watching, Glass wove her way through the crowd and back into the corridor. She didn't run into a single person as she made her way quickly to their flat, where she slipped out of her gown and into a pair of nondescript pants, piling her hair under a hat.

There was no designated observation deck on Walden, but there were a number of corridors with small windows on the starboard side, where the comet was expected to make its appearance. The Waldenites who didn't have shifts that day had begun gathering early in the morning to reserve the best seats. By the time Glass arrived, the hallways were flooded with crowds, talking in excited voices and clustering around the small windows. Some of the kids were already pressing their faces against the quartz glass or clambering onto parents' shoulders.

As she turned a corner, Glass's eyes settled on a group at the window a few meters down: three women and four children. She wondered whether the women were watching the fourth child for a neighbor, or if it was an orphan they'd taken in.

The youngest child toddled over to Glass and blinked up at her with a shy smile. "Hi there," Glass said, leaning forward so that she was level with the girl. "Are you excited for the comet?" The girl didn't say anything. Her large, dark eyes were fixated on Glass's head.

Glass brought her hand up self-consciously, grimacing slightly when she realized that her hair had fallen out of her hat. She began to tuck it back inside, but the little girl reached up and pulled at one of the loose strands.

"Posy, leave the lady alone." Glass looked up and saw one of the women walking toward them. "Sorry," she said to Glass, with a laugh. "She likes your hair."

Glass smiled but didn't say anything. She'd learned how to downplay her Phoenix accent, but the less she spoke, the better. "Come on, Pose," the woman said, placing her hand on the child's shoulder and guiding her away.

It was past 2100. The comet was due to appear any moment now. Up on Phoenix, the observation deck would be silent as everyone waited in quiet reverence. Here, children were laughing and jumping, and a couple of teenagers were yelling out a countdown.

Glass looked up and down the corridor, but there was no sign of him.

"Look!" a little girl called out. A white line was rising over the outline of the moon. Instead of fading away like most comets, it grew larger, the tail expanding as it blazed through space. It made even the stars look dim.

Glass stepped forward almost unconsciously, and a couple leaning up against the nearest window shuffled aside to give her space. It was so beautiful, Glass thought in wonder. And terrifying. It was growing larger and larger, filling up the entire viewing space in the porthole, as if it were coming straight for them.

Could there have been a miscalculation? Glass pressed her hands into the ledge so hard, she could feel it cutting into her palms. Around her, people started to step back, with a flurry of low murmurs and frightened cries.

Glass closed her eyes. She couldn't look.

An arm wrapped around her. She didn't even have to turn to know that it was Luke. She knew the scent of him, the feel of him, like a second skin.

"I was looking for you," she said, glancing back at him. Although the astronomical event of a lifetime was playing out right before his eyes, he was looking only at her.

"I hoped you would come," he whispered into her ear.

The crowd's anxious murmurs bubbled into exclamations of astonishment as the comet swept up and above the ship in a blaze of fire. Luke's arm tightened around her, and she leaned into his chest. "I couldn't imagine seeing this without you," she said.

"You didn't have any trouble getting away?"

"No, not really." Her stomach twisted at the thought of her mother standing next to the Vice Chancellor. "I just wish we didn't have to sneak around." She reached up and ran her fingers along his cheek.

Luke took her hand and brought it to his lips. "Maybe there's a way to change your mom's mind," he said earnestly. "Maybe I could talk to her. You know, prove that I'm not some barbarian. That I'm serious about my future—*our* future. That I'm serious about you."

Glass gave him a soft smile. "I wish it were that easy."

"No, I mean it." He took her hands in his. "She thinks I'm just some Walden jerk taking advantage of you. She needs to know that this isn't just a fling. It's real."

"I know," Glass said, squeezing his hand. "I know."

"No, I don't think you do," Luke said, pulling something out of his pocket. He turned to face her, his gaze unblinking.

"Glass," he began, his eyes glowing, "I don't want to spend another day without you. I want to go to sleep every night with you by my side and wake up next to you every morning. I want nothing else but you, for the rest of my life."

He held out his outstretched palm, with a small, golden object in it. It was her locket.

"I know it's not exactly a ring, but—"

"Yes," she said simply, because there was nothing else to say, nothing else to do but put on the locket and kiss the boy she loved so much it hurt, as behind them the comet streaked the sky with gold.

CHAPTER 29

Bellamy

Bellamy couldn't sleep. His mind was a jumble of thoughts all elbowing for his attention, making it impossible to tell where one stopped and the other began.

Staring up at the stars, he tried to imagine what was happening on the ship. It was strange to think of life going on as usual hundreds of kilometers away—the Waldenites and Arcadians toiling away while the Phoenicians complimented one another's outfits on the observation deck and ignored the stars. That was the only thing he'd miss about the Colony—the view. Before the launch, he'd heard of a comet passing, which would've been pretty spectacular to see from the ship.

He squinted into the darkness, trying to figure out how many days they'd been on Earth. If he'd counted correctly, then the comet was meant to appear tonight. There was going to be a fancy viewing party on Phoenix, and less-formal gatherings on Walden and Arcadia. Bellamy sat up and scanned the sky. He couldn't see anything from the clearing—the trees blocked too much of the sky—but he'd have a better view from the ridge.

Octavia was sleeping peacefully beside him, her glossy hair fanned out underneath her, her red hair ribbon tied to her wrist. "I'll be right back," he whispered, then took off at a jog across the clearing.

The thick canopy of leaves blocked most of the starlight, but after all his hunting expeditions, he knew this area of the forest well, anticipating every slope and turn and hidden log. When he finally reached the ridge, he paused to catch his breath. The cool night air had helped to clear his head, and the burning in his calves was a welcome distraction.

The star-filled sky looked just as it had every other night since they'd landed on Earth, and yet there was something different about it—the stars were pulsing, charged, as if waiting for something big to happen. And then, all at once, it did. The comet erupted across the sky, a streak of gold against the glittering silver, brightening everything around it, even the ground.

His skin sizzled as if some of the sparks had seeped into his own body, invigorating his cells with something beyond energy—with hope. Tomorrow he and Octavia would leave here for good. Tomorrow they would be free of the Colony forever, no one telling them what to do or how to be.

He closed his eyes and imagined how that would feel. Freedom from everyone and everything—even from his past. Even, perhaps, from the memories that had haunted him all his life.

Bellamy ran down the walkway, ignoring his neighbors' grumbles and the empty threats of the guards he knew were too lazy to chase a remarkably fast nine-year-old just to issue a reprimand. But as he got closer to his flat, his excitement slipped away. Ever since that terrible night when he caught his mom trying to hurt Octavia, he got nervous coming home.

He unlocked the door and burst inside. "Mom?" he called, carefully shutting the door behind him before he said anything else. "Octavia?" He waited, but there was only silence. "Mom?" he said again. He walked through the main room, his eyes widening at the overturned furniture. His mother must have been in another one of her bad moods. He crept toward the kitchen, his stomach wriggling like it was trying to escape through his belly button.

Someone groaned, and he rushed inside to find his mother

on the floor, lying in a sticky puddle of blood. A knife lay beside her.

He gasped and hurried over, shaking her shoulder frantically. "Mom," he shouted. "Wake up. *Mom.*" But all she did was flutter her eyelids and let out another faint groan. Bellamy leapt to his feet, gasping as he realized the knees of his pants were soaked with blood. He had to find someone. He had to get help.

He dashed back into the main room and was about to go run for a guard when a noise brought him skidding to a halt. His eyes fell on the closet, which was slightly open, a sliver of shadow creeping out of the gap between the door and the wall. He took a few steps toward it as a tiny tearstained face peeked out.

"Are you okay?" he whispered to his sister, reaching for her hand. "Come on." But she shrank back into the darkness, trembling. Bellamy's fear for his mother slid away as he stared at the little girl she'd made terrified to come into the light. "Come on, Octavia," he coaxed, and slowly, tentatively, she poked her head out again.

Finally, she toddled out of the closet, looking around the room with wide eyes. "Here," Bellamy said, picking up the red ribbon he'd given her from the floor of the closet. He tied it around her dark curls in his best approximation of a bow. "You look beautiful." He grabbed her hand, feeling his heart swell as her little fingers wrapped around his. He led her to their mother's bedroom, lifted her onto the bed, then curled up next to her, praying that he wouldn't hear any other noises from the kitchen.

They sat there together on the bed, waiting quietly, until finally their mother's moans stopped and there was only silence.

"It's okay, O," he said, holding his little sister tight to his chest. "It's okay. You'll never have to hide again."

As the comet's trail faded into blackness, Bellamy hurried back down the slope, eager to get back before Octavia woke up and realized he'd gone. But as he came around the bend, searching for the familiar collection of tents, all he could see were flames.

The entire camp was on fire.

Bellamy skidded to a stop, gasping as his lungs took their first breath of smoke-filled air. For a moment, his vision was filled with flames and shadows, but then shapes began to emerge. Figures were sprinting in every direction, some pouring out of the burning tents while others rushed toward the trees.

Only one thought consumed him as he jogged over to their blankets, his eyes searching the darkness for his sister's sleeping form. The knot of dread in his stomach told him what he already knew. Octavia wasn't there.

He called her name, jerking his head from side to side,

praying that she'd call to him from the edge of the clearing, from someplace safe.

"Octavia!" he yelled again, looking wildly in all directions, squinting to see through the smoke. *Don't panic*, he told himself, but it was no use. The flames tore through the darkness and Octavia was nowhere to be found.

Bellamy had come down from scanning the heavens only to find himself in the depths of hell.

CHAPTER 30

Clarke

For some period of time—minutes, hours, Clarke wasn't sure—all she could hear was the sound of their hearts, the whisper of their mingled breaths. But then a scream clawed its way out from the clearing, dragging them apart. Clarke and Wells jumped to their feet, Clarke holding on to Wells's arm for balance as the world slid back into terrifying focus.

He grabbed her hand and they ran back into the clearing. She heard more screams, but none were as frightening as the roar and crackle that made every nerve in her body stand at attention.

Flames rose up from the tents, some of which had already collapsed into smoldering heaps, like corpses on an ancient battlefield. Shadowy figures sprinted for the safety of the forest, pursued by tendrils of hungry flames.

Thalia, Clarke thought in horror, and started to run. She was too weak to make it out of the infirmary tent on her own.

"*No!*" Wells shouted, forcing his voice over the chaos of screams. "Clarke, it's not safe!"

But his words slid off her like a spray of ash. She made a beeline for the tent, smoke filling her lungs, blinking to see in the smoldering air.

His arm wrapped around her waist like a steel band, pulling her forcibly into the shelter of the trees. "Let me go," she shrieked, thrashing with all her might. But Wells held her tight, forcing her to watch helplessly as fire engulfed the infirmary fewer than a hundred meters away. The entire side of the tent was up in flames. The plastic tarp on top was melting, and smoke filtered out of the gap between the front flaps.

"Get *off*." She sobbed, twisting again as she tried to wrestle free.

He slid his arm under her and began dragging her backward. "*No*," she shrieked, feeling the sound tear her throat, pounding at him helplessly with her fists. "I need to get her out." She dug her heels into the grass, but Wells was stronger, and she couldn't hold her ground. "*Thalia!*"

"Clarke, I'm so sorry," Wells whispered in her ear. She

could tell he was crying, but she didn't care. "You'll die if you go in there. I can't let you."

The word *die* ignited a reserve of power that exploded through her. Clarke gritted her teeth and lunged forward, momentarily escaping Wells's hold. Her entire being had reduced to a single, desperate thought—saving the only friend she had left in the universe.

She screamed as her arm was wrenched behind her back. "Let me *go*." This time, it was more of a plea than an order. "I'm begging you. Let me go."

"I can't," he said, wrapping his arms around her again. His voice was shaking. "I can't."

The clearing was empty now. Everyone had made it into the woods, taking whatever supplies they could carry. But no one had thought to grab the frail girl who was now being burned alive just a few meters away.

"Help," Clarke cried. "Someone, *please* help." But there was no answer except for the roar and crackle of the fire.

The flames on the top of the infirmary tent rose higher, the sides collapsing toward each other, as if the fire were inhaling the tent and everything inside of it. "*No*."

There was a crack, and the flames shot up even higher. Clarke shrieked with horror as the entire tent collapsed into a storm of fire, then slowly crumbled into ash.

It was over.

As she walked away from the medical center, Clarke could almost feel the vial pulsing in her pocket, like the heart in the old story Wells had discovered at the library the other day. He'd offered to read it to her, but she'd flatly refused. The last thing she needed right now was to hear creepy pre-Cataclysm literature. She had enough scenes of horror playing out in her real life.

The vial Clarke carried in her pocket could never have a heartbeat, she knew; just the opposite. The toxic cocktail of drugs inside was designed to stop a heart for good.

When Clarke got home, her parents weren't there. Although they both spent most of the day in their lab, over the past few weeks, they'd conveniently found excuses to leave right before Clarke returned from her training and rarely came back until just before she went to sleep. It was probably for the best. As Lilly grew sicker, Clarke could barely look at her parents without feeling a surge of rage. She knew she wasn't being fair—the moment anyone protested, the Vice Chancellor would have her parents executed and Clarke Confined within days. But that didn't make it any easier for her to meet their eyes.

The lab was quiet. As Clarke wound her way through the maze of empty beds, all she could hear was the drone of the ventilation system. The soft buzz of conversation had faded as more and more bodies were secreted away.

Lilly seemed even thinner than she'd been the day before.

Clarke crept toward her bed and ran her hand gently down her friend's arm, shuddering as bits of her skin fell away. She slipped her other hand into her pocket and wrapped her fingers around the vial. It would be so easy. No one would ever know.

But then Lilly's pale lashes fluttered open, and Clarke froze. As she stared into Lilly's eyes, a cold wave of terror and revulsion crashed over her. What was she thinking? An overpowering urge to destroy the vial tore through her body, and she had to take a deep breath to keep herself from hurling it against the wall.

Lilly's lips were moving, but no sound was coming out. Clarke leaned forward and gave her a small smile. "Sorry, didn't catch that, Lil." She lowered her head so her ear was closer to Lilly's mouth. "What did you say?"

At first, Clarke could only feel the soundless wisp of air on her skin, as if there wasn't enough breath in Lilly's lungs to push the words out of her mouth. But then a faint moan escaped from her chapped lips. "Did you bring it?"

Clarke raised her head to look into her friend's panic-filled brown eyes. She nodded slowly.

"Now." The word was barely audible.

"No," Clarke protested, her voice shaking. "It's too soon." She blinked back the tears that had begun to fill her eyes. "You could still get better," she said, but the lie sounded hollow, even to her.

Lilly's face contorted in pain, and Clarke reached for her hand. "Please." Lilly's voice was ragged.

"I'm sorry." Clarke gave Lilly's fragile hand a gentle squeeze as tears began to trickle down her cheeks. "I can't."

Lilly's eyes grew wide, and Clarke inhaled sharply. "Lil?" But Lilly remained silent, staring at something only she could see. Something that filled her eyes with terror. The physical pain racking Lilly's body was terrible, Clarke knew, but the hallucinations, the demons who were with her every moment, hovering at her bedside, were worse.

"No more."

Clarke closed her eyes. The guilt and remorse she'd feel could never compare to Lilly's pain. It'd be selfish to let her own fear prevent her from bringing her friend the peace she wanted—the respite from pain she deserved.

Her whole body was trembling so hard, she could barely remove the vial from her pocket, let alone fill the syringe. She stood next to the bed and clasped Lilly's hand with one arm, using the other to position the needle over Lilly's vein. "Sleep well, Lil," she whispered.

Lilly nodded and gave Clarke a smile that she knew would be burned into her brain for the rest of her life. "Thank you."

Clarke held Lilly's hand for the few minutes it took for her friend to slip away. Then she rose and placed her fingers against Lilly's still-warm neck, searching for a pulse.

She was gone.

Clarke sank to the damp ground, gasping as her lungs reached desperately for the cool air, then rolled onto her side. Through the tears blurring her vision, she could make out the shapes of people standing all around her, their dark, featureless silhouettes still and quiet.

Her best friend, the only person who truly knew Clarke, who knew what she had done to Lilly and still loved her. Thalia had told her to make things right with Wells tonight—and then Wells had held Clarke back while they watched Thalia die.

"I'm so sorry, Clarke," Wells was saying, reaching for her. She pushed his hand away.

"I can't believe you," she said, her voice cold and quiet. Rage billowed in her chest, as if there were flames inside her that needed only fury and grief to blaze into an inferno.

"There was no way you'd make it," Wells stammered. "I just—I couldn't let you go. You would've been killed."

"So you let Thalia die instead. Because you get to decide who lives and who dies." He started to protest, but she kept going, shaking with rage. "Tonight was a mistake. You destroy everything you touch."

"Clarke, please, I—"

But she just stood up, shaking the bits of cinder from her clothes, and walked into the forest without looking back.

They all had ash in their lungs and tears in their eyes. But Wells had blood on his hands.

CHAPTER 31

Glass

"I'll get a ring as soon as I find one at the Exchange," Luke said to Glass, his hand on her lower back as he guided her through the crowded corridors back toward Phoenix. Most of the people who'd assembled to watch the comet were heading back to their residential units on the lower decks, making it difficult to move toward the skybridge. But Glass was hardly aware of which direction they were heading. Her heart was still thumping with joy, and she was shaking, holding tight to Luke's hand.

"I don't need a ring." She reached up to touch the locket, which seemed to be radiating warmth through her chest. Nothing could happen immediately, she knew. Although she turned eighteen in a few weeks, they couldn't risk getting married until the Chancellor woke up and confirmed her pardon—or never woke up at all. Her mother would understand eventually, once she saw how much Luke loved Glass. They'd get married and apply for permission to start a family, someday. But for now, just the promise of a future together was enough. "This is perfect."

They turned out of the stairwell and into the corridor that led to the skybridge. Luke stopped short and pulled Glass to him as a dozen guards jogged by, so close a few of their sleeves brushed against Glass's arm, although their eyes trained straight ahead. She shivered and leaned into Luke, who was watching them with a strange expression on his face. "Do you know what's going on?" she asked.

"I'm sure it's nothing," Luke said too quickly, his words at odds with the tension in his jaw. But then he raised their interlocked fingers to his lips and kissed her hand. "Let's go."

Glass smiled as they continued walking. The thud of the guards' boots had faded away, and they had the whole hallway to themselves. Suddenly, Luke stopped and raised her arm into the air. Before Glass had time to ask what he was doing, he'd spun her around and lowered her into a dip.

Glass laughed as Luke wrapped one arm around her waist and swept her across the empty hallway. "What's gotten into you?"

He paused and pulled her even closer to him, then leaned in and murmured into her ear. "I hear music when I'm with you." Glass just smiled and, in the middle of the hallway, closed her eyes as they swayed from side to side.

Finally, Luke stepped back, gesturing in the direction of the skybridge. "It's almost curfew," he said.

"Okay," she agreed, sighing. They walked hand in hand across the skybridge, exchanging knowing smiles that made every cell in Glass's body buzz with excitement. At the entrance to Phoenix, they stopped, reluctant to say good-bye. Luke ran his finger along the locket chain.

"I love you," he said, squeezing her hand before giving her a little shove. "Let me know once you get home. I'll come by tomorrow to talk to your mom."

"Okay," she agreed. "Tomorrow."

Finally, Glass turned and began walking across the skybridge. She'd made it halfway across when a shrill beep echoed through the empty space. She looked around, startled. The cluster of guards at the Phoenix end of the bridge broke apart, and she could hear someone barking orders. Glass froze as the sound grew louder and more urgent. She turned to look at Luke, who'd started taking a few hesitant steps forward.

"The bridge is closing," a disembodied woman's voice announced over the speakers. "Please clear the area." There was a brief pause, then the message repeated. "The bridge is closing. Please clear the area." Glass gasped as a barrier began to descend at the Phoenix checkpoint. She lunged forward and could see Luke running as well, but they were both too far away.

Glass reached the clear partition just as it locked into the floor, slamming her hands against it. Luke slid to a stop on the other side. He was saying something, but although she could see his mouth moving, no sound reached her ears.

Tears filled her eyes as she watched him bang his fists against the wall in frustration. She didn't understand. The skybridge hadn't been closed since the plague outbreak in the first century. She knew if it was closing now, it might not open again.

"Luke!" she cried, the word falling uselessly from her lips. She pressed her hand against the clear partition and held it there. Their eyes locked.

"I love you," Glass said.

Luke pressed his own hand to the wall, and for a moment, Glass could almost feel the warmth of his skin. *I love you too*, he mouthed. He gave her a sad smile and motioned for her to start walking. She paused, not wanting to leave without knowing what was going on, when she'd see him again. The alarm was still sounding overhead, ringing in her ears.

Go, Luke mouthed, his face serious.

Glass nodded and turned, forcing herself to keep her eyes straight ahead. But before she turned onto the hallway that led away from the skybridge, she glanced over her shoulder one last time. Luke hadn't moved. He was still standing there, his hand pressed against the wall.

Glass ran home, weaving through crowds of panicked civilians and stone-faced guards.

"Oh, thank god," Sonja said as Glass rushed into the flat. "I was so worried." She shoved a water pitcher into Glass's arms. "Go fill this up in the bathroom. I'm not sure how much longer the water will last."

"What's going on?" Glass asked. "They closed the skybridge."

"What were you doing near the bridge?" her mother asked, then blinked, taking in the clothes Glass had changed into after the comet viewing party. "Oh," she said flatly, a wearied understanding overtaking her features. "That's where you were."

"What's happening?" Glass repeated, ignoring her mother's look of disapproval.

"I'm not sure, but I have a feeling . . ." She trailed off, then pressed her lips together. "I think this is it. The day we all knew was coming."

"What are you talking about?"

Her mother took the pitcher back from Glass and turned to the sink. "The ship wasn't built to last this long. It was just a matter of time before things started to break down."

The water had reached the top of the pitcher and was now overflowing into the sink, but Sonja just stood there. "Mom?"

Finally, her mother shut off the water and turned around to face Glass. "It's the airlock," she said quietly. "There's been a breach." A shout rang out from the corridor, and her mother shot a quick glance at the door before she forced a smile and continued. "But don't worry. There's a reserve of oxygen on Phoenix. We'll be okay until they figure out what to do. I promise, Glass, we'll get through this."

Glass felt the realization dawning in her mind, twisting her stomach with dread. "What does that have to do with the bridge?" she asked, her voice so quiet it was almost a whisper.

"They're already running out of oxygen on Arcadia and Walden. We had to take security precautions to make sure . . ."

"No," Glass breathed. "The Council is going to let them all *die*?"

Sonja stepped forward and squeezed Glass's arm. "They had to do something, or else no one would survive," she was saying, but Glass barely registered her words. "It's the only way to protect the Colony."

"I have to find him," Glass said, trembling. She took a

shaky step back. Her head was a frenzy of words and images that bounced off one another, creating more panic than sense.

"Glass," her mother said, with something that sounded like pity. "I'm so sorry, but you can't. There's no way. All the exits are sealed." She stepped forward and pulled her daughter into a hug. Glass tried to wriggle free, but her mother tightened her hold. "There's nothing we can do."

"I love him," Glass sobbed, her body shaking.

"I know." Sonja reached out and took Glass's hand. "And I'm sure he loves you too. But maybe this is for the best." She gave a sad smile that sent chills down Glass's spine. "At least this way, you don't have to say a terrible good-bye."

CHAPTER 32

Wells

Wells watched Clarke stride off into the woods, feeling as if she'd punched through his sternum and torn away a chunk of his heart. He was only vaguely aware of the gleeful roar of the flames as they swallowed the supplies, the tents . . . and anyone who'd been unfortunate enough to be left inside. Around him, a few people had fallen to the ground, gasping for breath or shaking with horror. But most were standing shoulder to shoulder, facing the inferno, their figures still and quiet.

"Is everyone okay?" Wells asked hoarsely. "Who's missing?" The numbness at Clarke's words was burning away, replaced by a frantic energy. He stepped forward to the edge of the tree cover, shielding his eyes as he tried to peer through the wall of flames. When no one answered, he took a breath and shouted, "Did everyone make it out?" There was a ripple of vague nods.

"Do we need to go farther?" a small Walden girl asked, her voice trembling as she took a step deeper into the woods.

"It doesn't look like it's spreading to the trees," an Arcadian boy said hoarsely. He was standing next to a few battered water jugs and blackened containers he'd carried out of the camp.

The boy was right. The ring of bare dirt that bordered the clearing was wide enough that the flames engulfing the tents flickered just out of reach of the lowest branches.

Wells turned, searching through the darkness for a sign of Clarke. But she'd disappeared into the shadows. He could almost feel her grief pulsing through the darkness. Every cell in his body was screaming at him to go to her, but he knew it was hopeless.

Clarke was right. He destroyed everything he touched.

"You look tired," the Chancellor said, surveying Wells from across the dinner table.

Wells looked up from the plate he'd been staring at, then nodded curtly. "I'm fine." The truth was, he hadn't slept in days. The look of fury Clarke had given him was branded into his brain, and every time he closed his eyes, he could see the terror on her face as the guards dragged her away. Her anguished scream filled the silence between his heartbeats.

After the trial, Wells had begged his father to lift the charges. He swore Clarke had nothing to do with the research, and that the guilt she'd been carrying around had nearly killed her. But the Chancellor had simply claimed that it was out of his hands.

Wells shifted uncomfortably in his chair. He could barely stand to be on the same ship as his father, let alone sit across from him at dinner, but he had to maintain some semblance of civility. If he allowed his rage to break free, his father would simply accuse Wells of being too irrational, too immature to understand the law.

"I know you're angry with me," the Chancellor said before taking a sip of water. "But I can't overrule the vote. That's why we have the Council, to keep one person from becoming too powerful." He glanced down at the chip flashing in his watch, then looked back at Wells. "The Gaia Doctrine is harsh enough as it is. We have to hold on to whatever shred of freedom we have left."

"So you're saying that even if Clarke is innocent, it'd be worth it to let her die in order to keep *democracy* alive?"

The Chancellor fixed Wells with a stare that, a few days ago, would've made him sink into his chair. "I believe *innocent* is a relative term here. There's no denying she knew about the experiments."

"Rhodes *forced* them to conduct those experiments. He's the one who should be punished!"

"That's enough," the Chancellor said in a voice so cold, it almost extinguished Wells's rage. "I refuse to listen to this heresy in my own home."

Wells was about to launch an angry retort, but he was interrupted by the sound of the doorbell. His father silenced him with a final look as he opened the door and ushered in the Vice Chancellor himself.

Wells could barely contain his hatred as Rhodes gave him a curt nod in greeting. The Vice Chancellor wore his usual self-satisfied look as he followed the Chancellor into his study. After they closed the door firmly behind them, Wells stood up from the table. He knew he should go to his room and shut the door, like he always did when his father took meetings in their home.

A few days ago, he might have. A few days ago, he wouldn't have dared to eavesdrop on a private conversation. But now he didn't care. He crept toward the door and pressed himself against the wall.

"The dropships are ready," Rhodes began. "There's no reason to wait."

"There are plenty of reasons to wait." There was a note of irritation in his father's voice, as if they'd already had this discussion many times. "We're still not sure if the radiation levels are safe."

Wells inhaled sharply, then froze to keep his breath from disturbing the silence outside the study door.

"That's why we're emptying the detention center. Why not put the convicts to good use?"

"Even Confined children deserve a chance at life, Rhodes. That's why they're given a retrial on their eighteenth birthday."

The Vice Chancellor scoffed. "You know none of them are going to be pardoned. We can't afford to waste the resources. We're running out of time as it is."

What does he mean, running out of time? Wells wondered, but before he had a chance to think it through, his father broke in.

"Those reports are grossly exaggerated. We have enough oxygen for another few years at least."

"And then what? You'll order the entire Colony onto the dropships and just hope for the best?"

"We'll send the Confined juveniles in the detention center, like you suggested. But not yet. Not until it's our last resort. Unless the breach in sector C14 worsens, we've got a little time left still. The first prisoners will be sent in a year."

"If that's what you think is best."

Wells heard the Vice Chancellor rise from his chair, and in a flash, he ran silently into his room and collapsed onto the bed. He stared up at the ceiling, trying to make sense of what he'd heard. The Colony was on its last breath. They had only a few years left up in space.

It all clicked into place, why everyone was being found guilty: There weren't enough resources on the ship to support its population. It was a horrifying thought, but an even more terrible realization was making its way to the front of his brain. Clarke's birthday was in six months. Wells knew he'd never convince his father to pardon her. Being sent to Earth would give her a second chance. But they weren't going to start the mission for another year. Unless he did something, Clarke was going to die.

His only chance was to speed up the mission, to have the first group sent right away.

A terrifying plan began to take shape, and his chest tightened in fear as he realized what he would have to do. But Wells knew there was no other way. To save the girl he loved, he'd have to endanger the entire human race.

CHAPTER 33

Bellamy

Bellamy slid down the trunk of the tree and sank to the ground, feeling as hollow as the burned-out shell of the drop-ship. He'd been searching for Octavia for hours, tearing through the forest and screaming her name until his throat was raw, but the woods had answered him with nothing but maddening silence.

"Hey." A weary voice interrupted his thoughts. Bellamy turned to see Wells walking slowly toward him. Soot was smeared across his face, and the skin on his left forearm was badly scratched. "Any luck?"

Bellamy shook his head. "I'm so sorry." Wells pressed his lips together and stared at a spot on the ground just beyond

Bellamy for a long moment. "If it's any consolation, I really don't think she was here. We just searched the clearing pretty thoroughly. Everyone made it out in time except . . ." His voice trailed off.

"I know," Bellamy said quietly. "I'm really sorry, man. I'm sure you did your best."

Wells winced. "I don't even know what that means anymore." Bellamy looked at him in confusion, but before he had time to say anything, Wells gave him a small smile. "Octavia will turn up soon. Don't worry." Then he turned and trudged back into the clearing, where a few people were sifting through the ashes, looking for anything that had survived the blaze.

In the rosy dawn light, Bellamy could almost make himself believe that the horrors of the last few hours were nothing but a nightmare. The flames had long since died out, and while much of the grass had been burned away, the soil underfoot was damp. The fire hadn't reached the trees, whose flowers stretched out to greet the light, blissfully unaware of—or unconcerned with—the tragedy below. But that was the thing about grief, Bellamy knew. You couldn't expect anyone else to share your suffering. You had to carry your pain alone.

He heard a few of the kids arguing over what they thought had started the fire: whether the wind had carried a spark from their campfire to scorch the tents, or if someone had done something stupid.

But Bellamy didn't give a shit what had caused it. All he cared about was Octavia. Had she gotten lost while running for safety, or had she left camp before the fire even started? And if so, why?

He rose shakily to his feet, holding on to the tree trunk for balance. He couldn't stop to rest, not now, when every hour meant Octavia might be in danger. Now that it was light, he could search again. Farther this time. It didn't matter how long it took. He wouldn't stop moving until he found her.

As Bellamy moved deeper into the shade, he exhaled, relieved to be away from the insultingly bright sunlight. Relieved to be alone. But then his eyes landed on a figure winding its way toward him. He paused and squinted through the green-shadowed gloom. It was Clarke.

"Hey," he asked hoarsely, his stomach twisting uneasily at the sight of her pale, drawn face. "Are you okay?"

"Thalia's dead?" She said it more like a question, as though hoping he would assure her that it wasn't true.

Bellamy nodded slowly. "I'm sorry." She started to tremble, and he instinctively pulled her into his arms. For a long moment they just stood there, Bellamy holding Clarke's shaking form tight against him. "I'm so sorry," he whispered into her hair.

Finally, Clarke straightened up and stepped back with a sigh. Although tears were running down her face, the brightness had returned to her eyes, and a hint of color had snuck back into her cheeks. "Where's your sister?" she asked, wiping her nose with the back of her hand.

"She's not here. I've been searching for hours, but it's been too dark. I'm going out to look for her again."

"Wait." Clarke reached into her pocket. "I found this in the woods. Out past the stream, toward that giant rock formation." She placed something in Bellamy's hand. He inhaled audibly as his fingers closed around the familiar strip of satin. It was Octavia's red ribbon.

"Was it tied to a tree?" he asked faintly, unsure what he hoped the answer would be.

"No." Clarke's dirt-streaked face softened. "I saw it on the ground. It must've fallen out of her hair at some point. She was wearing it last night, wasn't she?"

"I think so," Bellamy replied, his brain frantically racing for snippets of memory. "Yes. She had it when she went to sleep."

"Okay," Clarke said with sudden firmness. "So that means she left the camp before the fire started. Look," she added, in answer to Bellamy's questioning look, "there's no ash on it. No sign that it was anywhere near the flames."

"You may be right," Bellamy said softly, rubbing the

ribbon between his fingers. "I just don't understand why she would have left before the fire started." He glanced back up at Clarke. "Weren't you outside the infirmary last night? Did you notice anything?"

Clarke shook her head, her expression suddenly unreadable. "I stepped away for a while," she said, her voice tense. "I'm sorry."

"Never mind," Bellamy said. He slipped the ribbon into his pocket. "I never got to apologize. You were right about O all along. I'm sorry." Clarke just nodded in acknowledgment. "Thanks for telling me about the ribbon. I'm going out to look for her."

He started to turn away, but Clarke reached out to lay a hand on his wrist. "I'll come with you."

"That's nice of you, but I have no idea how long I'll be gone. This isn't like when we went out to find the medicine. It might be a while."

"I'm coming with you," she repeated. Her voice was firm, and there was a fire in her eyes that made him hesitate to contradict her.

"Are you sure?" Bellamy raised an eyebrow. "I doubt Wells will be happy to hear that."

"He's not going to hear it from me. We're done."

Bellamy's brain buzzed with questions that never made it to his lips. "Okay, then." He took a step forward and gestured for her to follow. "But I should warn you . . . I'll probably take off my shirt at some point." He glanced over his shoulder and saw a smile flicker across her face, so small it might have been a trick of the light filtering through the heavy leaves.

CHAPTER 34

Glass

The Colony was eerily quiet, even for one in the morning. Glass didn't see anyone else as she dashed through the dark hallways, lit only by the dim glow of the blue emergency lights along the floor.

She'd slipped out after her mother had finally gone to bed, and now she tried to banish the image of her mother waking up and finding Glass gone. The hurt and horror that would contort her delicate features, just as they'd done countless times over the past two years. Glass would never forgive herself for the pain she'd caused her mother, but she didn't have a choice.

She had to get to Walden, and to Luke.

She paused on the landing to F deck, straining her ears for footsteps, but she heard nothing except the sound of her own ragged breath. Either the guards were on patrol in some other part of Phoenix, or they'd all been banished back to Walden and Arcadia, where they wouldn't steal any more of the air that had been reserved for Phoenician lungs.

Glass darted down the unfamiliar corridor, straining her eyes for the telltale silver gleam of an air vent. Nearly at the bottom of the ship, F deck was mostly devoted to storage. The air vent she'd crawled through after she'd escaped the dropship had led to the F deck on Walden. She just hoped that the same applied on Phoenix. Slowing to a walk, she scanned the walls for an opening, feeling dread seep into her with each step. What if she'd been wrong about the layout? Or perhaps the vent had once connected Walden and Phoenix, but it had been filled long ago?

Then a glint of metal caught her eye, and the tension building in her chest was swept away by excitement and relief. She quickly rose onto her toes, reaching for the edge of the grate, but it was too high up. She let out a frustrated sigh and turned to survey the hallway. None of the doors were marked, but they didn't seem to be protected by retina scanners. She grabbed the nearest handle and yanked. It groaned open, revealing a dark supply closet.

Glass's eyes settled on a small barrel, which she rolled out into the hallway. She stepped on top, removed the grate, and pulled herself up into the shadowy space.

Glass thought briefly of her last crawl through an air shaft, how the metal walls had seemed to press in on her from all sides, and shivered, reaching for her back pocket. At least this time she'd brought a flashbeam. She directed the feeble beam of light forward, but there was nothing in sight except the air shaft, stretching endlessly ahead.

It would end eventually, Glass knew. She just hoped she wouldn't run out of air before she got there. If she had to die, she wanted it to be in Luke's arms.

The scene on Walden was different than she'd expected. The lights seemed to be functioning normally, and as she hurried toward Luke's flat, Glass didn't see any guards. For a moment, she felt a brief surge of hope. Perhaps her mother had been wrong. The panic on Phoenix was all a misunderstanding. But as she climbed the stairs, she felt a strange tightness in her chest that only got worse when she paused to catch her breath. Her eagerness to see Luke might account for her racing pulse, but Glass knew she couldn't ignore the truth. Oxygen was already running low on Walden.

She forced herself to move slowly as she turned onto Luke's floor, breathing careful, shallow breaths to keep her heart rate steady. The corridor was full of adults speaking in low voices, shooting worried looks at the children scampering up and down the hall, so excited to be out of bed at such a late hour that they hardly noticed their labored breaths. Glass wanted to tell the parents to keep the children calm and still to conserve oxygen, but that would only create more panic, and there was nothing they could do, anyway.

Glass had barely started to knock on Luke's door before he'd pulled her inside and into his arms. For a moment, all she was aware of was the warmth of his body and the weight of his embrace. But then he broke away, and she could see shock and concern warring with the joy in his eyes. "What are you doing here?" he asked, running his hand along her cheek as if needing more proof that she wasn't an illusion. He glanced toward the closed door and lowered his voice before continuing. "It's not safe."

"I know," Glass said quietly, slipping her hand into his.

"I don't know how you even got here, but you need to go back," Luke said, shaking his head. "You have a better chance of surviving on Phoenix."

"I'm not going back without you."

He led her over to the couch with a sigh and pulled her onto his lap. "Listen," he said, as he wrapped a strand of her hair around his finger, "if the guards catch us sneaking onto Phoenix, they'll shoot me, and then they'll probably shoot you." He closed his eyes, wincing. "This is what they've been training us for, Glass. It was never said overtly, but . . . we all had a sense something big was coming, and we've been drilled on what to do." When he opened his eyes again, they were full of a cold fury she'd never seen in them. He must've noticed the worry on her face, because his expression softened. "But that's not any of your concern. You'll be fine. And that's all I care about."

"*No*," Glass said, startled by her own vehemence. "I *won't* be fine." Luke frowned and opened his mouth to speak, but Glass cut him off. "It'll kill me, knowing you're down here alone. It'll *kill* me," she repeated, suddenly frantic, gasping as she fought for air. "And if I have to die, I want it to be down here with you."

"*Shhh*," Luke murmured, running his hand down the back of her head. "Okay, okay." He smiled sadly. "The worst thing we can do is run out of oxygen arguing."

"Are you afraid?" Glass asked after a long moment of silence.

Luke turned back to her and shook his head. "No." He placed his finger under her chin and tilted it up, so that she was looking straight into his eyes. "I'm never afraid when I'm with you." He leaned forward and kissed her softly. She shivered, his breath making her skin tingle.

Glass pulled away with a smile. "Isn't this a waste of oxygen?"

"Just the opposite," Luke whispered, drawing her back. "We're conserving it." His mouth found hers again, and she parted her lips as his kiss grew deeper.

Glass ran her hand up his arm, smiling as he shivered. Without breaking away, she began to unbutton his shirt, telling herself that his unusually rapid heartbeat was a response to her touch. Her lips moved to his jaw, then trailed down his neck. She paused at his chest. There were numbers tattooed on his ribs. Two sets of dates that made Glass's stomach churn.

"What's wrong?" Luke asked, sitting up.

She lowered her finger toward the tattoo, then snatched it away, afraid to touch the ink. "What's that?"

"Oh." Luke frowned as he glanced down. "I thought I told you. I wanted something to honor Carter." His voice grew distant. "It's his birthday and the day he was executed."

Glass barely managed to suppress a shudder as she looked back at the second set of numbers. Glass didn't need a tattoo to remind herself of the day Carter had died. The date was branded as clearly in her mind as it was on Luke's skin.

Glass groaned as she brought her knees up to her chest. The sheets on her cot were twisted and damp with sweat. She was desperate for a drink, but it'd be hours before they brought her dinner tray and her evening water allotment. She thought longingly of all the years she'd spent blissfully unaware that water was rationed elsewhere on the Colony.

There was a low beep, followed by footsteps. Glass winced as she lifted her throbbing head from the pillow and saw a figure in the door. It wasn't a guard. It was the Chancellor.

Glass drew herself into a seated position and pushed a strand of damp hair away from her face. She braced for a flare of fury as she locked eyes with the man who'd ordered her arrest, but through the haze of pain and exhaustion, she didn't see the head of the Council. All she saw was the concerned face of her best friend's father.

"Hello, Glass." He gestured toward the other side of the cot. "May I?"

She nodded weakly.

The Chancellor sighed as he sat down. "I'm sorry about what happened." He looked more haggard than she'd ever seen him, worse even than when his wife was dying. "I never wanted to see you get hurt."

Without thinking, Glass brought her hand to her stomach. "I'm not the one who was hurt."

The Chancellor closed his eyes for a moment while he rubbed his temples. He never showed frustration or fatigue in public, but Glass recognized the expression from the few times she'd seen him working in his study at home. "I hope you understand that I didn't have a choice." His voice grew firm. "I swore an oath to uphold the laws of this Colony. I don't have the luxury of turning a blind eye just because the criminal in question happens to be my son's best friend."

"I understand that you need to believe that," Glass said, her voice hollow.

His face hardened. "Are you ready to tell me the name of the father?"

"Why should I do that? So you can lock him up in here with me?"

"Because it's the *law.*" The Chancellor rose to his feet and took a few steps toward her. "Because it's not fair that the father not be punished equally. And because it won't take my investigators long to go through the retina scanner records and figure out where you've been spending your time. We're going to find him either way. But if you help us, you'll have a much better chance of being pardoned at your retrial."

Their eyes met, and Glass turned away from him, wincing as she imagined Luke being dragged away in the middle of the night, the terror on his face as he begged the guards to tell him what was going on. Would they tell him the truth, allowing just enough time for the pain to register before they plunged the needle into his chest? Or would he die believing he'd been the victim of a terrible mistake?

She couldn't let that happen.

But the Chancellor was right. The Council wouldn't stop until they'd found the accessory to her crime. Eventually, one of the guards would trace Glass's movements to Walden, to Luke's floor—maybe even to his flat.

Slowly, she turned back to the Chancellor, knowing what she had to do. When she finally spoke, her voice was as cold as a death sentence.

"The father was Carter Jace."

There was a loud creaking noise in the hallway. She sat up, straining her ears in the darkness. She felt a coil of panic tighten around her chest. It sounded almost like the ship was moaning.

"Oh my god," Luke whispered, rising quickly to his feet. The sound came again, followed by a rumbling that shook the walls. "Let's go."

The corridor was still full of people, although now even the children had fallen silent. The lights began to flicker. Luke held Glass's hand tightly as he wove through the crowd toward his neighbor. Her face was grave as she whispered something to Luke that Glass couldn't hear, though Glass could tell from her expression that it was nothing good. Then another figure materialized next to them, and Glass inhaled sharply.

It was Camille. Her eyes narrowed as they settled on Glass.

Glass turned away, unable to look at Camille right now. She couldn't help feeling guilty about how things had turned out. She wouldn't blame the other girl for hating her.

A group of children was huddled on the floor next to their parents, who talked in low, worried tones. One of the little girl's lips had a bluish cast, and the boy whose hand she was clutching was struggling for breath.

The lights sputtered one more time, then went out. A series of gasps rose up in the thick, sudden darkness. Unlike Phoenix, Walden didn't have any emergency lights.

Luke wrapped his arm around Glass's waist and drew her closer to him. "We're going to be okay," he whispered in her ear.

But then another voice reached through the shadows. Camille had snuck over and was now standing on Glass's other side. "Are you going to tell him, or should I?" she said, too quietly for Luke to hear.

Glass turned to her, startled, but she couldn't make out the expression on Camille's face. "What are you talking about?"

"He deserves to know the truth. That his friend *died* because of you."

Glass shuddered, and even though she couldn't see Camille smile, she could hear it in her voice.

"I know your secret. I know what you did to Carter."

CHAPTER 35

Clarke

They had been walking for hours, making widening concentric circles through the woods, trying to cover every inch of terrain. The backs of Clarke's legs were burning, but she relished the sensation; the physical pain was a welcome distraction from her thoughts. The flames engulfing the sides of the infirmary tent . . . Wells's arms like handcuffs around her . . . the sickening crack as the walls collapsed.

"Hey, look over here." Clarke turned to see Bellamy kneeling on the ground near the spot where she'd discovered Octavia's ribbon, staring intently at what appeared to be footprints in the dirt. She was no tracker, but the marks of struggle were easy to read. Whoever had left the prints hadn't been on a pleasant stroll through the woods.

"It looks like someone was running, or in a fight," Clarke said softly. She refrained from finishing the sentence: *almost like someone had been dragged away.* They'd assumed Octavia had run away . . . but what if she'd been taken?

She could read the same terrible line of questioning on Bellamy's furrowed brow, and knelt down beside him. "She can't be far," Clarke said, meaning it. "We'll find her."

"Thank you." Bellamy nodded as he rose, and they continued walking. "I'm . . . I'm glad you're here with me."

They trudged on for what felt like hours, the sun rising and then sinking in the sky. As their circles grew wider, Clarke could tell they were approaching the edge of the forest. Through the outlines of the trees she saw a clearing and paused. There were more trees, but these looked different from the ones in the woods. They had massive, gnarled trunks and thick limbs covered with a canopy of green leaves. The branches sagged with round, red fruit. Apples.

Clarke approached the apple trees, Bellamy close behind her. "That's strange," she said slowly. "The trees are spaced so evenly. It almost looks like an orchard." She walked over to the closest one. "But could it really have survived all these years?"

Although the tree loomed over her, the lowest branch was fairly close to the ground. Standing on her toes, it was easy for

Clarke to stretch up and pluck an apple. She twisted around and tossed it to Bellamy before reaching for another one.

Clarke held the apple up to her face. They grew fruit in the solar fields on the ship, but those apples looked nothing like these. The skin wasn't just red; it had threads of pink and white running through it, and it gave off a scent unlike anything she had smelled before. She took a bite and gasped as juice began running down her chin. How could something taste sweet and tart at the same time? For just a moment, Clarke allowed herself to forget everything that had happened on Earth and let the sensation overtake her.

"Are you thinking what I'm thinking?" Bellamy asked, and Clarke looked over. While she'd been busy eating, he'd begun using fallen branches to measure the distance between the trees.

"To be honest, I wasn't thinking anything beyond how good this tastes," Clarke admitted, feeling the hint of a smile curl her lips. But Bellamy didn't laugh or tease her. He just kept staring at the perfectly spaced trees.

"These didn't survive the Cataclysm, and they didn't just grow like this," he said slowly, his voice filled with wonder and dread. Before he'd even finished, Clarke knew what he was going to say. Her chest tightened with fear. "Someone planted them."

CHAPTER 36

Wells

"Is this better?"

Wells turned and saw Asher, the Arcadian boy, pointing to the log he'd been chopping. The grass was covered with wood shavings and pieces that had been discarded after false starts—but this one actually looked promising.

"Definitely." Wells nodded and crouched down next to the log, running his fingers over the grooves Asher had carved into the wood. "Just make sure they're all approximately the same depth, or else the logs won't lock into place." As Wells stood up, Graham walked by, carrying a shred of melted tarp toward the growing mound of salvaged supplies in the middle of the clearing. Wells stood a little taller, bracing for a scoff or snide remark, but Graham kept his eyes forward and continued on without a word.

The fire had destroyed their tents, but most of the tools had been spared, and the medicine, too. It had been Wells's idea to try to build permanent wood structures. It was a thousand times more difficult than it sounded in books, but they were slowly figuring it out.

"Wells!" A girl from Walden ran over. "How are we going to hang the hammocks? Eliza says they're going to hang from the roof beams, but those aren't going to be ready for days, right? Also, I was thinking—"

"I'll come over in a few minutes, okay?" Wells said, cutting her off. A look of hurt flitted across her round face. "I'm sure you and Eliza are doing a great job," he added, giving her a small smile. "I'll be right there."

She nodded and dashed away, darting around a pile of melted tent rods that still looked too hot to touch.

Wells glanced over his shoulder, then started walking toward the tree line. He needed a moment to himself, to think. He moved slowly, the heaviness in his chest seeming to seep into his limbs, making every step laborious and painful. At the edge of the forest, he paused, breathing the cooler air deep into his lungs, and closed his eyes. This was where he'd kissed Clarke for the very first time on Earth—and for what was surely the last time in his life.

He thought he'd already experienced the most terrible kind of pain possible—knowing that Clarke hated him, that she couldn't stand the sight of him. But he'd been wrong. Watching her leave with Bellamy had nearly killed him. She hadn't even looked his way when she'd come to collect what was left of her gear. She'd just nodded silently at the rest of the group before following Bellamy into the forest.

If only she knew what he'd really done to be with her on Earth. He'd risked everything. And it was all for nothing.

None of the guards gave Wells more than a cursory glance as he raised his eyes to the retina scanner, then strode through the doors. Entry to sector C14 was highly restricted, but his officer's uniform, purposeful walk, and well-known face guaranteed access to pretty much any part of the Colony. He'd never taken advantage of his status, until now. After he'd heard his father's conversation with the Vice Chancellor, something inside of Wells had snapped.

His plan was reckless and stupid and incredibly selfish, but he didn't care. He had to make sure Clarke was sent to Earth instead of the execution chamber.

Wells jogged down the empty, narrow staircase, lit only by faint emergency lights. There was no reason for anyone to visit the airlock except for routine checks, and Wells had already hacked into the maintenance files to check the schedule. He would be totally alone.

The airlock in C14 was original to the ship. And despite the engineers' efforts to keep it in top condition, after three hundred years of facing the extreme temperatures and UV rays of space, it had started to deteriorate. There were tiny cracks along the edge and shiny squares where newer material had obviously been patched over the airlock.

Wells reached behind him for the pliers he'd tucked into the waistband of his pants. It would be fine, he told himself, his arms shaking. They were all going to be evacuated soon, anyway. He was just speeding up the process. Yet in the back of his mind, he knew that there weren't enough dropships for everyone. And he had no idea what would happen when it came time to use them.

But that was his father's concern, not his.

He reached out and began to pry up the flimsy edge of the airlock, wincing when he heard the faint hiss. Then he turned and raced back toward the stairs, trying to ignore the horror welling up in his stomach. He could barely stand to think of what he'd done, but as he hurried down the stairs, he told himself he'd done what he had to do.

Wells rose wearily to his feet. It was getting dark, and there was still a lot of work to do on the new cabins. They needed to finish at least some of the shelters before the next storm. As he approached camp, wondering if Clarke had taken enough blankets with her, if she would be warm when the temperature dropped, Asher came up beside him and launched into another line of questioning. He held one of the trimmed logs and seemed to want Wells's opinion on the size and cut.

Wells was too absorbed in his own thoughts to hear what Asher was saying. As they walked side by side toward the tents, he could see the boy's mouth moving, but the words never made it to Wells's ears.

"Listen," Wells began, ready to tell Asher it could wait until morning. Just then, something streaked past his face. There was a sickening thwack, and Asher flew backward. Blood bubbled out of his mouth as he fell to the ground.

Wells dropped to his knees. "*Asher*," he screamed as his eyes struggled to make sense of the image in front of him. There was an arrow sticking out of the boy's neck.

His first, mad thought was Bellamy. He was the only one who could shoot like that.

Wells spun around with a yell, but it wasn't Bellamy behind him. A line of shadowy figures stood at the bottom of the hill, the setting sun behind them. He gasped as shock and horror raced through his veins. Suddenly, it became clear who had set fire to the camp—and who had taken Octavia. It wasn't anyone from the Colony.

The hundred might have been the first humans to set foot on the planet in three centuries, but they weren't alone.

Some people had never left.

ACKNOWLEDGMENTS

I owe an immeasurable debt of gratitude to Joelle Hobeika, who not only dreamed up the premise for *The 100*, but whose imagination, editorial acumen, and tenacity were essential in bringing it to life. The same applies to Katie McGee, Elizabeth Bewley, and Farrin Jacobs, whose incisive questions and intelligent suggestions shaped the book at every level. I'm also grateful to the intimidatingly clever people at Alloy, specifically Sara Shandler, Josh Bank, and Lanie Davis, and the dedicated teams at Little, Brown and Hodder & Stoughton.

Thank you to my remarkable friends on both sides of the East River, the Gowanus Canal, the Mississippi, and the Atlantic for your support and encouragement. A special "shout"-out to my confidants and coconspirators at both ends of 557 Broadway, to the Crossroads crew, who first introduced me to science fiction, and to Rachel Griffiths for going light-years beyond the call of duty to help me grow as a writer and editor.

Most of all, I am grateful to my family—my father, Sam Henry Kass, whose writing overflows with unmatched wit and unparalleled heart; my mother, Marcia Bloom, whose art shimmers with the wisdom of a philosopher and the soul of an aesthete; my brilliant brother, Petey Kass, who makes me laugh until I can't breathe; my inspiring grandparents, Nance, Peter, Nicky, and David; and the Kass/Bloom/Greenfield clans, who make so many places feel like home.